Demon Crown 3

ROBERT E. VARDEMAN

A SYMPHONY OF STORMS

A TOM DOHERTY ASSOCIATES BOOK
NEW YORK

This book is a work of fiction. All the characters and events portrayed in it are likewise fictional, and any resemblance to real people or incidents is purely coincidental.

A SYMPHONY OF STORMS

A Tor Book
Published by Tom Doherty Associates, Inc.
49 West 24th Street
New York, N.Y. 10010

Cover art by Kirk Reinert

ISBN: 0-812-50084-9

First edition: May 1990

Printed in the United States of America

0 9 8 7 6 5 4 3 2 1

"Sef is a cunning whoreson; that I'll give him,"

said Kaga'klab, the Wizard of Storms. "He goes to stir up more trouble. He senses weakness within the castle walls." The scrying spell controlling Kaga'klab's window cloud began to weaken—an effect of the Demon Crown. He renewed the spell and changed the view to another portion of the mountains. Of Sef's troops, the wizard saw nothing until he found the village of Fron. Sef had retreated back to the Lesser Ty, toward Castle Porotane.

Kaga'klab shifted his view to the castle itself. The petty posturings and assassinations within had long since ceased to interest him. Only the majesty of storm-building and the symphony of the elements crashing together held his attention long. He cared little who triumphed; as long as the Demon Crown rested on a royal brow, no one else would sit on the throne.

Kaga'klab turned back in his chair, strengthening his scrying spell and looking once more to the Northeast and fair Ionia. The woman had concluded her treaty with Gaemock's ambassador and had moved on to more amorous conquests. The ambassador was willing.

The Wizard of Storms settled down to watch. He enjoyed storm-building more than Ionia's antics—but only barely. The fiefdom's ruler had proven inventive and diverting in the past. This time was no exception.

Tor books by Robert E. Vardeman

THE DEMON CROWN TRILOGY

The Glass Warrior
Phantoms on the Wind
A Symphony of Storms

THE KEYS TO PARADISE (writing as Daniel Moran)

The Flame Key
The Skeleton Lord's Key
Key of Ice and Steel

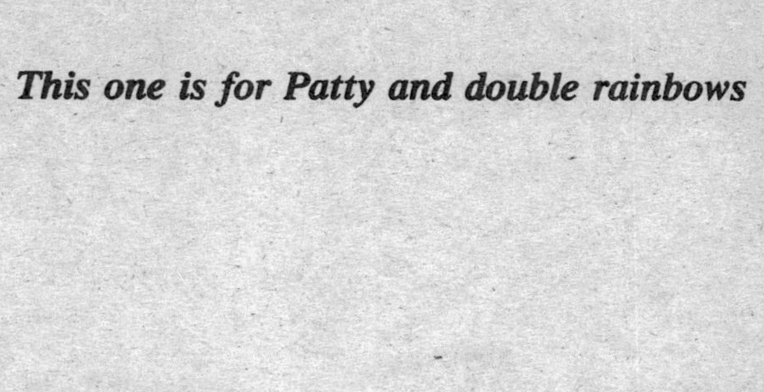

This one is for Patty and double rainbows

CASTLE OF THE WINDS
YORRAL MOUNTAINS
UVAIN PLATEAU
TUNNEL
CLAYMORE PASS
FRON
W
N
E
RIVER TY
CASTLE POROTANE
IRON RANGE
SWAMP
CITY OF STOLEN DREAMS
THE KINGDOM of POROTANE
50 MILES

Chapter One

Birtle Santon rubbed his withered left arm with his good hand and then drew his cloak around his body. The cold wintery winds whipping through the passes of the Yorral Mountains and sneaking into the pub where he sat sucked the warmth from him and made his joints ache. He was getting too old for this kind of adventuring.

The sight of the young woman across the room warmed him more than the cloak or the feeble fire guttering in the fireplace. She glowed with a beauty that made his heart pound fiercely. Her every movement was draped in grace and doelike litheness. Most of all she held the Demon Crown in her long-fingered hands and caused the diabolical device to shine with an emerald green that invigorated rather than enervated.

"A lovely sight, isn't it?" asked Santon's young

friend, Vered. The man's light brown hair had been blown into disarray, giving him a wild and dangerous look. The reflected gleam of the Demon Crown in his brown eyes caused Santon to sit a little straighter on the hard wooden bench and worry that much more.

"What is lovely?" he asked softly. "The woman or the crown?"

"Both," came Vered's answer. He laughed and slapped Santon on his good right shoulder. "Fear naught, dear friend. The crown is not seducing me. Oh, yes, I wish I could wear it. Damn the drop of royal blood flowing in my veins!"

"You miss its power."

"Aye, that I do," admitted Vered. "But the crown has found its rightful owner. She is Lokenna, daughter of King Lamost and heir to the throne of Porotane. There can be no question of that." Santon did not miss the wistfulness in Vered's voice. He *did* want the crown for his own.

"Titles mean nothing when dealing with magic of this order. You were unable to keep the crown from twisting you about. Can she prevent it or will she fall prey to its insidious call?" Santon knew this was no simple question. Lokenna had proven royal blood flowed in her veins; any commoner touching the Demon Crown died instantly. Santon considered this merciful. A member of the royal family wearing the crown became the focus of imponderable magic, power beyond belief, a weight too great to bear if the wearer showed any weakness.

Lokenna's twin, Lorens, had donned the crown and been broken by it. Would sister prove stronger than brother? Santon did not know. On that answer lay the destiny of the kingdom.

"What is all this madness about?" bellowed Bane Pandasso. "These two freebooters come dancing in here sweet as you please and give you this geegaw. Return it to them and get back to work." The burly man reached out to touch the Demon Crown. A sizzling spark of the purest green arched over to his fingertips. He yelped and backed off, sticking thick fingers in his mouth to soothe the burn.

"Do not attempt to touch the crown," Santon called. "It cannot be taken from your . . . wife." The word caught in his throat. Seeing such a lovely young woman married to a brute with heavy eyebrows wiggling like woolly caterpillars on bony ridges, a nose that had been broken too many times, pig eyes, a perpetual scowl, and a disposition to match his facial ugliness offended Santon. From the nervous stirrings of his friend, Santon knew that Vered's thoughts wandered down a similar path.

"He is good to me," Lokenna said, as if reading their minds. She sat between them, cradling the glowing crown in her hands. The ancient magical relic radiated a pure light unlike anything they had seen before. On Lorens' brow, it had produced a green the color of corroded copper. A mere glance had convinced anyone with sensibility that evil was afoot.

No longer. Santon relaxed in the light bathing him and knew that the Demon Crown could be turned to benefit rather than destruction. With the young woman he felt more at peace than he had at any other time since . . . Alarice had died.

Birtle Santon's thoughts turned to the Glass Warrior, the woman with hair of spun moonbeams, a beauty without peer. Tears beaded at the corners of his green eyes. He moved quickly to dab at the betraying droplets, but no one had seen this momentary weakness. Through the years of wandering Porotane he had found few women who affected him as strongly as Alarice.

She had been a warrior, a redoubtable wizard, a woman whose concern for the citizens of Porotane had led to her death. For almost two decades she had been entrusted with the Demon Crown. When Duke Freow lay dying, he had summoned her and sent her on a mission that would never be finished in the usurping noble's lifetime. Freow had been interred before Alarice had reached the Desert of Sazan to seek out the true heir to the throne.

Santon remembered her fighting the master wizard Patrin for Lorens' freedom. What a waste! Santon spat at the memory of Lorens. Lovely, courageous Alarice had died to place the youngling's worthless arse upon the throne of Porotane. He had misused the Demon Crown and plunged the kingdom into a civil war so intense that it beggared description.

"Do not mourn me, dear Birtle," came the whisper from outside. "I died so that the kingdom might prosper."

Santon jerked around, his withered left arm knocking the glass shield that Alarice had given him to the floor. The noise alerted Vered, whose hand shot to his dagger hilt.

"What's wrong?" Vered demanded.

Santon peered through the dirty pane of glass set into the wall. Outside a new winter storm raged, whipping up snow pellets and dirty rain.

"Nothing. Just the wind."

"There's more," pressed Vered. He moved

closer to his friend. "Did you see her again? Alarice?"

"I . . . I don't know. Perhaps."

"Does she approve of Lokenna?"

"It might have been a trick of the wind. Yes, a gust coming through the walls. Pandasso is not a good carpenter. Can you feel the draft, too?"

"Aye, that I can." Vered looked closely at Santon, then moved back to where he could talk quietly with Lokenna. Santon cast one last lingering look outside. Alarice's phantom had appeared to him several times before, but not now. Not this time.

He was not certain if that was good. He wanted to see her again, even if it was only her tortured phantom. The magics unleashed by Patrin in the battle of spells had prevented him and Vered from properly burying her. The Glass Warrior's body lay in the sand, her phantom roaming endlessly, seeking surcease and not finding it.

Selfishly, he wanted her to remain beside him, but his love—and pain—was greater. She had helped them find Lokenna. He would return to the Desert of Sazan, find her corpse, and give it the proper burial. It was the least he could do for a true heroine.

"I told you to get this pigsty cleaned up, woman!" Bane Pandasso stormed about, knocking over pewter goblets, breaking ceramic plates, spilling ale, and making twice the mess that had been this sorry inn's legacy when Santon and Vered had entered.

Santon motioned Vered to silence. The younger man's temper knew few bounds. Santon cleared his throat and said loud enough to be heard over the whine of the wind. "That is past. Lokenna must return immediately to the castle."

"What for?" Pandasso lumbered over, his long arms swinging like an arboreal animal's limbs. "She's my wife. She does what I say."

"She is Queen of Porotane."

"Please, I'll clean up. Bane is right. There is work to do." Lokenna gingerly placed the crown on the table. Its vibrant glow faded slightly but remained at a higher level than either of the adventurers had seen before.

Santon shook his head sadly. Things would change. He knew it by the way Lokenna touched the crown—and the way it responded favorably to her. Beside him, Vered heaved a deep sigh. He, too, understood what had yet to occur to Lokenna and her brutish husband.

"We should tend to the horses," said Santon. "The winds blow colder by the minute."

"I've had my fill of weather. How can anyone survive in this miserable place, much less prosper?" Vered looked around the shabby inn and added, "If this can be called prospering."

"The village of Fron is not the place one expects to find a queen," agreed Santon. "Only this isolation has kept her away from the madness gripping Porotane."

"We should ask how she eluded the wizard who kidnapped her. Lorens ended up the wizards's apprentice. What of Lokenna?"

"Is that to say you find this place less appealing than the City of Stolen Dreams?" Santon could not hold back a shudder of dread at the mention of Patrin's city and the horrors magically stored within its boundaries. Alarice had died there—and only her sacrifice had allowed him and Vered to continue their miserable lives.

"Fron has a certain charm. The war has left the village unscathed. There is no hint of starvation. Remember the coast?" Santon immediately regretted this riposte. Vered's handsome face turned to stone and a small muscle at the corner of his mouth began to twitch. The ebb and flow of the civil war had taken Vered's family—and had given him life, if Santon's suppositions were accurate. The drop of royal blood flowing in Vered's veins that allowed him to briefly touch the Demon Crown had not come from a common fisherman. Santon thought that a conquering noble had taken his pleasure with Vered's mother and left behind a bastard son.

"Lorens' soldiers might still haunt these passes," Vered said abruptly. "We should backtrack to be sure we have not been followed."

"We have left them behind. All that roam these mountains tonight are phantoms."

Santon stared out the filthy window once more in the wan hope of seeing Alarice's phantom fluttering past. He saw only swirls of white snow and a deepening storm.

He heaved himself to his feet and settled the glass shield on his withered arm before pulling the cloak tightly around him. He motioned to Vered and left the inn without a backward glance. Lokenna and her husband stood nose to nose in the kitchen arguing. It did not take a wizard of any ability to know what caused this disagreement. The woman had touched the Demon Crown. For her there could be no turning back.

Santon dropped chin to chest to keep out the cold fingers of winter trying to strangle him. His exposed skin rippled with gooseflesh, and the strong wind coming from the high peaks ripped at his cloak and made it seem inconsequential against the cold.

"There," came Vered's voice. "There are the horses. They've come loose from the hitching rail. Stupid animals should know better than to wander off in this storm."

Santon held out the shield and restrained the impetuous Vered. He had survived many years of conflict and treachery by listening to his inner voice. That voice now rose to a scream.

A deft flick of his wrist brought a heavy war ax swinging about on its thong. Vered bobbed his head in agreement. He drew the glass short sword Alarice had given him and slipped into the storm's white shroud. Santon waited a moment, then moved in the opposite direction. Lorens' soldiers had fought bitterly trying to regain the crown for their king. Lorens himself had arrived and shown startling magical ability. And what of others? Santon guessed that the bands of brigands preying on travellers in the Yorral Mountains came and went through Fron unhindered by the fearful locals.

Worst of all might be the rebels led by the likes of Dews Gaemock and Dalziel Sef. Although Santon's sentiments rode with Gaemock more than with Lorens, on a battlefield it was difficult to tell friend from foe—and with the Demon Crown as prize, betrayal would come all too easily.

Santon tossed his head and got his thinning hair out of his eyes. The snow pellets melted on his forehead and plastered down the hair where it lay. He ignored this. His every sense reached out. The crunch of heavy boots on the icy crust of snow alerted him to another's presence.

Crouching low, he moved with no more sound that a snowflake falling into a soft wet drift. Santon had barely recovered from an infected cut to his forehead and every joint in his body ached from the cold and travel. All that misery vanished and he became once more the deadly fighter of yore.

He came upon the man lying in ambush. Santon judged the distance, noted that he was attacking from behind, and, giving the man no chance to respond, then swung his ax in a short, vicious arc. The heavy, battle-nicked blade met the would-be ambusher's neck at the shoulder. He grunted, tried to stand and turn. Only then did he feel the full impact of the deadly cleaver. He turned slowly and sank into the snow. The hot blood gushing from the cut sizzled as it heated the frozen crust of the snowbank. Santon paid the fallen man no attention. One enemy lay dead.

He had no idea how many more would die before he could again rest easily.

A shout alerted him that Vered had found a worthy opponent. Santon hesitated, worrying about his impetuous friend. He shrugged it off. Let the youngling have his day. He had proven himself a staunch fighter over and over. Santon doubted they would find any in the Yorral Mountains who could stand against their skill and daring.

He circled, his clear green eyes roving, ever-watchful for attack. Even with such alertness, his ears gave warning before his eyes. He dropped to one knee, shoved out the glass shield, and deflected a sword slash from the rear. He pivoted on his knee, grinding it into the frozen ground as he brought his heavy ax around in a circle parallel to the ground and knee-high.

He grunted when the blade struck an armored thigh. Then the air was filled with screeches of pain as his adversary realized that his left leg had been cut to the bone. Santon gave the man no time to regain his wits. Lowering his shield, he shoved hard and bowled over the swordsman. The ax handle rose and fell, smashing the man's skull.

"Two," Santon said softly, panting, his breath turning to silvery plumes in the frigid air. "How many more?"

He continued his hunt and found three slain foe. He dropped the ax and let it dangle from its thong when he saw Vered sitting cross-legged on the hitching rail and daintily cleaning his glass sword.

"I do not understand the magic spells Alarice used to fashion this blade," Vered said, "but it has served me well this day."

"Three?" asked Santon.

"And two for you," answered Vered. "I have taken the liberty of examining the pouches of those I felled."

"And? What did you find besides a few paltry coins?" Santon joined his friend in cleaning his weapon. Now that the battle had ended, a heavy weight descended on his shoulders, turning him once more into a man pushed beyond his limits.

Vered looked at him in concern but said nothing about Santon's paleness. "A few gold coins among the lot, true," the brown-haired man said, "but also a strange document that authorizes these brigands to call themselves friend with Dalziel Sef's rebels."

Santon took the torn and heavily creased parchment and slowly read it. "A letter of marque granted by Sef," he said in astonishment. "I have never heard of such a thing."

"A license to steal, and to do it in the name of the rebels," said Vered. He pointed with the tip of his sword. "Actually, they are allowed to steal in the name of the future monarch of Porotane, good king Dalziel."

"He flatters himself."

Vered shrugged. "Who can say what happens in the land? Lorens' power is broken. We stole away the Demon Crown and robbed him of the only link he had to the throne. The pretender Duke Freow is dead. Between Dalziel Sef and Gaemock might lie bad blood. If they fight for the throne, who's to name the victor?"

"The true queen is there." Santon indicated the dilapidated inn with the edge of his shield.

"If unrest in the land extends even to pitiful Fron, we had better convince Lokenna to return quickly. Porotane cannot stand more of this vicious civil strife. What has raged for so long has almost broken the people's will to live."

A chilly blast of frigid wind blew down the pass and whipped Santon's cape like a garrison banner. He stared through the vee-notch of the pass and fancied he saw all the way to the Wizard of Storms' castle hidden away above the Uvain Plateau.

They found brigands and rebels with steel and glass. What weapons did a wizard use to conquer Porotane?

"Aye, let's see if Lokenna has convinced that

pig of a husband that she belongs on a throne and not in a scullery."

Santon threaded his way through the rapidly cooling corpses and caught the reins of their horses. The animals shied and tried to bolt, but the brigands had securely fastened the reins to a post hidden under the snow. Santon fumbled using his single good hand until Vered assisted him. They led the horses back to the inn and around to a small stable where they tended to grooming until their hands threatened to turn to ice.

"I'm for another mug of ale, even if it is thin and watery," said Vered. He tossed a small pouch into the air and caught it handily. "We have enough money to live on for some time, compliments of our clumsy ambushers."

"We were lucky. Less suspicious men would have gone directly after the horses and died in the snow."

"Not us, friend Santon. We will live forever!"

Vered threw open the door to the inn and was catapulted back into Santon. A heavy club had caught him squarely on the top of his skull. The pair tumbled into the snow, more brigands rushing from the inn. Flat on their backs and weapons useless, they stared at certain death.

CHAPTER TWO

Baron Theoll looked up and down the corridor before running his nimble fingers along the wood carving of an armored knight that graced the wall. A small click sounded and a secret passage through the thick stone walls of Castle Porotane opened for him. He darted inside, rat-quick, and pulled the panel shut behind him. His heart raced. The game he played this night was a deadly one, and the slightest mistake meant his death.

On boots with carefully padded soles, he walked gingerly along the narrow passage. Other nights he would have paused to peer through the dozens of spy holes. Theoll knew the value of intelligence and information gathering. Spying on the serving girls in their quarters often gave him insight into castle alliances and new treacheries.

But tonight he passed by such salacious pleasures. Only when he had reached a branching corridor and slipped into this musty, unused portion of the secret ways did he pause. Theoll cautiously pulled back a black piece of cloth and peered through the spy hole into Lady Anneshoria's quarters.

The sight of her undressing did nothing to arouse his lust. Her sleek limbs had opened for too many other nobles as she methodically worked her way to power for Theoll to care about her. He needed more this night—he needed to know Anneshoria's plan to assassinate him.

Theoll had heard rumors flitting about the castle; there were always rumors. This time, though, he had to give them credence. Anneshoria had seized equal power when he had killed Archbishop Nosto. The cleric had foolishly mixed religion and politics—and Theoll had foolishly permitted Anneshoria to share the throne as vice regent to hold back the tide of indignation rising against him.

He had made it seem that the dim-witted jester Harhar had committed the heinous crime. Anneshoria would have revealed the fool's part and betrayed Theoll if he had not agreed to her demands.

But he no longer could keep from moving against her. For weeks they had maneuvered for total dominance of the castle. What did the demon-cursed woman plot? He had to know!

Theoll pressed his eye closer to the spy hole and moved about slowly to scan the room. Another joined Anneshoria!

"Captain Squann," the woman said, barely loud enough for Theoll to overhear. "You do me a great honor with your presence this night."

"Lady Anneshoria, I seek only what is best for Porotane. The division of power in the castle weakens us. If we continue to fight among ourselves, the rebels will wash over us like a foul black tide."

"True," the woman said. She continued to disrobe, as if the soldier were not present. "Why do you come to me? Your ties are with Theoll. He has promoted you. You are his man."

"I am my own man," snapped Squann. He straightened his dark blue uniform jacket and touched the row of medals pinned to his breast. Theoll watched as the captain fought for control against Anneshoria's clever manipulation. "I seek only the best for the castle and the people of Porotane."

"How patriotic of you," the woman said scornfully. "No one else within these walls is so altruistic. What do you hope to gain? Would you become my consort when I depose Theoll? Ah, yes, that must be it. You like what you see now." Anneshoria pirouetted for him, naked. "You would like me the better if I were queen, wouldn't you, *Captain?*" She bore down on his rank to put him in his place.

Theoll prayed for Squann to whip out his dagger and drive it into the woman's foul heart. That would solve all the baron's problems. He could execute Squann as a traitor and need never reveal the reason for the noble lady's murder.

"Question my reasons, if you will, Lady," Squann said through clenched teeth. "I make a better ally than foe."

"No doubt, Captain," she said, softening her tone. She drifted to him, a lovely white speck carried across the room on a light summer's breeze.

Her hand reached out. Squann flinched. She tensed and caught at his cheek, drawing him closer. They kissed.

For the spying baron, time stood still. He raged and yet dared not shout. His hands clenched so hard that blood formed in the palms where fingernails cut into flesh. A big vein in his temple began to throb and hundreds of plans for revenge formed.

Theoll pulled himself back from the spectacle in Anneshoria's room. He did not wish to see them in rut. His time could be better spent consolidating his power base, finding those in the guard who hated Squann, getting promises of support from the other nobles. If he did not end this dual reign soon, the rebels would have all their heads on pikes outside the castle walls.

The diminutive baron slipped from his secret passage and into the main corridor once again. He walked quickly to his quarters, his left leg dragging slightly as old wounds made their presence felt. He massaged his arm where a sword thrust had nearly ended his life, and smiled. His disability was more feigned than real now, but he knew the value of having an enemy underestimate his prowess.

Nosto had made that mistake and he now lay in a crypt in the castle's catacombs.

He dropped into a chair behind a table strewn with papers. Theoll shuffled through them and carefully pulled out a single sheet covered with names connected by lines. The best place to hide battle plans in the castle was in plain sight. He had merely glanced toward the wall hangings concealing a spell-locked chest. Anneshoria's wizard was as adept as any Theoll could find. Small indications showed that the ward spells had been breached.

That mattered little. Theoll knew how to keep his secrets from prying eyes. He scanned the list, debating the loyalty of some and discounting others entirely. When he finished with his appraisal he vented a tiny sigh of disgust.

Squann had been his most powerful ally. Deposing Anneshoria and retaining the throne for himself would be doubly difficult without the guard captain's aid.

A tiny rap came at the door. Startled, Theoll looked up and moved worthless paper over the one detailing his coup.

"Enter," he barked. Dark eyebrows rose in surprise when Squann entered.

"Baron, I must speak with you."

Theoll eyed the soldier critically. The immaculate dress uniform now carried telltale wrinkles where Anneshoria had been less than discreet in stripping it from his broad shoulders. If he had not been watching through the spy hole, he would have assumed Squann had been on night patrol along the battlements.

He had been sheathing his sword, but Theoll knew it had nothing to do with duty.

"What is it?" Theoll tried to keep his tone neutral but a hint of his anger seeped around his words. Squann's eyes narrowed slightly.

"You know of my visit to Anneshoria this night?"

"What visit is this, Squann? Get to the point. I have much to do."

"I sought information from her, Baron. She is evil and must never rule Porotane alone. She will be worse than Lorens, even with the Demon Crown turning him down the road of madness."

"Fine words, Captain, but what do they mean to me?"

"You were watching. I know it, Baron. Nothing of importance escapes your alert eye. Anneshoria revealed her assassination plot to me."

"In the heat of fornication?" Theoll snorted in contempt. "She never loses control of her senses. What she told you was only what she wished to tell you. You pried nothing from her."

"The plan is a good one, Baron." Squann perched on the edge of the table. Theoll's hand moved toward the dagger he had sheathed at his belt. If Squann attacked, he would be greeted by cold steel.

"Please, Baron, I mean you no harm. You have done much for me when others turned away. I owe you everything and would never betray you. What I did was for you—and for the good of Porotane."

"You again beat the drum of patriotism?"

"I believe Porotane *must* have a strong ruler—soon. The kingdom will shatter into a hundred fiefdoms unless the civil war is ended and a king of great power and ability assumes the throne." Squann paused, his cold ebony eyes fixed on Theoll's. "You are such a man, Baron. Only you can unite a divided nation."

"Anneshoria offered to let you be her consort. What do you want from me in return?"

"Your trust. I know you can be generous to those who serve you well."

"Anneshoria knows of our past dealings. Why do you think she told you anything important that you wouldn't immediately reveal to me?"

Squann laughed. "I don't doubt that she mistrusts me. Her plan is a good one, though, and makes me think it is one she considered long and well."

"And?" pressed Theoll, interested in spite of his misgivings.

"She had discarded this one in favor of another. We know one route she will *not* take. That is valuable, as is some indication of the way she thinks."

Theoll leaned back and moved his hand from the sheathed dagger. He looked hard at Squann, then smiled slowly. "Porotane will need a new Marshal of Armies when I am king. Do you know where I might find a man suitable for such an exalted position, Squann?"

CHAPTER THREE

A hunting hawk swooped low, its talons dragging along the white drifts of snow. Lorens, King of Porotane, fugitive from rebels, screeched in fear and threw himself over an embankment. Hot streaks of red appeared on his back as the hawk tried to get a firm hold and lift him into the air. Lorens thrashed and screamed and lay in the frozen ravine until it became apparent that the bird of prey had left to find another, less taxing dinner.

Lorens stared into the pure blue sky framed by the razor-sharp peaks of the Yorral Mountains and laughed out loud. He laughed harder and harder until tears ran down his cheeks.

"You can never get me. Never! I am king! I am lord of all Porotane!" The tears fell from his cheeks and dropped to the crusted snow. There they froze after a brief fight with the cold.

Lorens heaved himself erect, tottered on the slick streambed, and finally wobbled along as if drunk. No man should endure what he had been through. Rebels. He cursed Dalziel Sef. The rebel had splintered what remained of his personal guard. Lorens had no idea what had become of his loyal followers and valiant soldiers.

He spat. None of this would have happened if those two worms had not stolen the Demon Crown. Shaking fingers touched his forehead where the magic crown had rested and given him limitless power. With its demon-granted magic he had been able to see anywhere in the realm.

More! He had *been* wherever he turned his magical senses. He overheard plots against him, saw troop movements, tasted the rebel's dinner, felt Sef's vile lover's caress, smelled the pungent wood smoke from campfires a hundred leagues distant, saw vistas locked away for too many centuries.

The demon Kalob had given the crown to King Waellkin three hundred years earlier as reparation for the horrors wrought on Porotane by demonic infestations. Lorens chuckled and wiped spittle from his lips. What treasure! What a prize! And it had been his!

He did not see the Demon Crown as another source of discord cast by the banished demon. All Lorens knew was the magnificent change. His entire life had been one of tedium and obedience. The tall, white-haired woman—the Glass Warrior his master had called her—had told him that he had been kidnapped when only a small child. Lorens cared little for this. He was a dutiful apprentice to the wizard Patrin and did not want to leave the City of Stolen Dreams.

He had not wanted to leave his apprenticeship until he touched the Demon Crown. Worlds opened for him—and even without the burning band around his head, some still stretched before him.

Lorens fought his way up the slippery ravine embankment and threw back his head, his shrill voice rising to challenge the heavens. "I see other worlds!"

And he did. His ringing words echoed not from lofty mountaintops but from dark and dangerous twisting corridors filled with sulphur fumes and timid beasts. Yellow eyes peered at him from the black depths. An occasional pink forked tongue slithered out and wiggled sinuously and suggestively in his direction.

Lorens laughed at them. They were powerless before him. The wedge opening their fearsome world to him lay in the Demon Crown, but he had no need of that magical device now. His power had grown. He had grown and he would use the denizens of this lava-and-volcano world as his soldiers. He would order them forth and their mere presence would cause the rebels to quake.

"When I regain the crown," Lorens muttered. His thoughts became incoherent and he drooled. "Nothing will be beyond my power." He turned to the dark world with its red-glowing lava twistings and beckoned. "Come forth, my little ones. Join me in this world and we will conquer!"

The deformed, grotesque beasts shuffled forward, talons clicking on hard rock, eyes darting and nervous.

"Come, come with me. Follow my banner and you will be rewarded! I, King Lorens of Porotane, will let you live!" He laughed harshly as the beasts recoiled. Lorens gestured. The beasts again shuffled toward him, ready to enter his world.

Lorens jerked about when a thunderclap rolled down from the uppermost reaches of the mountains. The sky remained unsullied by clouds. As lodestone draws iron, Lorens turned slowly until he saw a single lofty peak far away, looking over the Uvain Plateau. Eyes were not enough to see what came to Lorens.

"No, no, you won't rob me of this! You won't. Damn you, you hell-spawned fiend!" Lorens tried to use his feeble magical power to fend off the Wizard of Storms' most potent spells. He failed. The reclusive wizard had no need of the Demon Crown to make him whole and powerful.

A lightning bolt vaporized a large boulder a dozen paces away. Lorens threw up his arms to protect his face. Peals of thunder sounded constantly as the Wizard of Storms directed his attack from the distant Castle of the Winds.

"Come, come to me. Hurry, my friends. You must obey me!" Lorens shrieked when the first of the black-scaled reptilian creatures slithered through the portal he had opened for them. Sulphur fumes caused his nose to wrinkle and his eyes to water. He stood straight and tall and pointed. "There is the enemy. Destroy him! Do it for your lord and master! Do it for *me!*"

Another lightning bolt lanced down from the empty sky. This one touched the shimmering door into the netherworld that Lorens had opened. When the debris from the resulting explosion settled, only a dozen of the black reptiles had reached this side safely.

"Do not rest. Kill him. Kill whoever opposes me!" His shrieks turned incoherent. Lorens babbled and pointed. The reptiles dropped to all fours, then rose up in a parody of soldiers on parade. They formed a ragged rank and began marching toward the distant peak.

Lorens cackled. It might take them a month or a year or ten thousand years, but they would find the Wizard of Storms and destroy him. He, Lorens, son of Lamost, had ordered it!

Lorens fell silent when thick clouds formed directly overhead. Their leaden bellies split with flashes of lightning but no strikes reached the ground. In fascination he watched as raindrops formed—heavy-bodied, cloud-dragging raindrops unlike anything he had ever seen. The tendrils of cloud dipped lower and lower, their watery cargo glistening in the sunlight.

A sudden explosion knocked Lorens off his feet. From the cloud he saw four immense writhing blobs of water tumbling to the ground. When they touched the earth they did not spatter.

They grew. Slowly at first, then with great rapidity they grew into humanoid forms. Watery fingers reached out for the black, sulphurous reptiles. And every touch produced a soul-searing agony that caused the afflicted reptile to jerk violently, snapping important bones and dying instantly.

The Wizard of Storms' water warriors moved ponderously but managed to cut off all retreat by the reptiles. Lorens dropped to all fours and watched his alien army being destroyed by one born of pure magic.

Lorens scuttled off like a dog, leaving behind the unholy carnage. A league away, he dropped to his belly and lay panting. All concept of time had fled him. He could not remember if the battle of magic had been an hour or a year before.

His fingers worked weakly in the frosty soil until he touched a tuber. He smiled weakly and began digging. He ate the bulbous brown stem with an appetite that knew no bounds. When he had finished, Lorens belched and rolled over to stare at the sky and wonder what had caused his panic. He couldn't remember.

Everything was as it should be. Soon, very soon, he would regain the Demon Crown and again sit on the throne and rule Porotane. Soon. Soon.

Chapter Four

"He's dead. There is no need to search out his rotten carcass." Dews Gaemock glared at his brother, wishing Efran would show some sense. "You have played the fool overlong," the rebel leader said. "You still think like a court jester."

"That's not what you said when we engaged Lorens' troops. Whose plan did you select from all the ones submitted by your officers?" Efran Gaemock pulled his cloak tighter around him, thinking fondly of the warm corridors of Castle Porotane. The two years he had spent pretending to be Duke Freow's fool had not dulled his tactical sense. Once more in command of a company of troops, he had shown his skills.

He sneezed and looked around, as if he would find warm woolens awaiting him. The jester's motley he still wore provided almost no protection against the early winter winds blowing down from the highest reaches of the Yorral Mountains.

"You've not lost a bit of your talent," said Dews, clapping his brother on the back. "But prancing about in the midst of those royalist swine has made you too cautious. Lorens is dead. We routed his troops and scattered them from here to Porotane. I doubt if they've stopped running yet!"

Efran did not share his brother's confidence in either the soldiers' cowardice or the death of their king. Lorens' power was immense when he wore the Demon Crown. Efran had seen this too many times to lightly dismiss the demented wizard's apprentice-turned-king.

"The crown. Where is it?"

"The officer we caught and interrogated," said Dews. "He said that Lorens had lost it and sought those two you mentioned. What were their names?"

"The ones who installed Lorens on the throne. The ones recruited by the Glass Warrior." Efran frowned and began to pace in the snow, as much to keep warm as from nervous energy. Where did those two brigands figure into the power structure? They had aided Alarice and she had been a minion of Freow. But they had not supported Lorens, although they had returned with the young king and watched him mount the throne.

"They are petty thieves. You said so yourself. Come, brother. We have much to do. The kingdom is in disarray and awaits our tender touch to put it in order."

"There is still much to do here," said Efran. "Vered and Santon their names are. They might have recovered the Demon Crown."

"So? Neither can use it. Neither is of the blood royal."

Efran continued his aimless pacing, his mind turning over endless possibilities. In one thing Dews was right. The two could not put the Demon Crown to use. Efran had seen what happened when one not of the blood attempted to wear the crown. Lorens had amused himself too often by putting the crown on hapless prisoners. The agony etched on their faces before they died told of awful demonic worlds. No, Santon and Vered could not use the crown.

But they had found Lorens after fourteen years when all thought King Lamost's offspring had died. What other miracle were those two likely to perform?

"There is more that bothers me," said Efran.

"Brother, you try my patience now. We must ride for the castle. The defenders will throw open the gates and welcome us with garlands of flowers for our victory. Claymore Pass had been the scene of terrible slaughter in the past. It is now the site of our victory!"

Efran Gaemock shuddered at this. The phantoms drifting in and out of his peripheral vision appeared to be part of the swirling snow kicked up by gusty winds, but he knew better. Hundreds, perhaps thousands, had died in Claymore Pass and still roamed begging for their bodies to be properly buried. Efran sometimes could not tell the difference between the howls of the wind and the eternal pain of the undead phantoms.

To escape this he would gratefully leave the Yorral Mountains and Claymore Pass. But the feeling of duty undone gnawed at his guts. "I want Lorens' head as an ikon of our victory," he declared. "The head that wore the Demon Crown must now rest on a pike outside the castle walls for all to see."

"In this weather you expect to find a corpse?" Dews Gaemock's arm swept in a wide circle indicating the white curtains of blowing snow around them. "Not till spring thaw are we likely to find Lorens—or what remains of him."

"His phantom, then," said Efran. "His phantom will suffice."

"Who can capture a phantom and bend it to his will? Oh, a wizard of some power might. It was even said that the Glass Warrior controlled such a spell, but you would know that better than I."

"I knew little of her." Efran's eyes turned to the distant peak where the Wizard of Storms led his reclusive existence. He strained to see the fabled Castle of the Winds and failed. The snowstorm had worsened and threatened them with frostbite if they remained in this sparse bivouac any longer.

"We ride," Efran said. "I do not like leaving Lorens—or his body—behind. Remember that advice when it comes back to haunt us both."

Dews shook his head at such nonsense. They had routed Lorens' personal guard. The best Castle Porotane had to offer had run before them. What did it matter that the Demon Crown was again lost?

They mounted their horses and rode slowly down the winding path, the wind at their backs. Within a league they had re-formed. Of the hundred rebel soldiers who had entered Claymore Pass Efran noted only forty left. The toll had been great. His head sagged when he considered how few of those fallen had received consecration of their graves.

New phantoms to roam the rocky ways of the Yorral Mountains. So it had always been. Efran Gaemock wondered if this would ever change. He doubted it.

He rode, more asleep than awake, until a sharp noise brought him upright in the saddle.

"What is it, Dews?" he demanded. He blinked sleep and snow from his pale eyes and squinted. The banks of the River Ty stretched southward toward the castle and wended northward into their Yorral Mountain headwaters. What held his attention was a banner fluttering over a barge landing.

"I've never seen the likes of that before. No lord flies a gold-and-blue war flag." Dews motioned to a lieutenant, who nodded curtly and put the spurs to his horse. He galloped ahead, as much as emissary as a spy.

"Damn," cried Efran when he saw a single arrow arcing upward. The deadly missile found their lieutenant. From the boneless way the man fell from horseback, Efran knew he had died instantly.

"That was an unprovoked attack!" cried Dews. "How dare this lord of gold and blue!"

"Gold and blue," mused Efran. "That *is* familiar. A western province. A coastal city-state?"

Dews settled down in his saddle, his face turning stony. "Dalziel Sef hails from the westerlands. He calls the port city of Lih his home."

"Yes, Lih. Could he have mistaken our rider for one of Lorens' accursed soldiers?" Even as he asked the question, Efran knew the answer.

"Hardly. This can only mean that Sef has decided that, with Lorens gone and the castle defenses lacking a leader, the time is ripe for treachery."

"Sef was never noted for loyalty," Efran said sourly.

"I needed his troops. If we had continued to fight one another as well as Lorens's soldiers, we—"

"Brother, please. I *know* your reasons. They were good ones. We have this new problem to solve."

"No," said Dews Gaemock, his face turning even colder. "We are not the ones with a problem. It is Dalziel Sef. He must face us. And all the demons who once roamed this land will seem feeble when that treacherous son of a pig tastes my vengeance!"

Efran Gaemock nodded, his agile mind already working out the proper approach to the barge landing. Even with their handful of troops, seizing it would not be difficult against Sef's defenders.

And then? Efran would worry about that later. They had a skirmish to fight and win. He began ordering the rebel troops into position, again in his element.

Chapter Five

Birtle Santon struggled to roll to his left but he had become too tangled up with Vered for that. His eyes grew round as he saw death rising above him. The brigand-turned-rebel-soldier could crush a skull with a single swipe of his massive spiked club.

"Lokenna, wait, no!" came the cry from the inn. Santon recognized the voice as Bane Pandasso's. But that mattered naught. Not with death poised above.

A flash of lambent green caught Santon's attention. His eyes followed the arc of the Demon Crown as it came down over the blunt head of the raised club. The circlet spun about its new axis and descended. The rebel screeched in agony when the innocuous-looking crown touched the fingers gripping the club.

The brigand dropped his weapon and tried to back away. The Demon Crown stuck to his flesh as if it had grown there.

Santon shoved Vered aside and sat upright in the snow and mud, watching in helpless fascination. The soldier fought to pull the crown free. The more he struggled, the deeper the crown sank into his wrist. The green color of rotted flesh began to spread up his arm. The man's cries of terror were choked off when the rising tide of gangrene reached his neck and mouth. Putrescence destroyed further struggles. The bulky man sank to the snow and melted away.

"Never have I seen the like," muttered Vered. "And to think I put the crown on my own brow."

"Be thankful you've that drop of royal blood," said Santon. Lorens had tortured his prisoners using the Demon Crown, or so Santon had heard it rumored about the castle, but no one had described such a horrific action. He turned to the doorway of the inn. Lokenna stood there, face pale and hands shaking. Behind her Santon saw Pandasso, even more distraught.

"What d-did you do?" stammered Pandasso. "He melted away!"

Lokenna put a hand to her mouth and shook her head. Santon saw resolve filling her and color coming back to pale cheeks. "I couldn't let him kill those men."

"What did you *do* to him?" asked Pandasso, his voice firming now. A cunning look replaced the fear. "This is a skill that can make us a great deal of money."

"It's not for making money," Vered said briskly. He brushed himself off and frowned at the new dirt and tears in his clothing. "The Demon Crown gives power."

"Power," muttered Pandasso, as if this thought was totally alien to him. Santon snorted and got to his feet. Any thought might be lonely in that brutish head.

"We must return to Porotane immediately," Santon said. "These brigands carried orders from Dalziel Sef. With the crown in your hands, all will seek you."

"You are saying that this Sef wishes me harm?" asked Lokenna. "Because I have this crown?" She lifted the emerald-glowing crown and ran her fingers along its unadorned golden sides. "We know little of politics in Fron."

"My queen, politics comes to you," said Vered. "The brigands might have stumbled upon us by accident, but Lorens' soldiers still roam Claymore Pass. They would slay you instantly."

"Lorens?"

"Your twin brother," said Santon. He watched her reaction carefully. She did not believe him. "You and he were kidnapped when you were only children."

"Yes," she said slowly. "I was kidnapped. I remember escaping from an evil man who wanted to take me into a swamp."

"Tahir," said Santon. "He was a wizard of no real power and did Patrin's bidding. Patrin exiled Tahir when you escaped and took your brother as his own apprentice."

Lokenna shook her head. "This is all too confusing for me. I must begin supper. Not many in Fron patronize our inn, but they are the more important for their loyalty."

"Queen Lokenna, please," pleaded Vered.

"You are no longer a scullery maid. You are a monarch and must assume those duties."

"She knows nothing of being a queen," said Pandasso. "She is my wife and is needed here."

"With power comes money," Santon said. A foul taste rested in his mouth when he saw the avarice flare once again on Pandasso's face. "To reign supreme in Porotane means more money than you could count in a lifetime."

"With such power also comes . . . them." Lokenna pointed at the dead brigands. "Fron is isolated and peaceful because of that. I do not wish to change my life. I like it here. With my husband," she added, as if it had been an afterthought.

"With the Demon Crown comes duty. You are no longer your own person, Majesty," said Vered. "You can deny it, but others will continue to seek you out because of the crown."

"They cannot wear it, or so goes the legend. Why do they want it?"

"To prevent those in the royal house from using it," cut in Santon. "Nobles not of the royal blood hunger for power."

"Then let them take it. And you can take this, too." She tossed the Demon Crown toward Santon. Santon recoiled—but Vered moved faster. The young man dived and caught the crown before it touched his friend. The hue of green changed subtly.

For a moment, Vered stood juggling it. His face went slack when the crown's power began to insinuate itself into his brain.

"Vered!" snapped Santon. "Put the crown down. Now! *Do it now!*"

Vered reluctantly obeyed. He grinned sheepishly. "It was so nice to know real power again," he said. "I saw into Porotane. The castle is in turmoil. Baron Theoll and another I do not know vie for power."

"My bet is on the baron. He is a shrewd and ruthless man," said Santon.

"Wait," said Lokenna. "You, Vered, you can use the crown."

"I am of the royal line, but distantly. I use the crown—or it uses me. That is a better way of putting it."

"It uses him," agreed Santon, "even as it destroys him."

"Then it would destroy me, too," said Lokenna with loathing.

"No. You are linked together, you and the crown. See how its color changes when you are near it? You control it, not the other way around."

"It seems that way. I have no sense of it taking me over when I wear it." Lokenna lifted the crown and placed it on her head. The glow turned to a brilliance that dazzled the eye.

"We must go, Majesty. Dalziel Sef or others even worse will seek you out." Santon looked into the gathering blizzard and regretted the need to travel.

"She is not leaving Fron—or me." Bane Pandasso's words cut like a knife. "She belongs here and it's here she stays."

Santon motioned Vered back. The younger man would have driven his blade into Pandasso's fat belly to quell such opposition. Pandasso never realized how close to death he had come, but Lokenna did.

"My husband is right. I belong here." Even as she spoke, her eyes glazed over as if she focused on events far distant. Lokenna shook her head, as if denying what she saw.

"What is it, Majesty? What do you see?" asked Vered.

"Sef. Does he have cracked yellow teeth and a smile so evil that your blood turns to ice?"

Santon and Vered exchanged glances. They had no idea what Sef looked like. Their acquaintance with him came through rumors and stories told to frighten children.

"He is in the pass between Fron and the Lesser Ty." Lokenna turned toward the lower elevations. Santon and Vered followed her movement but saw only white curtains of blowing snow.

"How large a band does he command?" asked Vered. "We might be able to slip past in the storm and get to the Ty. A barge downstream will see us at the castle gates within a week."

"He moves well," she said. "His rebels allow no one past. They sweep upward. They travel quickly in the storm and will be here within the hour."

"We *must* leave," said Santon. "Sef will use the crown as a bargaining lever."

"There is more," said Pandasso. "You hold back. What?"

"He will try to capture Lokenna and force her to his will."

"She can slay with that magical thing," said Pandasso, shuddering as he glanced toward the fallen brigand. The flesh had stopped peeling from the man's bones, but the moaning of his newly released phantom rivalled that of the storm wind.

"If he puts her in a cell and magically binds

the door, he might be able to coerce her," said Vered. "Who knows what his plans are?"

"He wants to imprison me," Lokenna said. "Just as you said, he wants to use me—no, not *me*. He know Lorens no longer has the crown. He wants whoever can use *it*."

"How do you know this?" demanded Pandasso. "Look at me when I speak to you!" He shook his wife harshly, the Demon Crown tipping at an angle on her head. He stopped when he felt the sharp bite of Vered's knife.

"She is queen," he said softly. "We have sworn to protect her."

"As you protected her twin?" Pandasso edged away, glowering.

"Bickering accomplishes nothing," said Birtle Santon. "Sef will be here within the hour, if Lokenna is correct."

"The crown sees with crystal clarity," Vered assured him.

"The Lesser Ty affords us no escape. We must go back into Claymore Pass."

"But Lorens' troops will be between us and the Upper Ty!" protested Vered. "What does that gain us, other than the chance to freeze to death?"

"Yes, other rebels are there," said Lokenna. "Dews Gaemock fights a rebel band dockside on the Ty."

"Wait. Gaemock fights a rebel band? But he leads the rebels!" Santon held his head. The old wound throbbed mightily. He could not keep the elements in this battle from jumbling together and confusing him. The alliances shifted constantly—and all because of desire for the Demon Crown.

"Gaemock and his soldiers go south to the castle, but Sef's army will hinder them," said Lokenna. "There are others in the Yorral Mountains. Other soldiers. Uniformed officers work to re-form their ranks."

"Lorens's men," sighed Vered. "Everywhere we look, new armies pop up to oppose us. How will we ever get back to the castle?"

"The tunnel," said Lokenna. "I see it. North by northeast to Claymore Pass, then to the mountain tunnel. It emerges on the Upper Ty."

Santon groaned. "That tunnel is maintained by Ionia."

"And she and Dalziel Sef have formed an alliance," finished Vered. "Damn. What are we to do?"

"My brother. We must go to my brother. I want to see him face-to-face." Lokenna gestured vaguely toward Claymore Pass. "He is there."

"He'll kill you for the crown. We don't want him on the throne. He's mad!"

Vered's pleading did nothing to convince the woman.

"This is all so much pissing into the wind," spoke up Pandasso. "My wife's not going anywhere. She belongs here with me."

The rattle of metal on metal echoed up from the direction of the lower meadows. Dalziel Sef neared Fron.

"What you want is of no consequence," Santon said. "The war has come to you." He raced for the stables to see if there were more horses he could use. Two other animals looked at him curiously. When Vered joined him, he pointed. "Saddle them, too."

"Both?"

"Lokenna's not likely to leave her husband behind—and he'll be following when we ride out."

"I have no desire to again face Lorens."

"He is her brother and she's not seen him for fourteen years."

"He's crazed," Vered said hotly. "She's got the crown. She can *see* that."

"He's still her twin brother." Santon cinched the saddle as tightly as he could, then kneed the horse so that it exhaled sharply. Two more notches on the strap showed the horse's attempt to throw off saddle and mounted rider.

They led the horses outside. Pandasso and Lokenna stood in the inn's doorway arguing. He started to shake her again, then glance guiltily toward Vered. Pandasso balled his fists and let them dangle futilely at his sides. His need to strike out showed on every corded muscle but he held his temper in check.

"We do not leave Fron. This is our home. It's been good enough for you all these years."

"My brother hides in Claymore Pass," Lokenna said. "He needs my help."

"You didn't even know you had a brother until these two told you!" raged Pandasso.

"They did not lie." Lokenna jerked around, fear growing on her face. "The rebels! They're at the outskirts of Fron. Th-they're burning every house to find me!"

Through the swirling snowstorm rose orange tongues of flame from homes, from barns, from small businesses. The angry shouts of Fron's citizens carried on the wind.

Their death cries followed quickly. Sef gave no quarter as he slaughtered indiscriminately.

"We cannot fight him," said Lokenna. "There are too many—and we cannot sneak past. He has posted sentries to prevent any escape to the Ty."

"Back to Claymore Pass then," grumbled Vered. "I'd thought we were well quit of the place."

"Too many phantoms?" asked Santon, swinging into the saddle and flicking his wrist to bring his battle-ax to hand. He pinioned the reins with the edge of his glass shield and settled down. He did not ride and fight well—his useless left arm made anything more than a trot difficult, but he could manage if it kept them all alive.

"I don't want to add to their ranks," declared Vered.

Lokenna quickly mounted. The trio looked down at Bane Pandasso. Santon hoped that the man would stand his ground and refuse to join them. A battle cry from one of Sef's rebels sent Pandasso scuttling for the horse.

"Let's ride," said Vered.

"Wait," cautioned Lokenna. Her warning came simultaneously with Santon seeing two rebel soldiers emerge from the whiteness ahead of them. Sef had sent a squad to circle Fron to cut off even this risky escape.

"We can fight our way through, if there's not too many of them." Santon looked at the woman. Her face was pinched and drawn. Already the Demon Crown took its toll on her.

"There are only the pair," she said. "But they will slow us until the main force overtakes us."

Vered laughed and spurred his horse forward. The short glass sword gleamed from the light of burning buildings. His sudden charge took the two rebels by surprise. They killed peasants on foot and did not expect a cavalry attack. Vered ducked under one's clumsy swing with a lance. He rode inside and stabbed with his short sword.

Santon heard the glass screeching along metal body armor. Vered had not injured the rebel but had unseated him. The soldier fell heavily, struggling to regain his feet.

Santon used his good hand to loop the reins around the saddle horn, then guided his own horse forward using his powerful knees. A quick jerk brought his ax to hand and his shield into defensive position. He attacked the other rebel.

The rebel's lance danced off Santon's shield. Using all the strength locked in his powerful shoulders, Santon swung his ax—and connected with the rebel's torso. When the ax lodged in rib bone and flesh and did not come free, Santon found himself pulled from his saddle.

He landed on his back, the wind knocked from him.

"They come!" cried Lokenna. "Sef's troops are upon us!"

Cold wind blew across Santon's face and brought back life. He coughed and gasped and got to his knees. His fall had freed his ax but the leather thong around his wrist had cut deeply into his flesh. Blood flowed freely and made the ax handle slippery. Santon let the weapon dangle as he used the shield to lever himself to his feet.

"Did you lose this?" called Vered. The young adventurer tossed down the reins to Santon's horse. "You must be more careful with your belongings. It's hard stealing another in this wasteland!"

Santon heard a deep rumbling as a war cry rose in another's throat. He turned in time to see the man Vered had felled lift a mace. The glass shield deflected the blow. Vered turned his horse about and put spurs viciously to the horse's flanks, causing it to rear and paw the air.

One hoof caught the rebel and sent him crashing back to the ground.

"Are you coming, Santon? Fron is not my idea of a vacation spot." Vered laughed as he fought to regain control of his horse.

Santon mounted and looked back to the inn. Sef's men worked more diligently on setting fire to the buildings than they did in checking those who rushed into the storm to escape.

"My inn," moaned Pandasso. "My life is in that inn!"

"Your life lies ahead," said Santon. He did not look back to see if Pandasso followed. Ahead rode Vered and Lokenna, the Demon Crown glowing brightly and providing a beacon through the blowing snow.

CHAPTER SIX

Kaga'kalb, the Wizard of Storms, stood on the highest tower in his sprawling Castle of the Winds. Before him stretched a rocky mesa that dropped abruptly to the Uvain Plateau. His keen eyes watched the progress of a thunderstorm as it worked its way across the lower elevations. He smiled slightly. Those storms were not of his birthing.

Above his head swirled leaden clouds. *Those* were his. A thin arm raised. Lightning danced from the wizard's fingertips and lit up the tower with an eerie glow. As sudden as natural lightning, a bolt erupted from his hand and blasted asunder the dark clouds.

Rain fell. Kaga'kalb ignored it, secure and dry in a bubble of magic. His spells grew in potency.

His lips moved constantly as newer and more complex magics powered the storm forming.

Thunder rolled off his mesa and down the mountain slopes until all the Uvain echoed. He clapped his hands. The storm brewing exploded in a fury unseen in a score of years. More and more lightning sizzled and popped and exploded, reaching into the dark clouds and building them into a towering thunderhead.

When it seemed that the storm cloud would leave the planet, it began to shift away from the Castle of the Winds. Kaga'kalb guided its progress. He smiled broadly when his storm met the naturally occurring one and devoured it. For a brief instant, he was more powerful than the forces of air and sky.

Kaga'kalb leaned forward, his hands numb with the cold and frost forming on his thinning hair. The intricate spells he had woven collapsed. He watched the normal progression of wind and cloud with awe, as he always did. No matter how good he became, nature bettered his best.

Kaga'kalb straightened, amused with his handiwork now. His arms lifted again and he began to fashion tiny storms that darted about the perimeter of his larger creation. Here and there he formed lightning of varying colors and intensity. The thunderclaps met in counterpoint. He began directing them, moving lightning flashes into eye-searing patterns, sending cloud formations of dark and light into artistic forms. Like a maestro conducting a group of master musicians at the spring fair, Kaga'kalb created a masterpiece of sight and sound and feel.

Desiring more, he began snowstorms in the Yorral Mountains. A toss of his head created a hurricane far out at sea. A small tornado rose and fell, bucking and twisting and lightly touching ground in the far south of Porotane.

Kaga'kalb laughed aloud now. The power flowing through him this day revitalized and gave him fresh purpose.

"They have not learned," he said to himself. His vision was sharp but not good enough to focus halfway across the mountains to where the Demon Crown made its unsettling presence known to him. The magical device caused a darkness that both drew and repelled him.

Kaga'kalb would have the crown, not for his own use—that was not possible—but to keep the petty tyrants from ruining the kingdom. While the pretender Duke Freow had ruled, Alarice had kept the Demon Crown in safety. Freow's death and the search for the true heirs to the throne had upset the balance and disturbed Kaga'kalb's lonely meditations.

Like a black chancre growing within, he felt the crown's repeated misuse as Lorens tried to seize power. Kaga'kalb dared not allow such power to ruin Porotane. He cared nothing for the pretentious nobles or the petty peasants.

The land stretched out as a canvas to his cloudy paintbrush. The air filled with his watery artwork. Movements of storms both grand and small, those were his legacy, his duty, his pride. No wizard had formed the elements more cleverly or better.

Kaga'kalb would not allow fools to ruin land and sky, to render it unsuitable for his work through misuse of the Demon Crown. He had thought it gone forever when Lamost had died and he had convinced Patrin to kidnap the twins.

"I should never have trusted Patrin. The man always was a clumsy oaf. Never could weave a spell properly, even his dream specialties." Kaga'kalb dropped his arms and let the storms run their course. This day's work was not a masterpiece, but it served to soothe him. A more tranquil mind allowed him to work better. Tomorrow.

Or perhaps this night. His most interesting storms were created in the night, with silver moonlight and lightning vying for attention, with cloud patterns turning the world a dull gray and pitch-black, with raindrops giving a silvery sheen to the artificial and a pleasing smell to the natural.

Kaga'kalb pulled down the sleeves of his robe and wiped the frost from his hair. His fingers tingled. He put cupped hands to his mouth and breathed hard to warm them. He was getting old, but he was not yet ready to die. The true masterwork of his life had yet to be created.

"Can't create with the crown disturbing me." He turned and stared at a blank stone wall. Even through the dampening stone he saw the black pit of the Demon Crown. Not for the first time he cursed Kalob and all the demons for the disorder they had brought to this world. Then he cursed Waellkin for so foolishly accepting the crown as reparation.

"What kind of leader was he, anyway?" Kaga'kalb shook his head as he remembered Waellkin. The man had been vain and ambitious. Too ambitious for his own good or the good of Porotane. The lure of the Demon Crown had been too great.

Kaga'kalb shuddered and not from the cold. Lorens had again been stripped of the crown, he saw. But the two points of darkness, one intense and the other weak but growing, told of the disaster preparing to befall Porotane.

"The young fool could not control the crown—it controlled him and now the gateway to hell is open." Kaga'kalb sniffed and continued down the winding stone staircase until he came to a comfortably furnished room. He dropped heavily into a chair in the center of the room and looked around the circular space.

Subtle finger movements activated quiescent spells. Tiny clouds formed along the northeast portion of the wall. They billowed and roiled and turned from puffy white to ominous black. A miniature flash of lightning erupted from the storm he had brought into being.

Kaga'kalb smiled. "Ionia, Ionia, you magnificent slut. You always amaze me. You make a petty alliance with Dalziel Sef and then seek to betray it." The lightning flash closed the distance between the Castle of the Winds and Ionia's fiefdom. Through the magical cloud window Kaga'kalb watched as the noble parlayed with Dews Gaemock's emissary. Before this meeting concluded, Dalziel Sef would be neutralized and Ionia promised full control of Claymore Pass.

Kaga'kalb turned in his chair. The storm cloud spraying rain and snow pellets against the wall moved to follow the direction of his gaze. The Yorral Mountains stretched upward, harsh and rocky-sharp. The wizard studied this scene carefully. Blackness and blackness. The Demon Crown and Lorens. He studied the deeper speck of jet.

"Those two freebooters have found the other twin," he said in amazement. "That can be the only explanation for such power. Damn! Damn Alarice!

Damn them all! They will ruin a perfectly good kingdom. I'm too old to find a new spot to work my magic. Why should I move my lovely Castle of the Winds simply because they destroyed Porotane through ignorance and greed? Pah!"

The scrying spell controlling his cloud window began to weaken—the action of the Demon Crown. Kaga'kalb renewed the spell and changed the view to another portion of the mountains. Gaemock's troops met and defeated Dalziel Sef's at the River Ty. Of Sef's troops, the wizard saw nothing until he found the village of Fron. Sef had retreated back to the Lesser Ty and floated toward Castle Porotane.

"He goes to stir up more trouble. He senses the weakness within the castle walls. Sef is a cunning whoreson, that I'll give him." Kaga'kalb shifted to the castle itself.

The petty posturings and assassinations within had long since ceased to interest him. Only the majesty of storm-building and the symphony of the elements crashing together held his attention long. He cared little if Theoll or Anneshoria triumphed. As long as the Demon Crown rested on a royal brow, neither would sit on the throne.

Kaga'kalb turned back in his chair, strengthening his scrying spell and once more looking to the northeast and fair Ionia. The woman had concluded her treaty with Gaemock's ambassador and had moved on to more amorous conquests. The ambassador was willing.

The Wizard of Storms settled down to watch. He enjoyed storm building more than Ionia's antics—but barely. The fiefdom's ruler had proven inventive and diverting in the past. This time was no exception.

Chapter Seven

"We're lost," moaned Vered. "We'll never find our way in this storm. And worst of all, my clothes are ruined!"

"Quit complaining," called Santon, homing in on his friend's voice. The thick curtain of falling snow deadened sound and made vision beyond a few paces impossible. He urged his straining steed forward and bumped into Vered. Side by side they rode so that they could speak. A long, thin length of twine fastened to Vered's saddle extended tracelessly into the storm and connected with Lokenna's saddle horn.

"I know, I know," said Vered. "*She* can see where we are going. That does me little good—and my horse even less."

"Look on the bright side of this," said Santon. "There's no one to see how scruffy you look."

Vered snorted and sent silvered plumes leaping from his nostrils. The cruel wind caught the twin jets and mingled them with snow and polar air, as if saying that the same would happen to the warm body generating such steam.

"Some bright side. At the moment, I would settle for a warm side." Vered shifted in the saddle and rubbed his rear. "Especially a warm backside."

The twine went limp and dragged the ground. They stopped beside Lokenna and her mount. Another string went off to the right and connected to Bane Pandasso's saddle. The fleeting thought passed through Santon's mind that a careless swing of his ax would doom Pandasso to a frigid death.

"We cannot return to Fron," she said without preamble. "Although Dalziel Sef has personally left, he stationed a score of men to wait for me—for the crown." Lokenna self-consciously touched the glowing band of metal around her head. "I listened in to a meeting he had with his lieutenants. They hope to capture the crown and barter it away to the Wizard of Storms for the throne."

"What does he want with it? Even a spell-thrower of such power cannot wear the crown. Even Alarice couldn't." At the mention of the Glass Warrior, Santon fell silent, lost in thought. The white shroud wrapping him in its cold embrace reminded him of the white-haired woman and her cold undead existence as a phantom.

"What lies ahead?" asked Vered. "I do not want to ride forever in this storm. They will find us standing like ice statues come spring thaw if we do not stop soon and go to shelter."

"We are trapped between two forces," Lokenna said. "I have been watching, listening." Her eyes rolled up in a vain attempt to see the crown on her head. She touched the Demon Crown to reassure herself that it still sat firmly on her brow. "Dews Gaemock had forged a secret alliance with Ionia, one countering Sef's with the woman."

"I have never met this Ionia," said Vered, "but she must be a double-dealing witch."

"Then she's the only double-dealing witch you've not met," said Santon, coming out of his self-pity.

"Neither met nor bedded," Vered finished. He huddled forward, his entire body shaking with the cold. "A touch of warmth would be nice. Even one such as Ionia who would likely drive a knife between my ribs when it suited her."

"Her troops patrol Claymore Pass," said Lokenna, ignoring the men. "Gaemock's troops protect the ways to the River Ty."

"And you said she controlled the tunnel leading through to the Upper Ty," said Vered. "How can we escape the rebels?"

"I must see my brother," said Lokenna. "He can get us out."

"Lorens?" scoffed Santon. "He was a petty wizard at best. Only with the Demon Crown did he have any power."

"He is united with his troops again. Almost twenty soldiers ride behind his banner."

Santon and Vered both cursed. Santon said, "It is death to join ranks with him, Lokenna. He will kill you for the crown. He is demented. The crown has twisted him permanently."

"I see how he is," she said in a distant voice. Santon knew that she *looked* far beyond the range of human vision. What the Demon Crown revealed to her in this new foray he did not know. "If he is not shown the crown, he will not try to kill me."

"She might be right. Nothing but the crown matters to her brother," said Vered.

"There is no reason to let him know that she has ever worn the crown, either," added Santon. "You can hide a ways back while we parlay, then you can follow close as we get to the river."

"Yes, that is a good plan," Lokenna said without any inflection in her voice. Without another word she began riding. Santon and Vered watched her disappear into the whiteness as Pandasso rode up.

"What's going on here?" the heavyset man demanded in his gruff voice. "You been harassing her again?"

Neither man answered. Santon silently rode on when the string attached to his saddle began to draw taunt. He wished he had cut Pandasso's string when the opportunity had afforded itself. But he knew that would have done no good. Using the Demon Crown Lokenna could have located her husband easily.

The thought crossed his mind that she might not bother. Santon pushed that aside. From what he had seen of Lokenna, her loyalty knew no bounds. She might not love Bane Pandasso—Santon wasn't sure how even a mother warthog could—but Lokenna would not abandon him like castoff clothing.

Together they rode into the teeth of the snowstorm, each silent and lost in his thoughts.

* * *

"We cannot fight our way through," insisted Lokenna. "We see only the front of the patrol. Six others back these two."

Santon wiped the melting snow from his eyebrows and glared at the two riders. Dews Gaemock had again shown his cunning in stationing his men. Santon began to have a grudging respect for the man's ability and wished that they were not on opposite sides. Gaemock opposed any of royal blood sitting on the throne—and Santon had promised Alarice that one twin would ascend and rule.

"Birtle, they've sighted us!" Lokenna's cold grip on his shoulder tightened until it felt as if ice talons cut into his flesh.

"Damnation. May all the demons—and Lorens, too—take them!" He slipped from the shallow depression that had given them paltry shelter during their rest and moved quickly downslope. He had to position himself to keep these two from reporting back to the main patrol.

He and Vered worked well together. Past skirmishes had honed their instinct to the point that they knew how the other thought, what the other did, if the other needed help. Santon skidded and slid down a rocky slope, banging his shield and shoulder into the rocks. By the time he regained a precarious footing on a muddy patch, he faced both riders.

"What have we here, Tannay? Could it be the one Lord Dews sent us to fetch?"

Santon worked his glass shield into place and swung the ax up and into his grip. He winced at the pain this simple, practiced motion caused. The chaffed skin on his wrist had not begun to heal.

"Yes, Sergeant, he has the look about him.

Notice the arm. Look Efran himself mentioned that."

Santon frowned. Who was Lord Efran? He had no time to consider. Living took precedence over curiosity. He lowered his head, lifted his shield, and charged, his shining ax blade singing as it moved in an arc parallel with the frozen ground. The nicked edge caught one horse's leg just above the knee. Although he did not sever the limb, Santon heard fragile bones breaking. As the horse neighed in fear and tried to shy away, it threw its rider. All the way to the ground the sergeant of rebels cursed.

Santon had no time to finish off his fallen victim. Tannay attacked. The flat of a sword blade struck him on the side of the head and sent him tumbling. In the glass-slick mud Santon skidded farther than he anticipated. He had to struggle frantically to keep from falling over an embankment and down to a partially frozen stream.

Such determination to remain out of the water should have given an opportunity to Tannay. It didn't. Vered had attacked from the side, driving his sword through the rebel's armpit as he raised his weapon to kill Santon.

"You should be more careful, Santon," Vered told his friend. "That one intended to spit you." He carefully cleaned his glass blade in a snowbank.

"What happened to the other one? The sergeant?" Santon climbed to his feet and looked around. The unseated rebel had vanished into the whiteness around them.

"He has retreated to alert the rest of the rebels," came Lokenna's clear voice.

"Damn! We'll never elude them now."

"There is a way," said Lokenna, her voice as distant as her gaze. "We press on quickly, to the north, toward Ionia's troop bivouac."

"We might be able to confuse them, get them attacking each other!" cried Vered.

"No, they won't. They have established recognition signals."

"You know them?" Santon shared Vered's eagerness to learn this.

"They have exchanged soldiers and the codes are in their battle languages. I can mimic but not duplicate. They would know instantly."

"Why seek out Ionia, then?" asked Santon.

"My brother is near. He heads for the tunnel to the river. We can join him before he begins his fight through Ionia's forces."

"Always Lorens," muttered Vered. "If he sees either of us, we're dead. He *has* to know we stole the crown."

"He . . . he thinks his court jester is responsible. Harhar. He speaks of him with great rancor."

"Lorens would execute us on sight, just to stay in practice," insisted Vered.

"You will have the crown and follow. He will never see you. If you are afraid, Birtle, you can remain with your friend."

"You'd trust us together with the Demon Crown?"

"You did not have to give it to me. This Alarice of whom you speak so highly trusted you. I feel that I can, also."

"We ought to take the crown and throw it into the river—or bury it or somehow get rid of it," said Vered.

"No," snapped Santon. "Alarice said that the

crown was Porotane's only chance for peace, for unification."

"She had not met Lorens when she said those fine things." Vered went to the fallen soldier and began pilfering the body for anything of value. He tossed most aside until he came to a metal tag.

"What do you have?" asked Santon.

"A name tag for identification."

"Lokenna," asked Santon, "how long before the rebels overtake us?"

"At least an hour. Why?"

"There is time," said Vered. He began piling rocks to make a crypt. As he worked, Santon joined him.

From above came Pandasso's querulous voice. "What are you doing? We must ride to save ourselves!"

"We're going to bury him," said Santon. "Vered and I have seen enough phantoms wandering the pass to add to their rank. It won't take long and we know the man's identity."

Lokenna smiled. "You risk your lives to save a fallen enemy from eternal anguish? Indeed, I can trust you two with the crown—and my life."

Vered grumbled as he worked. Under his breath, he said to Santon, "Little does our new queen know that we plied our trade as thieves for many a year."

"Does that matter to a woman able to see any pilfering, no matter how well concealed?" Santon heaved the last rock into place and let Vered lower the slain soldier into the crypt. They began the tedious chore of piling the rocks backs. The burial site would keep out all but the most determined of scavengers.

Vered said the service laying the rebel's phantom to rest. He finished quickly, putting the metal tag on a rock above the grave.

"Rest well," Vered said softly. He vaulted onto his horse and never looked back as he rode off after Lokenna and her husband. Santon brought up the rear, his ears straining for some indication of pursuit by the rebels. Within minutes the softly falling snow blanketed out every sound but the *click-click* of his own horse's hooves on the rocky road through Claymore Pass.

Santon drifted, feeling as if he had entered a land without dimension or form. Whiteness greeted him in every direction. He rode along, nodding off and coming awake with a start, unsure of the passage of time. It might have been an hour or a day when he overtook Lokenna. Vered and Pandasso had already stopped.

"Ahead," she said softly. "Ionia's troops have set up guard posts to block travel. A league beyond lies the tunnel."

"What else?" asked Santon, hearing the edge in her voice.

"What else could it be?" Vered said with some bitterness. "Lorens lies between us and Ionia's troopers."

Santon looked at the Demon Crown perched on Lokenna's brow. The green was still warm and cheery rather than the corrupted color when Lorens had possessed it. Santon was unsure how to take this omen. Lokenna had worn the crown constantly since leaving Fron, but how long had that been? A few days, he was sure. Tiredness and hunger gnawing at his belly robbed him of his normal measures. How long must the woman wear the crown before it began to infect her as it had her twin?

"I feel nothing unusual, Birtle," she said, reading his expression. "I have seen what my brother has become. I've never known him but from all you have said, he was not always like he is now."

"Would that the tyrant were dead," grumbled Vered.

"He is my brother and I truthfully cannot say I remember him. If you say that we were kidnapped as small children—"

"Not that small," cut in Vered. "Alarice said you were five or six at the time. You should remember Lorens."

"I should," Lokenna said, "but I do not. This is all the more reason to see him. So much of my early memory is . . . gone."

"Magic?" suggested Santon.

"Perhaps. If the kidnapping was as brutal as you suggest, I may have simply blocked it out. If so, meeting Lorens might help return this part of my past." Lokenna smiled and Santon felt his coldness vanish in its warmth. "I do remember wandering and being taken in by an elderly couple who lived outside Fron."

"She married me when she was about fifteen," Pandasso added. "We've been happy till now."

Santon watched the gentle smile turn to wry amusement. He saw that Lokenna was content but not happy. With a man like Bane Pandasso how could any whose birth had been noble be happy?

"Let me wear the crown for a few miles more until we approach where my brother prepares his men."

"They are going to attack Ionia's position? In this blizzard?"

Santon couldn't believe it but Lokenna nodded slowly. She turned her horse and got it walking. Santon followed blindly, one direction no different from another.

Santon heard Lorens haranguing his soldiers long before he sighted them. The snow flurries had lightened and gave visibility of almost a hundred yards. For the kind of travelling they had done, this seemed extraordinary. He reined in and waited for Lokenna to decide her course of action.

"There he is," said Vered. "Your brother readies his men for a suicide mission. Without the crown, there is no way he can know how Ionia's troops are deployed."

"He might be crazy but he is not stupid," she said. She shivered. Santon did not think it was from the cold. "He still possesses a modicum of magical power. I see it boiling around—or swarming about his head. It is difficult to describe. He appears to be surrounded by hundreds of black insects."

"Those reflect his ability?"

"Who can say?" Lokenna took off the crown and held it out for Vered to take. He recoiled. "I am sorry," she said. "It is incredible to me that others find this wondrous device so deadly." The woman fumbled in her pack and came out with the glass box and carrying pouch. She put the Demon Crown within, closed the box, and handed it to Vered, who gingerly accepted it.

"I can feel its power, even through the case," he said.

"Resist, friend," urged Santon. "Remember what it can do to you."

"Aye, I remember too well. You need have no

fear on that. There are other matters that concern me more." Vered cleared his throat before continuing. "My queen, it pains me to ask this. What happens if your brother does not greet you with open arms and sibling love?"

"Lorens is incapable of either, but still I must meet him. He suspects another's presence. The Demon Crown is potent and he is hungry for it. If necessary, I can use it as a bargaining point."

"No!" Santon and Vered cried at the same time. Santon motioned his friend to silence. "You dare not, Majesty. Better the crown is destroyed and Alarice's quest dies."

"Along with it all hope for peace in Porotane," added Vered.

"Lorens is cruel and capricious and not in his right mind. All that is true." Lokenna stared down the slope. "There is much I must learn from him. He has worn the crown longer than I. Questions rise in my mind and asking another lessens the danger to me should I be forced to find out the answers by experiment."

Santon shook his head. Lokenna had seemed a simple serving wench in Fron. Such a comment from that woman would have been out of place. But it fit well with the different Lokenna, Queen Lokenna of Porotane, wearer of the Demon Crown.

"You will do nicely on your own, Vered. I trust you. Come along," Lokenna said, a hint of steel in her voice.

Santon and Vered exchanged glances. Vered shrugged and motioned for his friend to ride on. Santon rode slowly, his horse picking out firm spots in the muddy hillside.

Lokenna played a dangerous game, but he had to trust her. She had used the Demon Crown and seen the troop deployments in Claymore Pass. And he could understand her need to speak with her long-lost brother. But what other motives drove her?

He had no idea, and that worried him.

Chapter Eight

Birtle Santon looked over his shoulder to see if Vered watched, also. He did not. The younger man had wasted no time in finding cover. Santon hoped that his friend withstood the lure of the crown. The last time Vered had worn it, he had been drawn into a maelstrom from which return had been difficult—and without Santon helping, Vered would have perished.

The Demon Crown gave immense power. It also extracted a great penalty from anyone wearing it.

"Let me do the talking," said Lokenna.

"This isn't right and proper," her husband protested. "I speak for the family."

"She is queen. She speaks for the kingdom," said Santon.

"Queen," sneered Pandasso. "There you go

calling my Lokenna queen again. What does it mean? She puts on that fancy shining green crown and *that* makes her high royalty? Don't go giving me any of that. You been lying to me and her. I don't know what your scheme is, you petty cutpurse, but—"

"Silence." Lokenna's tone cut off her husband's tirade. Pandasso stared at her openmouthed with astonishment.

To the guard posted at the perimeter of the camp, Lokenna called, "We seek a truce. We have come to parlay with Lorens."

"Parlay?" came the skeptical reply to her request. "Who makes such a claim?"

"Let Lorens decide. I refuse to bandy words with a commoner."

The way she spoke startled Santon. Lokenna fell into the role of a monarch quickly. Too quickly, for his taste. Had the Demon Crown infected her as it already had her brother?

"Who causes such an uproar when quiet is needed?" Lorens came out of a crude tent and stood, hands on hips, glaring up at Lokenna.

All around the trio of riders the would-be king's soldiers fingered their weapons, unsure of what to do. But Santon saw—*felt*—that Lokenna and her brother were two poles of an immense energy. The others felt it, too, and this added to their uncertainty.

"Who are you?" asked Lorens. His face lost the rigidity and turned to a constantly flowing mass of conflicting emotion. Santon marvelled at the way Lorens' eyes finally bugged out and he exclaimed, "Sister! You are my sister! I feel the power in you!"

"I feel no kinship with you," Lokenna said

coldly. She sat stiffly in her saddle. "However, it seems that our paths have crossed and we travel side by side for a time."

"Kill her!" Lorens' face underwent another transformation, this time to stark hatred.

"Do so and you'll never recover the Demon Crown." Lokenna's voice was pitched so low that only Lorens and Santon heard. "What would you be then, brother? A nothing, as you are now." Lokenna spat. Beside her Pandasso protested this unladylike behavior. Santon silenced the woman's husband with a prod to the ribs with the edge of his shield.

"You have it?" Cunning came into Lorens' face, making him appear feral. "Yes, of course you do. You could never have found me this easily without it."

Lorens signalled his loyal guardsmen to close in. Santon allowed the soldiers to disarm him. Fighting a full score of them would accomplish nothing but a quick death—and he still thought that Lokenna had the upper hand.

"Do you think me foolish enough to ride into your camp with it? Hardly, brother. It seems that our parents birthed only one idiot—you."

Lorens held his madness in check through urgent need to again assume the supreme power offered by the Demon Crown. "Where is it? My torturers can make you tell."

"My name is Lokenna. And it will do you no good trying to force information from me that I cannot divulge. Another has the crown."

"Harhar!"

"You mean Lord Efran?" Lokenna asked. "Perhaps he has it. But that hardly seems likely, does it, brother? We must return to the castle. By the time we arrive, the crown will also be there. Other than this, I can tell you nothing about the crown's location."

"Who has it? If not Harhar, then it must be—"

"Lorens." Lokenna's voice cracked like a whip. "We share common goals at the moment. Both of us wish to return unharmed to the castle. To do so requires us to sneak past Ionia's troops. I know where they are posted."

"You've used the crown!"

"I have," she admitted. "Many days ago."

"You lie!" Spittle ran from the corners of Lorens' mouth. A lieutenant supported his liege. Santon saw how easily won over these fighting men would be. They had seen nothing but madness from their leader. Lokenna offered more than sanity—she offered safety and return to the protection granted by the castle walls.

"Officer," Lokenna said briskly. "Ionia has twelve men posted in the following locations. We must fight through her troops, but this is the weak spot."

"Yes, milady, it is," agreed the lieutenant, staring at the diagram Lokenna scratched in the snow with her boot. "What good does it do us to win through to the tunnel? Lady Ionia has hundreds of soldiers camped inside."

"Rumors, or lies. Take your pick. She is stretched thin. Her farmers refuse to give up their sons to be soldiers on winter patrol in Claymore Pass. We get past these paltry troops and the tunnel lies open before us."

"Why did you not bypass them and ignore us?" the lieutenant asked.

"She is a fool, that's why!" shouted Lorens.

"Consider," spoke up Santon. "For us to evade Ionia's guard positions is impossible, and we are too few to fight through. Together we *can* get to the tunnel."

"You are *my* officer," cried Lorens. "You will obey *me!*"

"Yes, Majesty." The office bowed low but his eyes remained on Lokenna and her serene acceptance of the situation. Santon knew that they had made an ally. The officer wanted only for his men to survive. Lokenna offered that and Lorens did not.

Lorens wiped the spittle from his lips and calmed. "Where is this weakness in the enemy line?"

Lokenna silently pointed out the posts once more, then erased it all with a quick stamping of her foot. She spun and mounted, not waiting to see if Lorens approved.

The former king did not but Santon did. Lokenna had handled both her brother and the situation with the skill of a diplomat. She had given away nothing, gotten much, and forged an alliance that would get them through the rebel lines. Santon hoped that Vered would be able to slip through the confusion unnoticed. Without him and the Demon Crown, Lokenna would find herself in dire straits at Castle Porotane.

"These posts. How many soldiers man each one?" asked the officer.

Lokenna quietly told him. Together they plotted, then the soldier nodded briskly and rode off to prepare his troops for battle.

"Your brother doesn't like you usurping his power. He might be crazy but he is not stupid. He knows what is going on," said Santon. Even as he spoke he watched Lokenna's husband. Bane Pandasso did not accept his wife's newfound power easily, either. Pandasso lacked Lorens' brilliance or magical ability and had nothing but jealousy to fuel him. That jealousy smoldering within Pandasso's breast would one day burst into flame.

Santon wasn't sure if Lorens' madness wasn't preferable—and safer.

They rode forward slowly, hugging one steep wall of rock until Lokenna lifted her hand as a signal for attack. Then all pretense of caution vanished. The lieutenant urged his troops on in a frontal assault on a small guard post positioned halfway up a gravel-strewn slope. The soldiers' horses slipped and stumbled but enough got through to overwhelm the post. Santon held back, watching carefully for sign that supporting troops came to regain the post.

"There!" he called to Lokenna. "One of them is escaping!" He didn't wait for Lorens' soldiers to give chase to the fleeing guard. Santon put his heels to his horse's flanks and sent the animal surging forward. He closed the distance between them quickly—almost too quickly.

The wily guard spun and put the butt end of his lance to the ground, thinking to impale Santon as he rode by. Santon swung the glass shield over and protected his right side. The steel tip of the lance bounded off the rounded surface and left him unharmed.

The impact also unseated him.

Hitting the ground would have knocked the breath from his lungs if he hadn't been screaming the entire distance from saddle to soil. Santon rolled and used his shield as a support to get to his feet. He immediately found strong arms circling him, carrying his backward, threatening to crush him.

Santon tried to get his ax into play. A powerful hand gripped his wrist. Santon's withered left arm proved no match for his opponent's right hand. Eye to eye they fought for supremacy.

If it had been a battle only of strength, Birtle Santon would have lost to his stronger, younger opponent. But over the years he had been in similar situations and knew brute strength was not the only way of winning.

Their faces pressed together, Santon strained to gain another fraction of an inch. When an ear came within reach of his mouth, he bit down hard. Gristle filled his mouth. The guardsman let out an agonized scream and momentarily faltered in his attack.

Blood flowing from his torn ear, the guardsman stumbled back half a pace. Santon judged distance and swung his shield. The edge caught the guard under the chin and knocked the man's head back. This put another pace between them. Santon's ax came to hand. The silvered downward arc ended in the guardsman's collarbone.

The impact rocked Santon—and killed his foe.

"Are you all right?" came Lokenna's worried call.

"Killing like this leaves a bad taste in my mouth." Santon spat again and wiped his lips on his sleeve. He needed a full quart of ale to wash away the taste. He wished Ionia would teach her troops simple hygiene like washing their ears.

"We must hurry. You have saved us from immediate battle with their reinforcements. It will take several minutes before they realize anything is awry," said Lokenna.

Santon got into the saddle but paused to look behind.

"I haven't seen Vered," the woman said softly. "We must trust to his skill."

"His skill isn't in question. He might beat us to the castle. It's that damned crown that worries me."

"It affects him as it did Lorens?" she asked, gazing at her demented brother. Lorens issued conflicting commands ignored by both officers and soldiers as they prepared to fight their way to the tunnel.

"Vered didn't wear it as long, but the effect was similar. He would have been driven crazy by the images crashing in on him."

"You must will them to slow and accept only the ones you desire," said Lokenna. "It . . . I don't know how I knew to do it. I just did. It surprises me that others don't have similar skill."

"Hurry, Majesty," cried the lieutenant. Santon wasn't sure to whom the officer called. Lorens thought it was to him and Lokenna didn't care. They rode quickly down a narrow ravine that opened onto a broad flood plain.

Deep canyons had been cut in the rock by spring runoff. Snowbanks piled head-high on either side of the plain turned it into an icy temple. Santon wanted nothing more than to worship within the dark circle he spied in the mountainside.

"The tunnel!"

"Aye, it is," said Pandasso, licking his lips apprehensively. "What do we want to go in there for? It looks dangerous."

"It's more dangerous staying here and waiting for Ionia to find that we've overrun a guard post."

"I don't like close places. I think me and Lokenna will go back to Fron. The brigands have left. We can rebuild the inn and everything will be fine again."

"You'll end up dead before you've ridden a single hour. Look." Santon pointed to steam rising from just inside the mouth of the tunnel.

"Soldiers," muttered Pandasso. "All the more reason to go home and forget this crazy scheme."

"Too late, too late," roared Santon. He swung his ax into his grip and kicked hard at his horse's sides. He led the assault directly into the tunnel, not knowing if the others followed. Santon saw no other course. If they hesitated now, they were lost. An all-out attack might take the guards posted within the tunnel by surprise, even if they outnumbered their attackers.

Santon's horse's hooves clattered on hard rock flooring and sent sparks skittering into the darkness. Santon's charge carried him deeper into the blackness, effectively blinding him until his eyes adjusted to the dimness. His ax swung to and fro but found no target. He reined back to wait for the others to catch up with him.

The bright circle of the tunnel mouth suddenly filled with soldiers—Lorens' soldiers!

"This way!" called out Santon. "There aren't any defenders."

He blinked and peered into the darkness, wondering at the source of the steam he had seen rising from the tunnel. In the distance he saw white, gauzy veils drifting along. Polar-cold fingers gripped at his heart. He hadn't seen steam or smoke from cooking fires; he had seen phantoms.

How many had died within these treacherous, rocky confines and had gone unburied? Santon counted no fewer than ten phantoms and more came and went untallied.

"Please help me," came one plaintive's cry. "My body is somewhere near. I know it. It must be . . ."

Santon did not answer. Phantoms could not detect their own corpses; they were souls cut adrift and lost between heaven and hell. Contact with those still living proved possible but they could not communicate with other phantoms. Santon had done his part in finding bodies and giving them the proper burial to put the shade to rest, but he dared not make that effort now.

Cocking his head to one side he heard the pounding of hooves—more hooves than Lorens' troops accounted for.

"Pursuit! Ionia sends her guardsmen after us!" He reined his horse around and plunged into the inky blackness, praying that Ionia had not littered her commerce tunnel with pits or booby traps.

The level floor proved slippery from seepage but otherwise safe. Still, Santon pulled back and let the others catch up with him. He strained to see if the guardsmen entered after them of if they considered pursuit futile. If they followed, Vered might never be able to get by them. They would form a plug that would effectively stopper him on the wrong side of the tunnel.

If that happened, the pressure to use the Demon Crown to see a way past would be overwhelming.

"Are they pursuing?" Santon asked of the lieutenant.

"They are moving slower but yes, they come after us." The officer frowned as he peered at Santon. The only illumination afforded them came from the feeble light of drifting phantoms. "You do not want them in the tunnel. Why?"

"I . . . Lokenna's husband is afraid of tight spaces. He likes to be able to see a way out." The lie came slowly to Santon. He did not prevaricate as easily as Vered. This sounded flat and both he and the lieutenant knew for what it was.

"Very well. We can send a small squad back to do what they can."

"Let me go with them."

"Lorens' orders are to see you and the woman through to the other end of the tunnel. I'll tend to this personally."

Santon watched the officer wheel around and go to the three nearest soldiers. The four rode back to do battle. Santon hoped that they succeeded in driving Ionia's men out of the tunnel. If they failed, Vered would never be able to get through. Santon wondered why Ionia had not placed a stronger guard at the tunnel mouth—but he knew she would after this.

"Come, we must hurry. There will be barges at the docks soon," said Lokenna.

"You saw this—before?"

"Yes. Cargo had gone upriver. The sudden winter storms prevented heavy loading on the return trip. We can get passage."

"And then?"

"Then we reach Castle Porotane and have other matters to cope with."

"How's your husband holding up?" Santon looked up and saw the arched vault of the tunnel coming lower and lower as they rode. The rocky roof soon brushed the top of his head, forcing him to ride hunched over. If it came any lower, he would have to dismount and lead his horse.

"Bane was trapped in a cave when he was a young boy. This must be frightening for him." Lokenna spoke in an offhand manner, no emotion tingeing her words. Santon wondered, not for the first time, how loyal she was to her husband. Love seemed to be lacking on both their parts; was devotion enough to hold Lokenna to him?

Santon didn't think it was, not when she had tasted the power granted by the Demon Crown.

Santon rode along in silence, trying not to hear the phantoms' wails or the steel-on-steel clanking from behind.

CHAPTER NINE

"I can't take more of this. I can't!" Bane Pandasso screamed and charged ahead wildly, leaving his protesting horse behind. Birtle Santon had seen the tension mounting in the man for the past mile. Pandasso's shoulders had hunched far more than needed to get through the low-ceilinged tunnel; it appeared that the innkeeper carried the weight of the entire mountain on his back.

The lieutenant, carrying a guttering torch that produced more noxious fumes than light, started after him. Lokenna held the officer back. "Let him go," she said. "He isn't going to run far, nor is he likely to hurt himself."

"Not in this tunnel," grumbled the lieutenant. "There's nothing in here except those bedamned phantoms."

Santon wiped the back of his neck to get off a

cold droplet of water that had dripped from above. Ahead he heard Pandasso running as if a horde of demons chased after him. He felt sorry for the man. Fearing tight spaces had to tell on his courage, and who was without some fear, but Santon scorned the man more. Others in the tiny band obviously disliked the low roof and tight fits through the tunnel with their horses, but they controlled themselves. Such weakness on Pandasso's part only shamed Lokenna.

Or so it seemed to Santon.

He paused and pressed his ear to the cold rock wall to detect any vibrations in the tunnel behind. The lieutenant had driven out Ionia's guard with a single frontal attack. Had this given enough opportunity for Vered to enter the tunnel? He could not tell. Between the noises made by the restless horses and the frightened, running Bane Pandasso, all hope of hearing a solitary man following vanished.

Without Vered, his and Lokenna's position became untenable when they reached the castle. Santon heaved a deep sigh and doggedly walked on. He estimated his chances for driving a dagger into Lorens' corrupted heart and did not like the odds for escape afterward. The mad king cavorted and bounced around like a child's toy, appearing boneless at times and then going stiff like a stone statue come to life.

The more Lokenna attempted to talk with her brother, the more Lorens spurned her.

Santon did not think there would be such difficulty in killing Lorens—except for the occasional cunning glint he caught in the wizard-king's eye. It was as if Lorens put on a small drama to keep the troops amused while his agile mind worked on, considering matters great and small. Santon ignored the antics. The problem Santon faced was the loyalty of Lorens's soldiers. They had gone through much with their king in the Yorral Mountains. Did this bond them strongly enough or could they be swayed to Lokenna's side?

Santon had no easy answer for that. In the officer he saw a chance for shifting allegiance to Lokenna. The lesser ranks might follow their lieutenant, who was personable and fair as a commander. Santon shook his head and gave up such speculation as a waste of time.

"It would not work," came Lokenna's soft voice. Santon jumped at the unexpected answer to a question he had not given voice to. The woman laughed gently. "No, I do not pry into your mind using some arcane magic spell. Your intentions are obvious to everyone."

"He is your brother. I meant you no disrespect."

"No disrespect to me or death to him." Lokenna's eyes fixed on her brother. Lorens dangled over the back of his horse, pretending to be a sack of flour. "Look at him. Child or madman? Who can say?"

"Madman. The Demon Crown did it to him."

"You've known him longer than anyone else here. I must believe you."

"Have you learned what you need from him?"

"No. He is careful when he speaks of the crown, not revealing enough to fill in the gaps in my knowledge. Lorens is also far more adroit a wizard than he lets on. The crown has brought out skills even his master did not possess."

"Patrin was the most powerful wizard in the kingdom, or so said Alarice."

"Alarice," mused Lokenna. "That is a name my brother refuses to mention. I have pointedly inquired after her and he turns the question to an insult."

"She died so that he could ascend the throne." Santon did not try to keep the bitterness from his voice.

"You loved her," stated Lokenna. "I see the way you examine each phantom as we pass. Do you think to find her among these poor abandoned souls?"

"She is—was—a wizard in her own right. She is not bound to the area where she died like these wights. She has spoken to me several times."

"I would like to meet her, even if it is only a dim shadow of her former self. There is so much I need to know that Lorens will not speak about." With a sudden animation, Lokenna asked, "What do you know of the Wizard of Storms?"

"Nothing more than that Alarice feared him—no, wait. Fear is too strong. She respected him but also strongly disapproved."

"He brings the storms to the mountains. These are not naturally occurring—you can sense that, can't you?"

Santon shook his head. "I guessed it."

"Magic," Lokenna sighed. "There is so much to learn and so little time."

Santon stopped and stared. Outlined in an arch of twilight stood Bane Pandasso. Tears of joy ran down the man's cheeks. He threw himself to the ground and dug his fingers into the rocky soil. "We have come to the end of Ionia's tunnel," said Santon.

"So it seems. The worst of the journey lies ahead of us," said Lokenna. She held her head up high and walked on, looking more like a queen by the instant.

"Too much. Too high," insisted Santon as he bargained for the use of the river barge.

"Then stay and freeze off your arses." The bargemaster stopped and inclined his head slightly in Lokenna's direction. "No offense meant to you, milady."

"So you think to insult the rest of us. Is that it?" demanded Santon, enjoying the haggling. Life pumped through his tired body and the argument gave him purpose once more. Lorens and the soldiers held back and let him ply his skills against those of the river man.

Santon took the bargemaster by the arm and led him to the side of the craft. "The soldiers I travel with—you know them?" The bargemaster shook his head. "They are King Lorens' personal guard."

The grizzled man laughed out loud. "You want me to think that *he* is our king? That's a rich one!" The bargemaster pointed at Lorens, then began to laugh even harder until tears ran down his ruddy cheeks.

"Do you deny we could seize this barge by force of arms?"

"You threaten me? Me? That's even funnier. I have Lord Dews' personal guarantee of safe passage."

"Indeed? Show it to me."

"Right here it is." The bargemaster fumbled beneath his heavy coat and pulled out a tattered slip of paper. He held it up for Santon to scan. "You see? I have the protection of Lord Dews himself."

"Alas, I do not see him or his sword here to aid you." Santon swung his shield around and caught the bargemaster's arm just above the elbow. The man yelped in pain as his arm went numb. With a deft grab, Santon took the pass.

"Here now, you can't do this!"

Santon swung the shield around once more, this time connecting just under the man's chin. The bargemaster's head snapped backward as he tumbled into the icy River Ty. He came to the surface sputtering and gasping for air.

"Best get into dry clothing before you catch your death," Santon said, unsmiling. Seeing the former bargemaster paddling for the far shore, Santon turned and signalled Lokenna and the others. "My liege, the craft is ours for the taking."

Santon showed the rebel pass to Lokenna, who handed it over to the lieutenant. She said, "Do with this what you must."

"Get us to the castle. Do it now, now, yes, do it now!" Lorens cut capers like a jester, trying a handspring that failed and left him upside-down against the rude shelter in the aft of the barge. Santon would have laughed save for the momentary impression of ugly black insects coming from Lorens's mouth. He remembered what Lokenna had said about her brother—darkness and evil surrounded him.

The expression on the king's face also bespoke of death. His lips moved and a spell formed.

"Brother, stop it!" snapped Lokenna. The sense of dread faded as Lorens righted himself and motioned imperiously to the officer and the few men remaining in his personal guard. They had already begun leading the horses aboard.

"You deny me my simple pleasures, sister. Do

not make that mistake again." His dark eyes blazed with hatred. Hardened though he was, Birtle Santon found himself moving away from the madman.

"Cast off the mooring lines," came the lieutenant's command. The movement of the barge into the sluggish flow of the river broke the tension. Lorens spun smartly and vanished into the bargemaster's rude quarters as his men started the tedious work of poling along.

The craft moved slowly at first, then gained speed as it neared the center of the current. Occasional ice floes banged hard against the hull. Each one startled Santon.

"You are no river man," said the lieutenant, laughing at his discomfort. "I grew up here. Makes me feel alive."

"Do you regret leaving to join the king's guard?" asked Lokenna.

"Of course. But the rebels must be put down." The lieutenant touched the rebel pass in his pocket. "Someone of royal blood must reign in Porotane." He issued a few more commands to keep the craft on a straight course in the flow, then asked Lokenna, "Is it true? Are you his sister? There is so little resemblance."

"We are twins." Lokenna stared at the distant, passing shoreline. "It is difficult for me to believe we are related, yet I know it is true. Even more than your word, Birtle," she added.

"She is a wizard, too?" the officer asked of Santon. Santon's voice failed him. All he could do was nod. The Demon Crown had awakened much in Lokenna—and it continued to grow. He looked to the land in hope of sighting Vered.

The young adventurer was nowhere to be

seen. Santon didn't know if this was for the good or not.

"Lieutenant," came an aggrieved cry from the stern. "There is a chain across the river ahead of us. Men with bows are positioned on either shore to keep us from cutting the barricade."

"Strip off your uniform insignia," the lieutenant ordered, obeying his own command. He heaved the betraying rank into the river, where it vanished tracelessly into a cold, watery grave. "We are filthy enough to hide the fact that the uniforms are of the same cut and color. Most of you, stay in the hold."

A tall man with a long red banner signalled them from the near shore. Santon waited anxiously as the lieutenant expertly guided the barge over, his soldiers poling slowly.

"Good day to you, Bargemaster," came the greeting. "You don't look to be laden with cargo this trip."

"We need drydocking. Sprung a leak in the hold, we did. Damn boat's going down on us slow," the lieutenant shouted back.

"You got the proper papers?"

The officer held up the pass issued by the rebel leader. Santon held his breath. He saw from the size of the garrison on the bank and the heavy stone fortifications that stretched around the river's bend that fighting their way free would be impossible. They had to bluff—and avoid a search.

"Can't see it from here. Pole closer." Behind the rebel moved archers. Santon saw one dip the arrow tip in pitch and wait beside a firepot. A single flaming arrow could send them to the bottom of the river.

"We can't get past the chain without using the

pass," the lieutenant said. "We'll be fine. Wait and see."

Two of his men worked a pole back and forth along the riverward side of the barge, complaining as they worked. When the barge was close enough, the lieutenant jumped across to the bank with the pass.

Santon waited impatiently, his barrel chest ready to explode from holding his breath. He panted harshly when the officer returned and signalled for his men to pole them back into the river.

"The pass was good?" asked Santon.

The lieutenant shook his head. "He never looked at it." The officer rubbed thumb and forefinger together to show what had convinced the rebel to let them pass.

Santon watched as the massive chain was pulled back from the river to let them by. He waved to one rebel on the shore, who waved back. The rebels weren't so much different, he decided.

How could the kingdom be any worse off in Dews Gaemock's hands when bribery still worked its own magic?

"There are the royal docks," said Santon, not sure if he was happy to see them. The barge had listed in a storm two days prior and the rocking motion had given him a continual case of seasickness. Even the lieutenant who professed to have been raised on the river had not fared well. Only Lokenna appeared untouched by the motion. But considerations other than his personal comfort nagged at him.

"You fear for me," said Lokenna, leaning against a thin pole and staring at the castle rising in the distance.

"I fear for my own life, too. Now that we have arrived, Lorens can tap into new reserves of troops. They still remember him as king, after all. Even without the crown, he is more formidable here than in the Yorral Mountains."

"What has happened in Castle Porotane in his absence?" Lokenna asked. Santon wasn't sure if she spoke to him or merely put voice to her inner thoughts. Changing subject abruptly, she said, "I remember it. The details aren't mine yet, but I remember the castle, but not in winter. In spring, with greenery surrounding the castle. An arbor?"

"Brambles for defense," supplied Santon.

"That the demon-damned place you been yearning for?" asked Pandasso. He had lost weight from his own bout with river sickness. Santon still considered him to be a pig.

"Her castle," Santon said pointedly. "It belongs to the ruler of Porotane."

"She's no ruler. She's my wife." Pandasso's tone had changed during the trip, though. He had seen Lokenna grow in stature until her regal bearing matched that of the proudest monarch. His words carried less belligerence even if he still protested the obvious.

"There is fighting on the shore," said Lokenna, interrupting the pointless squabble. "Rebels attack the royalist troops."

Santon did not need the woman to tell him this. The ragtag rabble attacking the uniformed ranks could be comprised only of rebels. They fought with the unity of a company, yet had the look of poor farmers and merchants. He found himself shaking his head in amazement. The rebels parted the approaching cavalry and began hacking the soldiers to bloody ribbons. For all their lack of military precision and beauty, they fought valiantly and well—and their officers knew tactics.

"We must make our own way to the castle," said the lieutenant. "We can expect no help from them. The fools! They ran into a trap as if they were led by the greenest recruit."

"They might be. Who can say what has—" Santon fell silent abruptly when he saw Lorens lightly jump from the barge to the dock. The man's eyes had glazed over. He held his arms in front of him as if blind and he had to feel his way along an unknown corridor. But the dancing sparks at his fingertips told of immense magic powers beyond an ordinary mortal's control.

"I feel it. The blackness rises within him," said Lokenna, her eyes clamped tightly shut. "How does he tolerate it? It . . . it makes my skin ripple with its evil."

The explosion knocked over those on the barge. Santon shook his head, trying to clear away the ringing in his ears. His vision had filled with dancing yellow and blue dots that only slowly faded. When his keen sight returned, his stomach turned over and over worse than it had during his bout of seasickness.

Wars had washed past him. He had seen destruction so bad that it dulled his mind. But this? Never had Birtle Santon seen such destruction of life. He wanted to vomit.

Lorens' spell had exploded *within* each of the rebel soldiers. As if a huge taloned beast had clawed its way free, their bellies and chests were left in mutilated, bloody strips. The snow-dusted landscape had turned an ugly red from their life's blood. Here and there spots sizzled as the superheated fluid cooled.

"There," said Lorens with some satisfaction. "That will keep the rebels in their place."

Santon found it difficult to stand. Only Lokenna's aid made it possible for his rubbery legs to begin walking. When they reached the dock, he waved her off, preferring to be on his own. How could such a fiend possess so much power?

Lorens had slain with the pass of his hand—and showed no remorse at the ghastly deaths. He acted as if he had stepped on a *mor*roach and nothing more.

The ambushed soldiers re-formed their ranks. Santon looked around the countryside, hoping to see Vered. Lokenna needed the Demon Crown to counter such immense power on her brother's part.

Santon walked, but he did not see his friend. Every step closer to the castle caused dread to mount that much more.

"The castle," Lorens said with gusto. "And it is mine! I rule with absolute power within its walls. Soon enough, that power will enfold the entire kingdom!"

Darkness had fallen. Watchfires along the battlements sputtered and sent sparks and smoke into the clean, clean air. They had not encountered any more rebels on their march from the docks, but many spies had been eliminated. Lorens licked his lips at the thought of those fools sending small children to spy on him.

He cared naught if they were grown or babes in arms. Traitors were traitors and he would kill them all!

If only he had the Demon Crown . . .

His hard eyes turned back to the castle walls. Fear leaped and died inside him when he thought of what he might find. Archbishop Nosto had been so powerful. But what of Theoll? The small baron had coveted the throne. And others? Lorens had spied on dozens of plots and counterplots when he had worn the Demon Crown.

The crown. He needed it now!"

"Majesty?" came a timorous voice. For an instant Lorens thought the voices that sometimes spoke within his head had returned. Then he realized it was only the whoreson married to his sister.

"Yes, my dear brother-in-law," he said with mock civility. Lorens pondered the spell that would remove this odious piece of garbage. Patrin had not taught him many useful spells, but that small grounding in magic had served him well enough. What he had not been taught by his master, he had learned wearing the crown.

Where was that wondrous magical device? Torturing Lokenna might be enough, but he doubted it. She spoke with the ring of truth in her voice when she said she did not know where the golden crown was—but could recover it.

"King Lorens?" Pandasso licked dried lips and rubbed his pudgy hands together nervously, as if to cleanse them of guilt. "We're almost at the castle, aren't we?"

Lorens held back his acid retort. Of course they were at the castle. Any fool could see it rising before them.

"Yes. What can I do for you?" he asked, his voice silken.

"Majesty, you see, it's like this. Between me

and Lokenna, it was all just as good as fresh cream until those two showed up with that damned crown."

Lorens said nothing. New schemes formed. He might have found an unexpected ally in this oaf. Torture might not be required, after all.

"I want things to be like they was between us. I'm a good husband." Pandasso shuffled his feet and averted his eyes. Lorens knew the man lied. "I just want us to go back to Fron and forget all this. I don't need to go into the castle—and my wife's no queen."

"True," Lorens said. "But there are problems with restoring your former life."

"The rebels burned the town and my inn with it."

"The crown, dammit," flared Lorens. He quieted down and went on, carefully choosing his words with studied calm. "With the crown, I could aid you immensely."

"I saw what you did this afternoon. The rebels . . ." Pandasso's voice trailed off.

"The King of Porotane has powers far beyond those granted by the Demon Crown." Even as he spoke, coldness gripped Lorens' innards. The power came and went, as did the voices. Now he felt hollow and alone—and weak. So weak! No matter how superior he was to this ignorant peasant, he was deathly alone and vulnerable.

"What if I told you how to get this crown back? What would that mean to me? To me and Lokenna?"

"My sister is stubborn, but I am gracious in my rewards. The crown is hardly necessary, but it is a symbol of power in Porotane." Lorens tried to arc sparks between his fingers to impress Pandasso. He hastily hid his hands under his cloak when nothing happened.

"You give me a new pub and some money—and Lokenna back—and I'll tell you how she intends to get the crown."

"It has something to do with the missing thief, does it not?" Pandasso jumped as if stuck with a needle. Lorens laughed at his simplemindedness. "Of course it does. Why else would one accompany us and never mention the other?"

"She's to meet this Vered outside the castle. He was following us all the way from the Yorral Mountains."

"How is she to signal him?"

"They don't know I know, but I overheard them talking."

"Yes, yes." Lorens stilled his need to recover the crown. He laid a hand on Pandasso's arm. "It's what Lokenna needs, even if she does not realize it. You see more clearly than she does in this. What is the signal?"

Bane Pandasso told him.

CHAPTER TEN

"The situation is critical, Baron." Commander of the guard Squann did not have to make this report to Theoll. The small noble had eyes. All he needed to do was gaze from the uppermost battlements at the gathering horde of rebels to know the peril. They came like flies to decaying meat. Getting rid of them would be harder than merely brushing them off.

"Captain, I appreciate your concern about external matters. What concerns me more is internal—and political. Lady Anneshoria grows bolder by the day."

"She has many believing her."

Theoll wondered if Squann played some duplicitous game. The captain had rushed from Anneshoria's arms to report that the woman plotted against him—but had the officer known that Theoll watched his every movement? Were Anneshoria and Squann engaged in triple-dealing?

In Castle Porotane those who merely worked plots within plots were novices—and usually perished for their inexperience. What game did Squann really play and whose pawn was he?

"She awaits you at dawn. The meeting is set so that the other nobles will appear minutes after you have been killed."

"What?" Theoll jerked his attention back from the ramifications of a traitorous guard commander to what the man really said about the plot. "Oh, yes, yes. I know this. I will not let her do away with me that easily."

"It might prove an excellent opportunity to remove Anneshoria," suggested Squann.

Again Theoll worried. Squann shared the woman's bed when she had pointedly refused such an offer from him. And he was regent king! That Squann played both sides to his own advantage, Theoll never doubted. What did he gain? What could Theoll lose?

"The rebels have infiltrated the castle," said Theoll.

"Who, Baron? Give me their names and I will have them beheaded!"

"Nonsense. We can use them. Anneshoria . . . has contacted them. She is a traitor in our ranks." Theoll watched slow realization dawn on the captain's face. The officer brightened at this lie that might rid the castle of Anneshoria permanently and with no chance of reprisal from her supporters.

"I had heard such rumors. I can find facts to verify this."

"Of course you can. Go and do so." Theoll dismissed Squann with a wave of his hand but called out before the captain had left, "A moment, Captain. Who commands the rebel forces at this moment?"

"We have been unable to find out, but from the deployment and tactics, I believe Dalziel Sef faces us. There are none of the subtleties Gaemock always employed."

"What has happened to Gaemock?" Theoll wondered aloud. "It is no matter. Let the rebels diminish their own rank. We have problems of our own with traitors, don't we, Captain Squann?"

"I'll look into it immediately, Baron."

Squann had barely vanished when Theoll sprang up from his paper-strewn desk and went to the ward spell–guarded box behind the tapestry. For the hundredth time, he ran his fingers over the oak lid. It had been tampered with, he saw. A slow smile crossed his thin lips. Anneshoria knew what lay within—and it was all part of his own trap to snare her. The diminutive baron did not care if Squann allied himself with Anneshoria or not.

What had to be done would be accomplished by his own hand.

Theoll spun and went to the far wall. His dagger scraped away mortar to reveal a tiny lever. Prying it free with his dagger tip produced a grating sound. Part of the wall pulled back to reveal a small, dark tube leading into the depths of the castle. Theoll travelled the secret passages of the castle but had only once used this crawlway. It did not pay to advertise all he knew.

As surely as his eyes spied on others, he knew Anneshoria spied on him. Theoll touched the dagger point with his forefinger and decided the weapon was too nicked for use. He threw it across the room and fetched a new, shiny-bladed dirk.

The weapon's gleaming perfection would soon be marred with drying blood.

Theoll sheathed the dirk and dived headfirst into the small tunnel. On hands and knees he made his way quickly through the maze that spiraled ever downward. Only when he came to the dungeon level did he slow down enough to peer through the frequent spy holes in the walls.

A shiver of anticipation passed through him. Anneshoria had brought two soldiers to the dungeons for questioning. He listened to her torturer asking, "Tell us of Theoll's plan. Tell us all you know about the secret niche in the garden wall."

Theoll smiled broadly. Anneshoria *had* penetrated his spell-locked chest! Fake plans showing a hiding place in the castle wall had been part of the trove left for her eyes. The rest told of how he would kill her this morning when they met—just as she planned to kill him, if Squann was to be believed.

A loud shriek of pain echoed through the chamber. The soldier had died denying any complicity in Theoll's assassination scheme. Theoll felt a pang of guilt for the man's death; he had been innocent. But in Castle Porotane everyone took the risk of becoming involved in plotting. The innocent, most of all, became embroiled because of their naivete.

Theoll slipped forward into a hollow space behind a torture device. His hand rested on the dirk. Anneshoria ought to be here watching the torture. She always sat on a special chair back far enough to prevent blood from spattering on her fine gowns. The chair back had been made specially to Theoll's specification. When she sat with her back to a wall, secure that the chair was constructed of heavy wood, he would strike. The blade would slip through the thin false back in a single stroke.

Anneshoria would die in the torture chamber. It might be long minutes—even hours—before anyone discovered it. And who escaped from the dungeon? Her guards had supplanted those of the late Archbishop Nosto. Only a traitor in her own rank could perform such a feat of murderous magic.

Theoll peered through tiny eyeslits in the device. He frowned when he failed to see her head outlined by grim flame leaping on the torturer's brazier.

Did she know? Had Squann alerted her? No, no, it was impossible. This scheme had never been put to paper. No one save Theoll knew the details. He had done it all himself.

Where was the slut?

Theoll pushed open the compartment lid and dared a quick glance into the dungeon. The second soldier's life swung on a thin cable, and the torturer methodically sawed at it. The burly torturer and the sweaty, bloody, naked soldier he took in with one look. Nowhere was Anneshoria to be seen.

His plan had failed!

Theoll wanted to shout, to strike out, to kill. He contained his destructive impulses. With the well-muscled torturer and his many assistants nearby, anything other than a silent retreat would be self-destructive. Theoll crept back into the narrow tubelike tunnel and sat, legs crossed and mind racing.

Something had gone wrong. Anneshoria never missed her amusements in the torture chamber. She was as bad as Archbishop Nosto had been on this point. Theoll's mind turned from the woman's absence to the reasons that might cause it.

A slow smile replaced the worried frown. The only thing that would draw her away from a particularly toothsome torture session would be—Theoll's death!

The Baron scampered up the tunnel and got into the upper levels. He turned and twisted and forced himself past tight-fitting blocks and came out in more familiar ways. He dusted off his filthy clothing, then forgot about it entirely. He heard Anneshoria and Squann arguing.

Pressing his eye to the spy hole in Squann's quarters, he saw the commander of the guard and Lady Anneshoria.

". . . on the battlements, I swear it, lady!" protested Squann.

"You lie. You play at his game, not mine. You lured me here to kill me. You are in his pay, after all I have given you! After all you have meant to me!"

Theoll smirked. He knew what she had given the captain. He had watched enough times.

"So be it!" Squann reached under the bed and drew his sword. Theoll wanted to cry out and warn the captain; he held his tongue. Fighting Anneshoria in this manner would never work. He was startled that Squann did not realize this—and he was even more surprised that Squann supported him over the lovely lady.

Squann launched a decent attack that would have spitted any other unarmed woman. Anneshoria moved with the speed of a striking snake and danced back. Theoll watched her fumble with a large ring and twist off a jewel. She held the ring to her mouth, her pink tongue darting out to sample the white powder within the tiny compartment revealed.

She had moved with the speed of a viper before. Now her reactions were blinding. The drug she had taken speeded up movement tenfold. Try as he might, Squann found it impossible to do more than put a single slice in the woman's shoulder.

Theoll knew the drug wore off quickly; Anneshoria made the most of the brief acceleration. A small dagger hardly longer than her middle finger came from her bodice. She danced inward, past Squann's flailing, slow thrust and drove the point into the man's belly.

Squann gasped and folded over, clutching his guts.

"You will be dead soon enough, fool," Anneshoria said. "The point was poisoned against your treachery."

Squann peered up at her with glazed eyes. "I wanted only for Porotane to be united. Too much war. Too much." He gasped and dropped to his knees. Theoll felt a pang of sorrow for the man he had underestimated. Squann had seen the true ruler of Porotane in him and had tried to eliminate Anneshoria. Theoll realized that he ought to have trusted the captain. Anneshoria would not have been diverted from the torture chamber this night if he had let the man know his plans.

Theoll discarded such a chimerical notion. He dared not trust Squann, even now as the man died. Events had forged this course of events and they must now run their course.

"Where is he?" demanded Anneshoria. "I came here to kill that little whoreson and I will! I will not spend another night sharing the throne with him!"

"He . . . on the battlements. The northern tower looking out over the rebel front." Squann began writhing on the floor in obvious pain. Only an incoherent gagging sound came from his mouth now.

"Very well. I will see him dead on the battlements." Anneshoria jerked her gown away from Squann's feebly clutching fingers and left.

Theoll watched her walk carefully. A slight falter came to her step. The drug had taken its toll. Although it imparted fantastic speed for a few seconds, it left the user drained. He had heard of the drug but had never found any magician able to concoct it. He wondered at Anneshoria's contacts in obtaining such a valuable spell-laced drug.

Theoll used the tip of the dirk he had intended to drive into Anneshoria's back to force open a small portal into Squann's chambers. The guard captain moaned softly and opened his eyes.

"Baron?" he croaked.

"I listened at the wall," said Theoll. "I believe I know the nature of Anneshoria's poison. Be still and we shall see if it can be countered. I have some small knowledge in such matters." He did not tell Squann that he had systematically poisoned Duke Freow and had made a careful study of all possible deadly drugs.

Theoll went through Squann's quarters until he found spare fire liquid for the table lamp. He poured a generous portion onto the wound, then ignited it. Squann screeched in pain.

"Endure, Captain," ordered the baron. "This is for the best. In this you must trust me."

Squann's face turned deathly pale and his eyes remained clamped firmly shut. His twitchings slowed and he lay as still as he could.

"Good." Theoll looked at the large ring on his own thumb and considered the risks in giving Squann the countering agent hidden within. Anneshoria had shown herself to be adept at the use of poisons. Theoll might need this antidote.

Captain Squann had shown himself to be loyal. Theoll realized the need for allies in the coming battle for supremacy within the castle walls. He knelt and forced open Squann's mouth. He opened his ring and knocked a few grains of the yellow powder onto the officer's tongue. Blisters appeared where each grin touched moist flesh. Theoll clamped the mouth firmly shut as Squann went into convulsions.

"Relax. Trust me. This is the antidote. The fire burned away part of her poison at the wound. This attacks the rest of Anneshoria's poison in your body."

Squann slowly relaxed and his eyes opened, the glaze gone.

"You'll live. I'll send the chirurgeon to tend you."

"Baron, I sent her to the battlements."

"I heard. I had intended to eliminate her in the dungeon, but I have no reason to shun the towers."

"Take guards. She is dangerous."

"Rest. I will return when I have finished with her."

Theoll left through the door into the outer corridor. Finding a chirurgeon he could trust at this time of night would take too long. Squann might be weak now but the danger had passed. The guard commander had shown himself to be strong and brave; a few more hours of pain would not do him irreparable harm.

Theoll had an assassination to complete.

As his short legs took him even higher in the castle and onto the exposed battlements, his mind worked out a different plan. Anneshoria expected to find him—he would hunt her down. Everything she intended to do, he would do first. The element of surprise would be his.

He smiled wickedly. He hoped she tried to use her drug again. His reading had shown that two uses within the circuit of the sun left the user a mindless husk.

Cold wind blew into his face and pulled lank, dark hair away from his forehead. He had not realized until this moment how much he perspired. He did not fear Anneshoria, he told himself over and over.

Theoll was not sure if he lied to himself on this point. After Lorens had vanished to hunt the Demon Crown and Archbishop Nosto had been killed, the woman had risen to power quickly by skillfully manipulating the other nobles. Theoll had been unable to use her to further his own goals and had agreed to the ridiculous division of power.

Two sitting simultaneously on the throne? Absurd!

The snap of fabric in the strong wind alerted him to her presence. She moved in shadows ahead of him, stalking him, thinking that Squann had spoken the truth in his death throes.

Anneshoria might be expert at stalking in the

boudoir; out here she proved herself a rank amateur. Theoll closed the distance between them quickly and silently.

Stars shone down from the crystal-clear night sky and provided enough illumination for Theoll to see the woman's face. It was drawn as if she experienced considerable strain. For the first time, Theoll let confidence rise within his breast. She feared him!

The dirk came into his hand. Two quick steps closed the distance between them. With his weaker left hand, Theoll reached out and grabbed a handful of the woman's hair. He jerked hard, snapping her head back and forcing her off balance.

"You thought to kill me, lovely Anneshoria. How foolish of you." He lashed out with his dirk, trying to slit her taut throat. The woman twisted around and lowered her chin in time to take the edge of the knife along her cheek. Dark blood spurted in the moonlight, but Theoll saw instantly that this was not a killing stroke. It would leave her disfigured, but he did not want her beauty marred.

He wanted her dead!

She snapped at his wrist, like a caged animal. Theoll pulled back, dagger ready for a second thrust. Anneshoria slipped free, kicking and screaming for the guard. Theoll lunged and missed—and almost died.

Anneshoria grabbed the back of his cloak and tried to heave him over the battlements to the ground below. For a brief instant, Theoll hung suspended, staring out and down.

Below stretched the deadly brambles that protected the lower portions of the castle from ground attack. And beyond? He saw the glint of silvered moonlight off battered armor as the rebel troops changed positions. His mind worked on a dozen items simultaneously. The rebels prepared for a dawn attack. He had to devise a counterplan or the castle might fall.

Fall. Theoll stared back at the brambles so far below and knew fear. He shrieked and lashed out once more with the dagger. The tip caught the woman's hand and opened a deep gash that sent black blood pouring over him.

She tried again to boost him up and over the stone crenellation but her own blood robbed her of purchase on his clothing. Cursing, Anneshoria backed off to launch a new attack.

This time Theoll was ready for her. She gave voice to a battle cry and rushed him. He dipped under the outstretched arms, got his hands on her waist, and heaved.

"Theoll, wait, no!" she pleaded. They had reversed positions. Where he had hung suspended over the edge of the battlements the woman now struggled. "We can come to an agreement. I will go to the western provinces. I will be content with ruling a maritime—"

His dirk moved upward along her belly, but he did not drive the blade into her softness. He let her feel the deadly steel point, to know true fear.

"Theoll!"

"Good-bye, Anneshoria." He dropped the dagger with a loud, ringing clatter to the stone walkway. She relaxed, thinking he had relented and would allow her to go into exile.

Theoll's muscles bunched as he heaved her up and over the side. Anneshoria cartwheeled through the air to her death below, screaming as she fell.

Theoll retrieved his fallen dirk and put it in his belt. Only then did he look.

A contorted body hung on the brambles below, the foot-long thorns piercing the tender, unmoving body. Theoll stood and stared, drained of all emotion. Then he turned and went down the winding stairs to find a chirurgeon for Captain Squann. If the rebels attacked at dawn, he needed an able leader to mount the defense.

A good king never wasted resources.

King Theoll, he said to himself. *King* Theoll!

Chapter Eleven

"We must not delay getting into the castle, Majesty," cautioned the lieutenant. "The rebel patrols are everywhere. They form their ranks for a dawn attack. We must not be caught outside."

"You mean we should get inside the castle to regain the throne," said Lorens. His dark eyes scanned the edge of the forest for the sign that Vered and the Demon Crown had arrived. Losing the castle to the rebels meant nothing if he could recover his magical crown. Nothing but this mattered. Nothing. *Nothing!*

"We will meet opposition."

"Doubtful." Lorens chuckled. "I put an impostor on the throne in my place. They believe I have never left the castle. The fools believe I still rule!"

The lieutenant said nothing. Lorens faced the

man and studied him. Sparks of the growing darkness within his soul rose and for a brief instant he saw with more than eyes.

"You think they dared try to depose me? Impossible! I took too many precautions."

"It is dangerous in our exposed position. We have too few men left to properly defend you, Majesty. If we were inside the castle, we could call on the entire army for protection."

Lorens barely listened. The secret entry to the castle lay less than an hour's walk away. They could be inside long before Dalziel Sef launched his morning offensive. What Lorens needed above all else was the Demon Crown. If that cowardly traitor Pandasso hadn't lied, the other thief would bring it directly to his hand.

"There!" he cried when he spotted the one long flash and the two short ones. "Get a lantern. Quickly, fool, a lantern!"

"We don't have any, Majesty. And I advise against showing light. The rebels . . ."

"May the demons take all the rebels!" Lorens reeled as blackness swelled around him and the voices within his head began their incessant shrill howling. He blinked and saw a red-glowing land of jagged black rocks and torments beyond his imaginings. As suddenly as it appeared, it vanished—but the stench of death and decay lingering caused his nostrils to flare.

"If you must signal," spoke up a soldier, "we can use the campfire and this shiny bit of metal."

The lieutenant turned and knocked the soldier back. "Showing our position means death!"

Lorens paid them no attention. He drew a short dagger and walked to the banked campfire. He positioned himself and turned the silver blade in such a way that he reflected back two short flashes and a long—the combination Pandasso had told him. No matter what signal came, send back the reverse.

A long and a short. Lorens sent a short and a long.

"Majesty, this is a dangerous game to play."

Lorens spun on the lieutenant, dagger in hand. He jerked and sent the blade up under the officer's lowest rib and into his heart. The lieutenant convulsed once, then slipped silently to the ground.

"You." Lorens pointed to the soldier who had offered the reflecting metal to him. "Take his rank. You are now lieutenant of my personal guard."

Lorens turned back to study the dark terrain between the edge of the forest and his position on the low rise. A ravine afforded the best spot for ambush. "There," he told the soldier struggling to accept his new rank. "A lone man will ride through that ravine in a few minutes. I want him and what he carries."

"Should we take him alive, Majesty?" the new lieutenant asked.

"Yes!" Lorens' command came out a snake's hiss. He dared not lose the crown again. Vered might have hidden it. Torture would loosen his lips, if he had secreted the crown elsewhere.

The newly commissioned officer rushed off to obey. When he returned with half the force, Lorens stopped him. "These are the ones you have chosen?"

"They are the best of those remaining, Majesty."

"Good. I will command them. You are to remain in camp and take my sister and the ancient thief into custody."

"What of your brother-in-law?"

"Dear Bane will be my honored guest. Chains for the other two, royal treatment for my new ally." With that, Lorens motioned the lieutenant off his horse and got up in his place. This mission was too important to trust to a green officer and one who would probably be put to death soon for incompetence.

It was so hard finding good officers.

Lorens held back the demonic cackling that rose to his lips. For a brief, sobering instant, the red-lit land of death and pain appeared in front of him. Demons cavorted and pointed. Lorens shook off the vision. He was going to recover the Demon Crown. He could deal with the demonic presence later.

The ravine provided better cover than he'd dared hope for. Lorens positioned his men and sat quietly, waiting for Vered and the crown. In less than ten minutes he heard the clicking of a horse's hooves against the rocky ground. The dark figure that rose on the far bank of the ravine made Lorens catch his breath.

The green glow from the Demon Crown was visible even through the carrying bag and the crystal case holding it. Lorens wiped sweat from his upper lip. Did he truly see it or did he *see* it? Whichever it was, Lorens sensed victory close at hand.

He stood, hand on his dagger. There would be no need to let this miserable worm live. He had the crown with him.

Vered rode down the steep embankment. In the instant his horse struggled to keep its footing,

Lorens' guard attacked. The horse neighed loudly as a long pike was thrust in front of its hooves. The horse crashed to its knees and sent rider and crown into the air.

By the time Vered had recovered his breath, he stared up into Lorens' smirking face.

"We meet again, you and I. Give me the crown."

Vered tried to kick Lorens' legs from under him. He failed. Lorens dropped to one knee and pressed his dagger against Vered's throat.

"The crown," repeated Lorens.

Vered reached slowly for the rucksack containing the crown and its case. He opened the flap and revealed the crown. Seeing the Demon Crown again, Lorens forgot everything. Like a greedy youngling given a new toy, he grabbed for the crown with both hands. Vered tried to wiggle free but the guards surrounded him.

"It will destroy you if you put it on again," he warned Lorens.

The wizard-king did not hear him. Hands trembling, he lifted the crown and gently placed it on his brow. Lorens jerked stiffly erect and his eyes glazed over. The crown changed from the verdant, lush, alive hues it had assumed when Lokenna wore it to the all-too-familiar corroded copper green bespeaking decay and death.

"It is Sef who mounts the attack against the castle," Lorens said. He turned toward Castle Porotane. His face hardened. "They killed my double. They killed Nosto. Anneshoria and Theoll now rule—no, wait. Theoll just murdered Anneshoria. Theoll thinks to usurp my power. The sniveling whoreson!"

Lorens spun about and stormed off.

"Majesty, what of this one?" called a soldier with a sword point at Vered's throat. He received no answer from the king, but the lieutenant remembered his orders.

"Never mind him. We ride straight for the castle."

Vered did not question why Lorens had ordered his life preserved for the moment, but he doubted it meant he would die of old age. The question foremost in his mind was the fate of Santon and Lokenna. Nothing would make Santon reveal the signal; he would die first. But what had Lorens done to his sister?

The guards dragged Vered back to the temporary campsite. Another small knot of soldiers told Vered where Santon and Lokenna were. He was shoved against his friend; they went down in a pile.

"Vered, they caught you!" Santon moaned at the disaster that had befallen them.

"The crown. Tell us, Vered. What of it?" Lokenna's fear spread through Vered like wildfire.

"You didn't betray me? But how did he know? Does Lorens still retain the power given him by the crown?"

"No, impossible. But he has the crown now. I saw him ride past. He didn't even look in our direction," said Santon.

"Why bother? He can see anywhere in the kingdom using the magic of the crown. Eyes and ears are feeble in comparison. But I rode into a trap. How did he know?"

Lokenna's face went pale. "My husband. He must have overheard and betrayed us to Lorens."

"But why? This means our death—*all* our deaths." Vered grunted when a soldier poked him with a lance. They moved slowly toward the castle and its towering walls.

They spoke softly as they were herded forward. Santon said, "He and Lokenna are . . . drifting apart."

"Sailing apart is more like it," said Vered. "She has become a queen and left him a poor innkeeper."

"But he loved me!" protested Lokenna, still shocked. "How could Bane turn me over to certain death?"

"Where is he?" asked Vered. "Do you think Lorens has already killed him?"

"Pandasso lives," came the new lieutenant's voice from behind. The officer poked them again with a sword to keep them walking briskly. "He thought to barter with King Lorens."

"The crown for a return to the way it was in Fron," guessed Santon.

"No, not even Bane is that stupid," said Lokenna.

The derisive snort from the young lieutenant contradicted the woman's claim.

"I came through heavy rebel troop emplacements," said Vered. "We are going into the teeth of a new storm."

The lieutenant grunted and prodded harder in way of an answer. Vered was not to be denied his chance to talk. To Santon he said, "There is no way the castle can survive the force Dalziel Sef has mustered. Even if the political will is there, the castle must fall this time."

Santon explained briefly what he had learned of the conditions within Castle Porotane. Nothing his friend said made Vered feel any better.

"I came so far with the crown and not once did I so much as touch it," he said.

"I must know," said Lokenna. "How did you follow us? We saw no hint of you in Ionia's tunnel or on the river."

Vered laughed at this. "I had help. Someone showed me the way through the mountains. It was not easy, but I survived and actually came out below you on the river. I might have arrived here before you."

"Help?" Santon's voice almost cracked with the strain. He knew Vered would not trust any casual meeting with strangers in the Yorral Mountains. "Did Alarice's phantom aid you?"

Vered nodded. "She is drawn by the power in the crown. She sensed my weakness and gave me the will to resist its lure."

Lokenna looked from man to man, not sure if they made fun of her. Their solemn expressions and the way Santon turned away and stared forward fixedly assured her that this was no mere jape on their parts.

"Can we rely on her aid inside the castle?" she asked in a whisper.

Vered shook his head. "She told me that Lorens' power repels her. She is a wizard—but she is also a phantom. Her control over things living is diminishing."

A sudden lightning bolt arched across the vault of the clear nighttime sky. Everyone in the small party looked up in surprise.

"Where is the storm cloud that generated *that?*" Santon wondered aloud.

"It builds over the Castle of the Winds," said Vered. "Alarice fears the Wizard of Storms and his meddling in the kingdom's affairs."

"It's raining from a clear sky. How is this possible?" marvelled Lokenna.

They trotted toward the thick brambles surrounding the castle and, at the officer's goading, pushed aside a wall of thorns to reveal a small highway through the thicket. Lorens dismounted and rushed ahead, the glow from the Demon Crown lighting their way.

"See how it possesses him totally? He is its slave, not its master." Vered hesitated before entering the bramble tunnel. With Lorens ahead and the soldiers behind, their chance of escape would be diminished. A hard blow to the back of his head sent him stumbling forward.

"Move along now," came the cold command. "You've got a tryst with a torturer in the dungeons."

"I would go happily to my death," said Santon, "if I could have only a moment alone with Pandasso."

"I join you in that fond wish," said Vered. Rain pelted down from the empty sky, blown down from storms raging over the northern Uvain Plateau. He jumped again when a clap of thunder rolled across the kingdom. It sounded to him as if the reclusive wizard hidden away in his mountains fastness had just declared war.

"We'll never see our way free of this," he grumbled. "Lorens' soldiers have us bound for the dungeon, Sef attacks at dawn, and the Wizard of Storms sends his own weapons against the lot of us. Even if we escape, we'd likely be frozen in his blizzards or beaten to death by his wind or drowned by his floods."

"That's the Vered I know and love," said Santon. "Always looking on the bright side."

"What's worse, my tunic is getting ripped apart by these damnable thorns!"

They came to the castle's stone wall and paralleled it for half a mile. Neither had seen this entry point. A large gate yawned wide and dark before them. The soldiers crowded them through and into a small courtyard Vered identified as being near the southwestern corner of the castle.

When they were forced together in a tight knot by the soldiers, Bane Pandasso rode in. From his precarious perch on horseback he stared down at them. His eyes had turned to saucers and his hands trembled.

"Lokenna, I never meant for this to happen. I wanted only for it to be the way it was between us. The inn. The—"

"Silence," snapped the lieutenant. "I have no orders concerning you. The others go straight to the dungeons."

Pandasso turned and swung awkwardly, trying to hit the lieutenant. The officer ducked easily and used the flat of his sword to knock Pandasso to the ground.

"Put him in with them," the new officer ordered his squad.

"But King Lorens said he was to be treated as an honored guest."

"Go tell Lorens, then," snapped the lieutenant. "Very well," he continued when he saw that no one in this small command had the nerve. "Get the four of them to the dungeons." A wicked smile crossed the man's lips. "And put them all in the same cell." He saluted Santon and said, "I have no great love for traitors, either."

* * *

Lorens erupted into the main courtyard and looked around wildly. Only a few patrolling sentries saw his dramatic entrance. Hurried whispers passed among them and finally one daring guard rushed off to find the commander of the guard and report this unseemly entrance of a man they had thought dead.

Lorens settled down and used the power of the crown to shift his senses through the castle, examining it room by room, listening and watching and learning. He trembled with rage by the time he spied the frantic guard helping Captain Squann down the corridor and out into the courtyard.

"Squann, where is Theoll?"

"Majesty," the captain said, almost doubled over from his injury. "He and Lady Anneshoria—"

"I know," cut in Lorens. "I know about that. Where lies Baron Theoll's loyalty? To himself or to me?"

Captain Squann straightened painfully. "I am sure he will greet your return. We thought you had died."

"Liar! You saw my double assassinated. You knew it was not I who died!"

"Majesty!" the officer protested. "How could I have known? The double was too good. Until this moment, I thought you had perished and with you the power of the crown." The captain's eyes fixed on the blazing ring of green-glowing gold circling Lorens' head.

"I will deal with you later. First, I must find Theoll." Lorens pivoted and faced the eastern portion of the courtyard. "There, He is there, trying to ascend the throne and take the power and title that belongs to *me*. How dare he!"

Lorens trembled as he felt power welling up within. He tried to form the spell that would cause Theoll's guts to erupt from every orifice in his body. What had worked against the rebel soldiers now failed him, even with the augmenting power from the Demon Crown.

To cover his frustration, Lorens shouted, "I'll kill him with my bare hands!" He ignored the sudden downpour of rain and snow from the clear sky; his attention fixed totally on Baron Theoll.

Lorens saw the castle grapevine at work. Theoll learned of his return almost as quickly and surely as if he had used the Demon Crown. The baron blanched and ran. Lorens watched—*saw*—his every move using the crown's power. Theoll darted down one hallway and up another, finding back staircases and pushing through dormitories where soldiers slept noisily. No matter where he ran, Lorens followed magically.

Theoll fearfully looked up and down a broad corridor before opening a secret carved wood panel and slipping into the myriad ways built between walls. Even the thick stone did not prevent Lorens from seeing where Theoll ran.

Step firm and face cold as his anger grew, Lorens began to close the distance between them. Theoll used the secret passages that had given him power. Lorens relied on the ultimate magic in the Demon Crown.

Lorens came to the throne room. At one end of the immense audience chamber rose the dais holding the throne that so many coveted. He stared at it, as if seeing it for the first time. Since his father King Lamost had reigned from that throne, a usurper, a double, Theoll, and Anneshoria had occupied it. Their rule had been brief.

Lorens would rule for a thousand years!

The power erupting from sources found by the crown, he turned and laid his hands on a blank stone wall. Fingers glowing with an ugly green light, he pulled back suddenly. The wall collapsed and revealed a cowering Theoll.

"You thought to depose me, Baron. I cannot tolerate that."

"I only meant to hold the throne as regent, Majesty. I meant you no harm."

"Liar!" raged Lorens.

Theoll saw death in Lorens' eyes and glowing touch. He stood and stared up at the magic-possessed wizard-king. Fear evaporated in the face of certain death.

"I wanted the throne," Theoll said defiantly. "And the brief time between Freow's death and your return I governed Porotane well. I would do it again!"

Theoll lunged, dirk gleaming in the greenish glow cast by Lorens' hands and the Demon Crown.

The spell conjured by Lorens caught the small baron and threw him high into the air. Theoll crashed to the floor, burned by the magical fires and crushed by the height of his fall. Rebellion still flickered in his dying eyes.

"You mock me. You, you little worm!" Lorens launched a burst of magic so intense it burned the flesh from the left side of Theoll's body. The monarch struggled to create the spell that would make the baron explode. That spell eluded him again.

"I would make a better king," sobbed out Theoll. The baron clawed his way up the steps to the throne. Before Lorens could cross the room and drive the dagger deep into his heart, Theoll sat on the throne.

For the span of a heartbeat he was King of Porotane.

Chapter Twelve

"Don't kill me. Please don't!" begged Bane Pandasso. His eyes had turned wide with fear when the cell door slammed behind them. Birtle Santon and Vered glared at the man. Lokenna stood to one side, not willing to interfere if the two adventurers decided to strangle her husband, as they had promised.

"You betrayed me—us!" roared Vered. "I don't lose my temper often. I am losing it now!"

"Wait, Vered," cautioned Santon. "This will do us no good."

"Killing this slug? It'll make me feel better at being tossed in this stinking dungeon. *That's* what good it will do."

"Lorens is watching with the crown," said Lokenna. "I feel the blackness about it. It . . . it tickles—or burns. It is difficult to describe its vile magic."

"Then let him see what becomes of his toadies."

Santon grabbed Vered's arm and held the younger man back. "Did it ever occur to you that this is exactly what Lorens wants? He'd love nothing better than to see us rip one another apart in our anger."

"Let it be *his* blood that flows." Vered spat at Pandasso.

"I did not mean this to happen. I only wanted life to return to the way it was before you came to Fron." The man's bulky belly rolled to and fro as he talked. "If anyone's to blame, it's the pair of you!"

"You betrayed us to my brother," said Lokenna. "Even one as naive as you, Bane, ought to have known what that meant."

"Lorens *enjoys* wearing the crown," Vered said coldly, his anger beginning to fade. "Or hadn't you noticed?"

"How was I to know?" Pandasso wiped at the tears forming in his eyes. "Do you think an innkeeper knows of such things? Or an innkeeper's wife?" He spun on Lokenna. "What do you mean calling me 'naive'?"

"You are, my husband."

"And you, the wife of a simple innkeeper, have somehow gained the wisdom of the world? Pah!" Pandasso spat and moved from the trio, hunkering down in a corner of the straw-littered stone cell.

"I have," Lokenna said softly. "The Demon Crown educates its wearer quickly."

"But it hasn't taken control of you." Santon

formed the words as a statement, but he almost turned it into a question. Lokenna was vastly different from the woman they had met, and the crown had been the only instrument capable of such change.

"The crown does not force change. It allows it. I lack the proper words to make you understand. If there is weakness, it destroys you through them, but if you use your strength with the crown, you become invincible!"

"Lorens' problem is ambition," said Santon. "He served as Patrin's apprentice for too long. He never learned to handle power because his master failed to train him in its use. Given this boundless magical power, he runs wild."

"There is that," said Lokenna, "but he is also weak and abuses what he has. The crown makes it seem as if it caused the change." She frowned. "It does something more, too. There were hints."

"These were the matters you wished to discuss with Lorens?" asked Vered, who paced the cell like an animal. He rattled the bars in the tiny door window and found no weakness.

"I received hints of a door . . . opening. The door overlooked a perilous land populated with hideous creatures."

"Demons?"

"Yes, perhaps. I don't know." Lokenna turned and leaned against the wall, her head bowed. "It matters naught. He will kill us. He has the crown."

"In case you missed it, we're under siege," said Santon. "The rebel army is going to keep him busy. Knowing where they place the troops, where they attack, where their weaknesses lie, does nothing if Lorens cannot mobilize the castle's defenses."

"Theoll will have tried to regain the throne. He tasted power once after Duke Freow died. He wants it permanently."

"And I am sure others, such as this Lady Anneshoria the guardsmen mentioned on the way down to these fine quarters, see themselves as ruler." Vered peered through the bars, then wiggled his hand down the front of the metal door trying to find the lock. He gave up when cramps caused his arm to twitch.

"Do you think the rebels will win?" asked Lokenna. "I noticed one in particular while using the crown. He seemed a decent sort."

"A decent rebel? Pah! Goes to show how much you've to learn," cut in Pandasso. "They burned my inn. They destroyed your home. *That's* how decent they are!"

"That was Dalziel Sef," she said. "No, another caught my attention. Efran Gaemock."

"Lord Dews' brother," said Santon. "His name is unfamiliar."

"He's supposed to have died years ago," said Vered. "Or perhaps he turned tail and ran."

"He served as jester," said Lokenna. "In the court of the duke."

"Efran Gaemock was Harhar?" Santon and Vered exchanged bemused glances. Santon grinned crookedly. "I always thought more lay behind those mad acts of his than need to make others jolly."

"Why did he have truck with Duke Freow?" asked Vered. "Why not go along with Theoll's scheme to assassinate him?"

"He and Dews Gaemock parted on their desire for stablility in the kingdom," she said. "Efran wanted one of royal blood on the throne and Dews wanted only change."

"Both have their wish now," Vered said, grumbling. He dropped to his knees and examined the lock carefully. From inside the lining of his once-fine tunic he took a slender piece of springy metal. He worked it into the lock and sat patiently, working it about inside the mechanism.

"Can he get us free?" Lokenna asked.

"If anyone can, Vered is our man. He's quite good at this."

Lokenna stared, but Santon saw that she did not watch Vered. Her thoughts drifted elsewhere. She said suddenly, "We need an ally. Against Lorens we have no chance. He is too powerful—and he knows how to use the crown."

"The crown is using him. Don't care what you say," Vered said as he worked at the lock. "You want us to join up with Harhar?"

"Efran?" The woman smiled mysteriously. Santon wondered what thoughts ran through her mind. They were completely closed to him as he studied her face. "No, he lacks the power. We must find another."

"Who can possibly oppose Lorens?" asked Santon. The answer came to him before Lokenna spoke.

"The Wizard of Storms. He is all-powerful while he remains within his Castle of the Winds."

"You mean he cannot leave or he loses his power? No one's ever even hinted at that," exclaimed Santon.

"I don't know how I know it. My senses spread out across Porotane and I touched on many bits of information. But I do know this. He can aid us. The storms he sends cloud Lorens' power—and the wizard commands an army more powerful than any of flesh and blood."

"There!" called Vered. He drew the steel strip from the lock and pushed open the cell door. "Let's go find our wizard."

"You agree we should ally ourselves with him?" Santon asked, startled at his friend's easy acceptance. Vered had never shown any trust of any wizard.

"If the Wizard of Storms is across Porotane, across the Uvain Plateau, and high in the Yorral Mountains, I'm all for seeking him out. I just want to be free of this stinking prison!"

Vered stepped out of the cell and screeched in pain. Santon bulled his way forward and kicked hard at the metal door. It groaned as it swung on its hinges—and the abrupt exit saved Vered from a sword thrust by a jailer.

"Where did he come from?" wondered Vered as he got his feet under him and danced away from the armed man.

Santon's meaty fist crashed into the side of the jailer's head, knocking the man to the floor. Vered pounced like a hunting cat and grabbed away the sword. A single quick lunge ended this threat to their freedom.

"I know where he came from," Lokenna said from inside the cell.

"Another insight from using the crown?" taunted Vered.

"He came with the rest of the squad."

Santon and Vered spun. Facing them were six armed and armored soldiers ready for a fight.

"Here!" called Vered, tossing the nearest soldier the sword he'd captured. The soldier reacted as Vered had hoped. He grabbed for the sword hilt. As he moved out of position, Vered dived low and caught the guardsman just above the knees, bowling him over.

Santon lost track of what happened then. A soldier taller and burlier than he bellowed and charged. Santon's good hand caught the soldier's thick wrist and forced the mace away. The soldier's left hand drove hard into Santon's exposed midriff.

The air erupted from Santon's lungs and he sank to the cold stone floor, gasping for breath. He was aware of Bane Pandasso rushing past him. A single blow from the huge soldier sent Pandasso crashing back into the cell.

By the time his vision cleared and his lungs did not protest air seeping in and out, Santon saw that they were lost. More than a dozen alert guards crowded around, weapons drawn and ready to kill. It took him several seconds to realize that Vered was nowhere to be seen. Hope sprang up inside.

"Don't worry about your friend," the big guardsman said, peering down at Santon. "He cannot get far."

"Even if he does escape us, he'll never run far enough to get away from King Lorens," boasted another.

With a sinking sensation, Santon knew how true this was. A booted foot cut off his ruminations on the subject and drove him back into the cell.

"Oow," moaned Pandasso, nursing his face. Blood flowed freely from his broken nose and split lip. Santon wasn't sure if this didn't improve the piggish man's appearance.

"Are you hurt?" asked Lokenna.

For an instant Santon thought the woman spoke to her husband. Lokenna ignored Pandasso's moanings and had knelt nearby. Santon nodded. "I'll live—at least until they see fit to execute us."

"Vered got away," she said.

"There is still a chance, then," he said, but he doubted it. Vered was a single light against the darkness gathering around them. The entire squad of guards had stayed on duty outside. And what the one soldier said rang all too true. Whenever Lorens saw fit, he could use the Demon Crown to examine every niche in the castle and find Vered. The wizard-king need not leave the safety of the throne room.

"I tried to help," moaned Pandasso. "They were too well armed for me to do anything."

Santon said nothing. Pandasso's attack had been ineffectual. Santon found Lokenna's reactions more interesting. She ignored her husband totally and ran light, probing fingers over the spot where the guardsman's fist had struck him in the chest.

"Bruised ribs," she said, not telling Santon anything he did not already know. "But there is nothing broken."

"It takes more than that to stop me," he boasted. A moment of giddiness passed when he heaved himself to his feet. He peered out and saw even more guards entering the cell block. Even if Vered recruited half the rebel army, there would be no chance of escaping this cordon of steel unscathed.

"What's wrong?" Lokenna asked.

"Your brother might have remembered that there is no need to keep us around," Santon said truthfully. He recognized an execution detail when he saw it. The sight of the commander of the castle guard personally in charge meant their deaths had been ordered.

Santon watched curiously as Captain Squann dismissed most of the men present and positioned the few remaining at the entrance into the dungeons, well away from the cell. Hope flared until the commander spoke.

"Your deaths have been ordered by King Lorens," Squann said loudly.

"It is as I suspected," said Lokenna. Tears welled at the corners of her eyes, but it was her husband who took the sentence the worst. Wracking sobs shook Pandasso's bulky body.

"When?" asked Santon. He had lived on the edge of life overlong. He had known for some time that only luck kept him alive. Now, at least, he would join Alarice in her phantom wanderings across Porotane. Santon did not think that Lorens would allow a proper burial for enemies of their magnitude.

"Keep protesting loudly," whispered Squann. "I am here to release you, but the others do not know."

"What treachery is this? Do you hope to instill hope in us, then dash it to make the torture worse?" Santon studied Squann's pain-etched face and again dared hope.

"I have been ordered to kill you."

"Becoming a traitor to your kind is preferable?" asked Lokenna.

"He cannot be my kind. He is cruel. I . . . I thought Baron Theoll might be able to unite the kingdom and stop this war. I was wrong."

"Lorens might be listening to us. You place

yourself in jeopardy even speaking to us in this way," warned Santon.

"I know. It matters little to me." Sweat beaded on Squann's face. He pulled back his shoulders and winced. "I may be dying. Theoll tried to save me from a poisoned blade, but I fear his magic remedies failed."

"You do this to strike back at Lorens?"

"I do this in the hope that you will be able to bring peace to Porotane." Squann looked over his shoulder, then said in a voice so low that Santon almost failed to hear it. "You must not attempt to escape. Only then can I justify the minimum number of guards."

"What is your plan?"

"There is a secret way from the castle." Santon almost laughed at this. Alarice had known of one and revealed it to him and Vered. Lorens had reentered the castle though another secret door. Did Squann know a third way? Castle Porotane leaked secret passages in and out.

"We agree. Do you understand, Pandasso? We can get out of this with whole skins if you obey. Do you understand?" Santon kicked at Pandasso, who cowered in a corner.

"I'll go. Just don't harm me."

"It means all our lives if you disobey the captain."

Santon and Lokenna exchanged glances. Her eyes were unreadable, but Santon hoped she could control her husband's cowardice. Squann had no reason to lie to them. Lorens had them completely under his power and the giving of hope, then dashing it through a cruel twist did not seem his style of torture.

"Out, prisoners," ordered Squann in a loud

voice. The cell door swung back. The guardsmen turned and drew their weapons, instantly wary. Squann signalled them to proceed. "They won't try to escape. They are resigned to their fate."

"Never seen a prisoner going to his death who was resigned to it, Captain," said one.

"Ruvary, go on ahead and make sure the strangling posts are ready in the courtyard," Squann ordered. The soldier who had spoken started to protest, then turned and left.

Squann walked boldly forward toward the three remaining guards. "You, check the corridors to be certain no one obstructs our progress. You two, follow along behind to make sure they don't dally on their way to execution."

As one turned, Squann drew his dagger and swung the handle down hard on the soldier's head. A sick crunch told of a crushed skull. The other guard turned and for an instant ignored Santon. Santon's powerful right arm circled the man's throat in an unbreakable hold.

"Should I finish him?" asked Santon. A curt nod from Squann spelled the guardsman's death. Santon jerked and broke his neck, then cast him aside.

"Hurry. We have little time before Ruvary wonders what's become of us. He's loyal to Lorens."

"You mean he's after your job."

For the first time Squann smiled. "In other circumstances, I could like you. You understand what happens within these walls."

"I was here long enough to see how you people live," said Santon. He started after Squann, then stopped. "Wait. Vered! We've got to find him!"

"The one who tried to escape earlier?" Squann shook his head. "There is no time. Ruvary is suspicious of me. We dare not waste an instant reaching the tunnel."

"Vered might have already gotten free," said Lokenna.

Santon hesitated. He did not like the idea of abandoning his friend. The clank of heavily armed soldiers patrolling the corridor spurred him into action he did not like.

"Let's get out of here. If we're caught, we're no good to Vered."

"He might have escaped. He remains free, at least," Squann assured him.

They went through the dungeons and up stairs clogged with cobwebs and bold vermin larger than Santon's hand. They came to a small arch that had been sealed years ago.

"This is the spot. Begin pulling down the blocks," ordered Squann. He tossed his dagger to Santon and turned to drag his sword blade along the lines of crumbling mortar.

Santon balanced the dagger in hand for a moment, considering again the chance that this was a complicated trap set by Lorens. Again he had to assume that Squann had nothing to gain by such a charade—and neither did Lorens. The wizard-king took his amusement from other sources.

"Where does this lead?" Santon asked, pushing a block through into the tunnel beyond. Fetid air gusted into his face and bespoke long years of entombment.

"I don't know. I came across it on an ancient map of the castle."

"What became of the map?" asked Lokenna.

"I destroyed it. There's no reason to let others

know of this." Squann grunted as he lifted down a block. His face had grown increasingly pale, but he motioned Lokenna away when she went to aid him. "There's no time. We must get away from the castle. It matters naught if Lorens can see us unless he has the power to reach us."

Santon started to tell the captain about the king's magic spells that had exploded the rebel troops into sausage, but Lokenna shook her head and silenced him.

"Get into the tunnel," urged Squann.

"It's dark in there. And I see red eyes staring out. There's vermin inside bigger'n me!" Pandasso backed away. "You can't make me go in there. I went through that damned tunnel in the mountain. But I won't go here."

"Go or stay and die," said Santon. He had no time for the man's fears. He saw that Lokenna agreed. She stepped over the fallen blocks and went into the tunnel.

"We need a torch to see," she called back.

"There's nothing around here," said Squann. "We dare not find one, either. I hear them searching for us."

Santon cocked his head to one side and strained. From the dungeon came sounds of pursuit. Ruvary had returned and found their handiwork. Two dead guards—and Squann missing. An ambitious man would see his chance and seize it. No matter what happened, Ruvary would have Squann's rank afterward.

"I'll lead the way. My night vision's good," said Santon. "Squann, bring up the rear."

"What about me?" cried Pandasso. "You can't leave me here to die. They want to kill me!"

"Tunnel or death—you choose." Santon

ducked his head and entered the tunnel, squeezing past Lokenna. He heard Pandasso sobbing as he swallowed his fears and entered the tunnel. Proceeding cautiously, Santon checked the floor for sudden pits or deadfalls. The musty odor increased as he walked, however, and he decided that any mechanical traps laid in this corridor had long ago fallen apart. All they needed to worry about was behind them.

"You coming, Squann?" he called back.

"Go on," gasped out the commander of the guard. "I . . . the poison works faster at my guts. Get away. Do what you can."

His voice cut off suddenly and was replaced by the clash of steel against steel.

"We have only minutes before Ruvary follows," said Lokenna.

"Longer," said Santon. "Squann is dying but he has heart. Ruvary won't find him an easy target."

Santon plunged on into the inky tunnel, worrying about what lay ahead and behind—and most of all about Vered's fate.

Chapter Thirteen

Lightning danced along the chipped stone battlements of Castle Porotane. The vivid purple and green discharges blew away shards of stone and made walking patrol impossible. The guards protested to their officers, who dared not carry the complaints further, fearing what King Lorens might say. Along with the lightning came intense rain and a wind so strong that it ripped away the wizard-king's banner and sent it fluttering into the night.

"Bring the traitor up here," ordered Ruvary. The soldier hesitated; Ruvary did not. He struck the soldier squarely on the side of his head, sending the man tumbling down a flight of stone steps. "When I give an order, you will obey it without question. The next time you think to disobey, you die!"

He had to shout to make himself heard over the intense storm boiling around the castle walls. Ruvary settled down to stare into the turmoil, wondering if he had properly chosen his road to power. Supporting a demented soul like Lorens might mean death if a powerful enough wizard opposed him.

But Ruvary had yet to decide if this storm was the product of magical opposition or the result of a spell conjured by Lorens himself. If the wizard-king brought on such a potent defense of his castle, it would never do abandoning him—betraying him.

Ruvary had been tempted to join Squann in the secret tunnel and escape. Ambition burned too brightly within him for that, though. The idea of bringing to justice such a traitor in the ranks of King Lorens' guard assured him of a secure post.

"As secure as I can get," he muttered to himself. The gusts of wind drowned out his mumbled words and insured that no one overheard. In spite of this isolation caused by the elements, Ruvary looked around guiltily. Lorens knew everything. They said the Demon Crown gave these powers, but Ruvary cared little for such speculation. That the king knew anything was proof enough that he had cast his lot with the winning side.

"May the demons take all rebels!" he shouted in the teeth of the storm. As if answering, a jagged bolt edged down from the sky and blew apart the landing above him. Ruvary threw up his arm to protect his face from flying fragments.

Doubt assailed him again. Did Lorens conjure this storm to protect the castle from the rebel forces or did another, more powerful wizard send it as a screen for the rebel attack?

"Captain, here he is," came a frightened voice. Ruvary turned to see two guards supporting Squann. His predecessor as commander of the guard twitched feebly. One eye came open and peered at him, but Ruvary did not care about Squann's condition.

"Take him to the battlements."

"But the storm!" protested the one who had given him trouble before. This time Ruvary lashed out with his heavy boot. The man lost his balance and tumbled backward down the stone steps. Halfway down the flight bright red spots began to appear. By the time the soldier landed, neck broken and face destroyed, at the foot of the stairs, his blood colored every worn step.

"Take the traitor to the battlements," Ruvary ordered again. This time fear of his punishment outweighed fear of the storm. They dragged a limp Squann to the walkway.

"Over there. Put him by the pole that supported the banner." Ruvary felt uneasiness growing. He stripped off his metal armor and cast it down the steps. He did not allow his men to follow his lead in this. If a lightning bolt came down from above, let it seek out his underlings. They existed only to serve him—and to die, if necessary.

"Ruvary," croaked Squann. "This does no good. I am dying. Poison. Anneshoria poisoned me with a blade."

"You allowed the prisoners to escape. No," said Ruvary, enjoying this moment of superiority to the utmost. "You didn't *allow* the prisoners to escape. You *helped* them."

"The kingdom." Squann's next words vanished in the sonic assault from the thunder. "We must stop the war. It is destroying us all."

"You sell out to rebels? That is your way of ending the fighting? You should have obeyed our liege lord. Only by following King Lorens can we unite Porotane." Ruvary looked around self-consciously, wondering if his noble speech went unheeded by his monarch. He had no hint to the effect of his words, either on king or storm.

"Captain, the storm worsens," protested a soldier. The lightning blast limned him and turned him into something less than human. For a brief instant, Ruvary thought the flesh had been stripped from the guardsman's body and only his skeleton was left. He blinked and wiped the rain from his eyes. A chill worked down from the Yorral Mountains and threatened to turn this cold rain into sleet.

"Tie his hands to the pulley," he ordered. Ruvary watched as Squann was bound to the flagstaff. "Raise him."

The soldiers exchanged glances, then hastened to obey. The thunder deafened them; it also drowned out Squann's cries of pain as they jerked him slowly upward on the staff. The wind caught his thrashing body and pulled him away. Ruvary wondered if he could estimate the wind's velocity by the angle Squann's body made with the flagpole.

Such a notion vanished when the very heavens opened with a powerful jagged sword thrust of lightning that ripped asunder clouds and terminated on Squann's torso. A cascade of burned offal rained down. Again Ruvary tried to protect his eyes but the afterimages remained—and they frightened him.

He did not see yellow and blue dots dancing

merrily. He saw demons cavorting as they feasted on Squann's cremated flesh.

"Down. Get out of the storm. Now!" Ruvary was first down the stairs. He heard the others behind him, but he dared not turn to see if they were uninjured. The image of the demons had burned itself into his brain as surely as the energy bolt had seared Squann's body. Ruvary slipped and almost fell when he came to the foot of the stairs; he had forgotten the pool of blood left by the other unfortunate soldier.

Boots leaving bloody prints, Ruvary went to report the traitor's execution to King Lorens.

"I cannot see. I cannot feel. I am blind and deaf. Who puts me into this black existence?" Lorens paced back and forth, wailing piteously and struggling to set the crown more firmly on his head. No matter how he twisted or turned it, no images from afar appeared.

"Calmness. I must not panic. Why doesn't the Demon Crown work? What have I done wrong? What? A spell? *What?*" He spun in fright when a strong rapping sounded at the door to his chambers. "Who is it?" he called.

"Captain Ruvary reporting, Majesty."

"Enter and be damned."

Ruvary came through the door more timidly than his knock had intimated. Lorens took some small pleasure in being able to frighten an underling. Not a year ago, Ruvary would have terrified him, a poor apprentice wizard never straying far from his master. Now the powerful soldier feared him!

"Majesty, the traitor has been put to death. On the battlements."

"Yes, yes, I know," Lorens said. "I watched." He kept the panic from rising in his voice. Anything within the castle appeared perfectly to the magic of the crown. Nothing beyond the boundaries of Castle Porotane could be spied upon. He was blind and deaf when he needed his power most. What caused this blackness?

Who caused it?

"Do you think the rebels will attack in the storm, Majesty?"

"They are fools if they do. Dalziel Sef might consider it a bold stroke, though."

"Gaemock is not their commander?"

"I could not locate Gaemock." Lorens bit his tongue to keep from revealing more of his weakness. He had concentrated on Sef's troop placements, his weaknesses and his strengths. Of Dews Gaemock he had not seen a trace. If the rebel leader plotted elsewhere in Porotane, such a move had been hidden by the sudden storm.

"Do we prepare to repel or do we mount an offensive of our own and sally forth?" Ruvary shifted restlessly from foot to foot while trying not to seem nervous in the presence of his liege. "I need to know so that I can prepare the formations and have the horses saddled and ready by dawn."

"Attack or defend," mused Lorens. He tried to remember what he could about the rebel position. "Ask Squann. He knows such things."

"Sire, Squann is dead. You witnessed his execution for treason against you."

"What? Yes, of course, I knew that. Yes." The winter cold that had crept into the castle didn't matter; Lorens experienced a sudden fever. His hold on the soldiers seemed tenuous. He dared not let this ambitious whoreson take over. Squann had tried to do that. Squann had died. He remembered that now. He could kill Ruvary, too. Yes, that was what he had to do. But later. After the rebels were defeated.

He smiled crookedly. Ruvary might die a hero in battle. That would solve the problem of another ruthless, relentless soldier trying to usurp power as Baron Theoll had done.

"Defense is out of the question. Dalziel Sef will never launch a direct attack. He will attempt to lay siege to the castle. The early winter favors him, diminishing our stores more quickly."

"Then we attack?" Ruvary sounded uncertain of this approach.

"I know the precise location of every cavalry unit Sef has in the field. Is that not good enough for you to defeat him?"

"He is entrenched on the upper slopes."

"They are not slopes. They are hills. Less!"

Ruvary started to speak but Lorens' mood quieted him. The king did not have to charge up a fortified slope wreathed in falling snow; his men might have to in the morning.

"You worry needlessly, Ruvary." Lorens regained his confidence. Sef would not move his troops in this storm. His position would be unchanged from the last scrying with the crown. "I will show you their troop concentrations, their weaknesses, how you will attack and win."

Lorens pulled out a map of the surrounding countryside and began marking the positions for his new field commander. By the time he left, Ruvary's confidence had soared.

Lorens watched the officer leave, sure of his victory. The longer Lorens thought about it, the less certain he became that he properly remembered the images he had seen. He spent the remainder of the night listening to the storm and worrying.

Why wouldn't the Demon Crown function?

"The storm is lifting, Majesty. Thank you."

Lorens looked at his new captain and almost asked what he meant. Lorens held his tongue in time. It would not do to admit that he had not been the author of the prodigious storm that had hammered away at the castle walls all night.

"You will ride directly to glorious victory. Nothing can stop you. Go now!"

The heavy castle gates cranked open and the line of mounted soldiers stirred in anticipation of the coming battle. When the gates had opened enough to allow a double column through, Ruvary gave the command and they raced out to meet the rebels.

Lorens walked up to the battlements and stared across the countryside to where the major battle would occur. The storm had left the land damp and the sky cloudless and blue. The uneasiness he had felt at being in the storm and blinded by it evaporated when he saw how proud and strong his troops looked. They rode into battle at his order. And they would triumph this day for his glory!

The Demon Crown warmed to his touch and glowed its familiar off-hue green. He closed his eyes, then slowly opened them and both saw and *saw*. Sef had not repositioned his troops during the storm. Everything he had told Ruvary remained true. There was no way he could lose if his soldiers fought valiantly!

Using the magic given him by the crown, Lorens relished the sight of blood flowing as the front of his assault force met the outer fringes of the rebel defense. The enemy drew back, then turned and ran in complete rout. His forces pushed on, the double column splitting, one half going to the east and the other plunging westward.

The rebels to the east had the chance to escape into the farmlands. His cavalry spent needless time tracking down the fleeing cowards. The true battle occurred to the west where his soldiers pinned the rebels into a fork in the river. If Sef were to escape, he would have to cross the River Ty.

Lorens watched and saw that the rebel leader could not do it. He had made no provision for escape, thinking his position secure. That cost Sef the battle. The rebel fought well enough, Lorens *saw*; but to no avail. He had lost the high ground, he could not flee across the river without boats, and the river effectively hemmed him in.

He had to fight like a cornered rat or die.

Lorens laughed aloud, the sound that of a madman. Sef had no choice. He would die even if he fought!

"Squire!" the wizard-king bellowed. "Prepare my steed. I will ride to the scene of battle and personally lead my troops."

The frightened squire hurried to obey. Lorens flicked the hem of his cape up and dangled it over his left arm. Head high, crown giving him minute by minute intelligence about the fight, he went to the courtyard, allowed the squire to help him mount, and then rode quickly for the front lines.

Lorens marvelled at the change that had come about in him. While under Patrin's tutelage, he had feared all things beyond the ordinary. Now he rode through the rebel-infested countryside to take his place at the front of troops fighting a desperate enemy. Courage came with the Demon Crown.

Lorens also knew that there was no one along the road to waylay him. A quick survey using the crown had shown only barren land denuded by troops and the ice storm of the night before.

He sucked in a lungful of crisp, cold air and rode with head held high, as befitted a conqueror. He had led his men to conquest over the rebels. He had vanquished them. Duke Freow had failed. Theoll had made a botch of it. No one else in Porotane could have succeeded.

"Majesty, you shouldn't be here," came Ruvary's harsh words. "It is too dangerous in the field. They fight with the savagery of a force twice their size."

"You attack in the wrong spot, fool," snapped Lorens. He knew the source of his commander's irritation. The rebels held back his troops, true, but Ruvary did not want the soldiers seeing their king leading. He wished to snatch away all the glory for this victory.

"You!" bellowed Lorens. He signalled to a sergeant leading a small company of lancers directly up the hill and into Sef's main force. "March to the west, then cut north and attack their flank. They will collapse totally."

"Majesty, we have few enough troops. To divide—"

"Silence, worm! Obey or die!" Spittle ran down Lorens' chin. Only the wind turning it icy caused him to notice. He swiped at it and adjusted the crown on his head. Black powers welled up within him. He swallowed hard when he saw the peculiar red-lit land peopled by the grotesque dancing figures of demons. Using the magic power locked within the Demon Crown, he directed his senses deeper into his new and daunting world rather than denying its existence.

No, came a booming voice that caused his bones to quake. *Not yet. Your time for this world will come. But not now.*

Lorens wobbled and almost fell from the saddle. Only a gust of frigid wind that brought him to his senses saved him from embarrassment in front of his men.

"You obey or you die." Lorens used the blackness and the denial of his power to form a spell that quickly grew beyond his control.

Lorens recoiled in horror as the swirling terror he created spun and stalked up the hill toward the rebel forces. One rebel, braver than his comrades or less fleet of foot, vanished into the whirling magical pillar. His shrieks of agony were blotted out almost instantly. Left behind was only the memory of the man.

The tornado dissipated but its dire effect on his troops remained. The frightened sergeant ordered his men around the hill in the flanking maneuver, as his wizard-king ordered. "Captain Ruvary be damned," Lorens *heard* the sergeant say. "All he can do is flay me alive. The king can do *that!*"

The sense of power mounted in Lorens. He turned to Ruvary and smirked. Once he would have been frightened of the powerful soldier with the steel sword and battered shield. No longer. He had found a power transcending anything a mortal could command.

"Dalziel Sef," he said suddenly. "The rebel leader is escaping across the river. He has found a small boat. After him, fool. Don't let him escape!"

Lorens threw caution to the winds and rode directly up the hill into the concentrated might of the rebel forces. Following so closely after the cyclonic death he had sent broke the will of the rebels. They threw down their weapons and fled screaming.

King Lorens was first atop the hill where the rebels had been strongest. He watched, eyes sufficing, as the lancers caught the retreat on the tips of their weapons. Nowhere did a rebel remain with defiance in his heart. All knew fear.

All feared Lorens!

"There," he called to Ruvary. "That small boat making its way across the river. Stop it!"

Two men rowed frantically in the tiny boat to get Dalziel Sef away safely. Lorens tried once more to tap the power that had brought the cyclone into existence. As before, he found only impenetrable darkness that defied his attempts to use another spell. He could do nothing but use the Demon Crown to watch Sef flee.

"Archers. Get archers here. Shoot him out of the water. He must not reach the other side alive!"

The archers tried, but Dalziel Sef had gone beyond their range. The swift current of the snow-fed river carried the tiny boat along quicker than usual for this time of year. But even if it hadn't, Sef's escape would have been assured. His head start was too great.

"All the rebels have surrendered, Majesty," Ruvary reported. "Where do you wish them imprisoned? There's a small village, long deserted, not a half day's travel from here."

Lorens brushed off the suggestion. "Kill them. Kill them all."

"But, Majesty, I recommend—"

Lorens swung on his officer, grabbed the man's tunic and pulled him close. Bowing his head allowed the crown to touch Ruvary's forehead. The office gasped and died instantly from the brief contact. Lorens jerked and threw the body to the ground.

"Let him rot. No one is to touch his foul body," Lorens called out. "Let him remain a symbol to all those who would disobey or question my command!"

A hush fell over the conquering army. Lorens smiled crookedly. He had established complete dominance. He waited for the slaughter of the captured rebels to begin before turning slowly to survey his new kingdom, a kingdom unified under his control.

Only when he stared across at the uplift of the Uvain Plateau did he hesitate. Fierce storms clawed along the buttes leading up to the plateau—and the Demon Crown's power faltered again.

He could not see anything on the Uvain Plateau . . . except for a castle perched high on a pinnacle.

Chapter Fourteen

"Light!" exclaimed Birtle Santon. "I see light ahead."

"How long have we been in this demon-haunted tunnel?" asked Pandasso. He pressed close to Santon, making the adventurer move more quickly to avoid his touch. He could not forget that Pandasso had betrayed Vered to Lorens. Nothing in the man's behavior since had worked in his favor, either.

"Long enough for there to be light outside," said Santon. Then he frowned. The light had vanished. Pandasso ran full into him again. Santon winced as his withered arm scraped the rocky tunnel wall. He wished he still carried the glass shield Alarice had given him. That device had proven useful, not only in saving his life in battle but for protecting his weak arm. It would have been a true boon in this tunnel when the only guidance he had had was a hand along the wall and his sense of direction.

"I hear a storm. Thunder." Lokenna moved to join them. He did not mind her presence. If he had been able to see in the pitch-blackness of the escape tunnel, he would have killed Pandasso and left his body for the vermin.

"There!" he cried. "Light again."

"It's lightning," Lokenna said. "The brilliance shines against rock and reflects into the tunnel."

"It lasts so long. The storm must be incredible. We might be better off in the tunnel until it blows away," suggested Pandasso.

Santon shook his head, then realized they could not see except in the flashes. "We leave immediately upon finding the exit. I don't know why Ruvary didn't pursue us. He might have been too interested in showing off what a traitor Squann was, but the tunnel is open behind us and a squad with a torch can cover the distance in a matter of minutes."

"I don't like the tunnel, but getting wet would be even worse," complained Pandasso.

"Birtle is right," said Lokenna. "It is dangerous remaining in the tunnel. We are captives limited to travel in only two directions—one, if you consider that we dare not return to the castle."

Santon continued his cautious advance until he came to the tumble of stones blocking the exit. He began pushing the rocks away with his good arm. Lokenna joined him. Only when he saw his wife struggling with the huge chunks of stone did Pandasso lend a hand. In a short while they had cleared a crawl space large enough even for Santon's broad shoulders and Pandasso's girth.

"It's been many years since this tunnel was used," said Santon, looking over the stone. "Let's hope the rebels don't have a guard posted outside to watch."

"They don't," Lokenna said positively. "There is no feel of human presence."

Santon peered at her but the woman's face was still cloaked in shadow. Even the purple flashes of lightning outside failed to show her expression. He wondered if she had become infected with the evil carried by the Demon Crown or if this was a knack she'd always possessed.

"Birtle, you worry so," she said, putting a gentle hand on his shoulder. "The crown has awakened much in me, but it has not harmed me. Truly, it hasn't."

"Wait here while I scout and see where we've come out." Santon wiggled through the hole and tumbled out into a raging storm. Wind caught at flesh and chilled him. Rain mixed with snow battered his face. He tucked his bad arm into his belt to keep it from blowing wildly in the gusty winds.

For a minute, he sat hunched over, squinting into the night. The storm gave occasional glimpses of a surreal land populated by creatures from a demented nightmare. Santon slowly recognized those creatures as trees blown over by the storm, rocks strangely limned by the lightning, naturally occurring formations in the land itself. In the distance he heard the gurgling passage of the River Ty and knew his sense of direction had been accurate. The tunnel had twisted around but had eventually headed due east. He walked slowly to a rise and peered into the night. The ice floe–racked river lay a bowshot away—a perfect escape route for any wishing to flee Porotane.

Santon turned and looked back at the castle. The wind and rain chilled his body. The sight of Castle Porotane locked in the grip of the storm chilled his soul. That could not be a naturally occurring storm. The sharp delineation between calm and storm showed that. It was as if a wizard had positioned the storm to strike only at the castle and those within it.

"The Wizard of Storms shows his power," Lokenna said at Santon's elbow. He jumped. He had not heard her approach.

"I thought you were going to stay in the tunnel until I scouted the countryside."

"There is no danger to us. Not when the Wizard of Storms directs his full wrath against my poor brother." The woman tossed back her head. The wind caught her hair and sent it rippling in a long banner. Rain dotted her face and turned Lokenna into a being more than human. She looked at Santon and saw his expression. She smiled and it was the smile of a goddess.

The night had turned infinitely colder for him.

"I hurt my leg. Help me!" came Pandasso's whining voice. "I can't walk. You'll have to carry me."

"Walk or we throw you into the river," Santon said. "I'm in no condition to carry you and your wife's not strong enough." Santon continued to grumble, saying under his breath, "A full team of draft horses might not be strong enough, you giant fat oaf."

An explosion knocked them flat. Santon shook himself and dared to look at the castle. A jagged bolt of purple and green lightning unlike anything he'd ever seen had smashed the uppermost castle turret. He blinked. He thought he saw a body fastened to the flagpole being whipped about by the storm.

"The Wizard of Storms shows his distaste for Lorens this night," Lokenna said. "Come. Let's see if we can't convince him to join us against my brother."

"We're going all the way to the Uvain Plateau?" protested Pandasso. "My leg's turning game. Can't walk that much. It's too far!"

"Then stay." Santon helped Lokenna to her feet and started walking in the direction of the rebel force. He would have preferred skirting their encampment but time pressed in on him like a weight. The Uvain Plateau lay a hundred miles to the northwest and, once on the plateau, reaching the Castle of the Winds meant another two hundred miles of travel. If they had to fight the wizard's storms every second of the way, they might never get there.

"I sense your uncertainty in asking help from the Wizard of Storms," said Lokenna. "I do not like the idea of entreating a wizard of such power to help us, but Lorens and the Demon Crown are too strong to oppose in any other way."

"The rebels will deal with him. What good does the crown do him if he has no followers?" Pandasso hiked along behind them showing no sign of an injury.

"The power lies within, not in his soldiers," said Lokenna. "He can cause great woe if he uses the power of the crown for his own gain."

Santon fell silent. He remembered how Lorens had exploded the rebel troops when they had landed at the royal docks. Such magical power had not been present when they'd found the frightened apprentice wizard in the Desert of Sazan. The crown had greatly augmented his power and had turned him into a vicious, mad killer.

Santon looked over his shoulder at the castle, wondering at Vered's fate. He held back the tide of guilt mounting within but at great emotional cost. He stopped and stared. The huge flashes of lightning lit the landscape in a continuous, if flickering, display brighter than day. At the bramble barrier, near the spot Alarice had shown them, Santon saw movement. He strained and saw four figures emerging from the tunnel of thorns.

"Lokenna, can you make out who that is?"

She shook her head. "Not at this distance. If I wore the Demon Crown, it would be simple. But now?" She again indicated silently that she could make out no details of the four.

Hope flared. Vered knew only the secret ways in and out of the castle shown them by Alarice and Lorens. The tunnel had been discovered by Squann and would be unknown to Vered.

"We should wait. He might find us. That might be Vered."

"Who're the other three? Friends? More'n likely, he's traded us for his own hide."

"Spoken by one who knows true treachery," said Santon, his shoulder muscles bunching tightly. His hand clamped so firmly around the hilt of the dagger that his knuckles turned white and the veins stood out in bold relief.

"We are surrounded by the rebel army," Lokenna pointed out. "Is this the place to wait to see if that is your friend?"

The four emerging from the secret tunnel through the brambles mounted horses and rode at an angle from the castle. Wherever they went, it would require considerable hiking for Santon to catch up.

His guts churned with indecision. He had no reason to believe that any of the riders was Vered. He only hoped that his friend had eluded Ruvary's guardsmen and had escaped the castle walls. The notion that Vered had perished trying to rescue them, when they had already won free of the castle, pained Santon the most.

"We need horses," he said, still watching the riders battle their way through the storm. "Even if none of them is Vered, we need horses to reach the Uvain Plateau. I have no desire to walk all the way—and listen to *his* complaints."

Lokenna's eyes locked with Santon's and silent agreement passed between them. He found himself liking the woman more by the minute. She displayed courage and good sense, but the feelings he held for Alarice were not replaced by those for Lokenna. He admired Lokenna; he could never love her. She held herself apart, aloof, as if she were a spectator to all that happened around her rather than a participant.

Santon glared at the woman's husband. Bane Pandasso would never merit even grudging respect from him. Santon gestured for them to continue their slow march through the rain. The mud sucked at his boots and made walking a trial. Before they had gone a mile, Santon's feet had turned to lumps of ice and he knew he would be unable to continue much longer.

They needed food, shelter, fire—and horses.

"The rebel lines must be ahead," he said. He stared at the way the hillside had been torn up by scores of horses. Even the drenching rain had not been able to mask this spoor. "I'll see what I can find."

"See what you can steal, you mean," grumbled Pandasso.

"So you want to dance into the rebel camp and ask them nicely to give us what we need? How far will that get us?"

"Didn't mean nothing by it."

Santon tried to tell himself not to get angry at Pandasso, but he refused to take his own advice. He could not forget the man's continual whining—and past treachery. Even if Pandasso had betrayed Vered and the crown to Lorens for what seemed a good reason, Santon could never forgive him. They had lost the only bargaining lever they had with the wizard-king by that simple treason.

"Do you want me to go with you?" asked Lokenna. He saw that she meant what she said. She *would* accompany him, if he thought it would help. How unlike her husband Lokenna was.

"I'm safer alone. Wait a while. If I'm not back by sunrise, you go on toward the plateau. You don't want to be caught between rebels and the castle. Better to be behind their lines where they are less apt to keep a sharp lookout."

Seeing that Lokenna agreed with his reasoning, Santon walked off into the storm-cloaked night. A dozen paces placed him in his own world, cut off from everyone else. Santon used his good hand to wipe the rain from his eyes, then bent over and advanced cautiously.

His hunting sense worked for him again. He would have stumbled across a small sentry post if he had continued walking. He dropped into the freezing mud and wiggled on his belly, ignoring the filth. A moment's thought about Vered and how his friend would have been complaining about ruining his fine clothes passed. Santon concentrated on the guards in the post.

He counted five in a crude lean-to. Two slept, one snoring noisily. The other three huddled around a guttering fire continually assaulted by rain and the occasional snowflake.

"Freezing our arses off and for what?" groused one. "We sit and wait when Sef knows that nothing will happen. Not in this demon-cursed weather."

The other two concurred. Santon made his way around the camp, careful not to make too much noise. The wind and rain and snoring drowned out any stray sounds he may have made. He got to the rude corral where they had penned their horses. Under a tiny shelter of limbs he found their tack.

Santon wasted no time. The sky would begin turning pearly with dawn soon—if the storm allowed such light to show. He got a bridle and saddle from the shelter and outfitted the largest horse. Two more trips saw two more animals ready for travel. They whinnied loudly, but the storm prevented the miserable rebel sentries from hearing. Santon felt sorry for them. When their superiors learned that they had allowed a thief to make off with three horses—why not all five?—they would be disciplined severely.

The thought of spare horses appealed to Santon. He readied a fourth and a fifth. In this way they could ride and allow two horses to rest. Lokenna was so light her horse might not need respite, but Santon and Pandasso both weighed down any animal with their bulk.

Santon vaulted into the saddle and led the other four saddled horses from the corral. The rain lessened, then stopped. He urged the animals to greater speed. The sudden lightning of the sky told him that dawn would soon break over the Iron Range.

"Birtle, we're so glad you came back. There is trouble in the castle." Lokenna was beside herself with worry.

He stood in the stirrups and stared at the castle. The storm had disappeared quickly, again betraying its magical origin. The main gate of the castle caught his attention.

"Lorens launches an assault on the rebel line. We've got to be away quickly!"

"The storm blinded him. I felt him trying to use the crown and failing, but with the magic storm past, he can see everything."

Santon helped Lokenna into the saddle, wheeled his steed about, and put his heels to the heaving flanks.

"We're riding into the rebel camp!" cried Pandasso. "We cannot go there. They'll kill us!"

Santon hunched over his horse's neck and spurred the horse on. The two spare animals raced along easily behind. He heard Lokenna's horse and knew they would survive. Of Pandasso's complaints he heard nothing. His plan would get them safely through the rebel ranks and to the plains beyond.

With luck, they would ride unmolested. With luck.

"Halt!" came the challenge. "Who goes there?"

"Messengers for Dalziel Sef. There's cavalry

from the castle on the road. Lorens has launched a full attack. Spread the word!"

The effect exceeded Santon's wildest hope. The rebel guards vanished as they rushed to spread the word and awaken the sleeping camp. They had planned on siege, not defense.

Through the center of the camp rode Santon, Lokenna, and Pandasso. As they went, Santon called out his warning. He had no real love for Dalziel Sef, but his sympathies lay more with the rebel, in spite of all he had done to Fron and other villages, than with Lorens.

Sef showed cruel ambition—Lorens wore the Demon Crown. That made the wizard-king the more dangerous.

Even as he rode, Santon saw the type of soldier Sef had recruited. For the men, he felt a pang of sorrow. They were poorly equipped and did not react to this dire threat in a trained and military fashion. Most would die if Lorens' field commander kept a tight control over his own troops.

The damned civil war had raged far too long. Santon prayed that Lokenna was right and that some alliance with the Wizard of Storms could be forged.

Santon reached the northernmost limits of the rebel camp, his voice hoarse from shouting the warnings. He heard the first clash of steel against steel. Lorens's soldiers had advanced quickly to engage the rebels this soon after leaving Castle Porotane. Santon had no stomach for staying and lending his single strong arm to the fight.

"Santon!" came Lokenna's cry. "To the left. Lorens' men!"

He had no idea how they had penetrated this far through the rebel line in such a short time.

Two armed and armored riders urged their horses on to cut off his escape. Santon cursed his stupidity. When he had sneaked into the rebel sentry post he should have stolen more than tack. The dagger Squann had given him remained his only weapon.

"Keep riding, Lokenna. I'll slow them down." He tossed the reins of the two spare horses to Pandasso. The man had the good sense not to let them drop. With his wife, Pandasso rode on as hard as he could. Lather already flecked the sides of his straining horse.

Santon hoped the animal wouldn't die of exhaustion. When he spun about to face the two royalist soldiers, he hoped he wouldn't die. The dagger seemed an even more pitiful weapon now that he faced one rider with a lance and the other with a battle-ax.

He gauged his chances, then spurred hard so that he rode between the two. At the last possible instant he jerked on the reins and dodged to the left, effectively cutting off the rider with the ax and engaging the lancer from his weak side. The soldier fought to lift his weapon and get it to his left.

Santon ducked under the descending shaft and backhanded the rider, knocking him from his saddle.

With one foe down, Santon kept riding, heading for a stand of trees where a rider with an ax would be at a disadvantage. He veered to the right and for an instant vanished directly behind the rider, who struggled to get his galloping horse turned for the pursuit.

Santon grunted as a tree limb flashed past at head level. He kicked free of his stirrups and used his powerful left arm to swing like an ape. A sudden heave got him onto the limb. Panting, he lay flat and waited for the soldier to follow his trail.

So intent was the soldier on the hoof marks in the muddy ground that he failed to look up. Santon slipped off the limb and looped his arm around the rider's throat. A spiked gorget cut into Santon's arm, but he cared less for strangling the soldier than he did with unseating him. They crashed to the ground, the armor putting the fallen soldier at a disadvantage.

Santon used his dagger, driving the sharp point into an exposed armpit. The soldier died instantly.

He sank to his knees and unfastened the ax from the soldier's wrist and put it around his own. He still railed against the loss of his glass shield but having an ax once more made him feel complete.

Santon got his horse and spent a few minutes rounding up the other two horses. He checked them for trail rations and found little. Lorens expected this attack to be a quick one. From the decreasing sounds of battle, Santon guessed that Lorens' bold attack had crushed the rebels' spirit.

He headed north and west and found the fresh trail left by Lokenna and Pandasso. Within an hour he had overtaken them. Within two they had left the battleground far behind.

But Birtle Santon kept looking over his shoulder, sure that someone watched their flight.

Chapter Fifteen

Vered moaned as he rubbed his bruised ribs. He had rolled into the guardsman and used his rib cage as a battering ram—but it had been worth the minor injury. The guards had fallen and spent too much time stumbling over one another to catch him. He didn't like leaving Santon and the others in the cell, but their main hope of rescue lay with him if he stayed free.

He dashed to the door leading from the dungeon and found it open—but nonetheless closed to him. An entire squad of guardsmen rattled and clanked down the stairs in front of him.

Vered spun and looked for somewhere to hide. He shuddered when he saw a torture cabinet door propped open. He ducked into the coffinlike device and pulled the lid shut. He almost screamed in horror when it locked into place.

The click of the lid shutting echoed and drowned out the pounding of the soldiers just a few feet away.

Vered struggled violently and found himself falling backward. He banged his head against a low stone ceiling. For a few seconds he simply lay stunned, wondering what he had gotten himself into. Then a slow smile crossed his lips. The torture cabinet had a false back—he had blundered into a secret passageway.

He got to his hands and knees and peered at the dirt under him. Someone had been here recently if he judged the footprints properly. Vered turned his attention back to the torture cabinet. Spy holes gave a good view of the dungeon; his heart leaped to his throat when he saw the guards pushing Santon and the others back into their cell. Even worse, the squad did not depart. They stayed on duty, posted in such a way that he couldn't hope to overcome one without two others seeing.

Vered decided to explore the secret passage rather than waiting for the guards to become lax and trying to pry open the coffin lid. He felt naked without a decent weapon to hold—and his clothing hung in tatters. He wondered if a bath and a new tunic and breeches might not be available before he tackled the job of rescuing Santon.

He crawled along the dirty passage, bumping his head often on the low ceiling. Whoever had passed this way had been much smaller—Vered wondered if it hadn't been Baron Theoll. The small noble had tried spying on him and Santon from a similar secret passage. They had nearly poked out the baron's eye.

The first exit was blocked. Vered moved on, following the spoor left by the previous traveller in these secret ways. When he emerged from the wall, Vered found himself in a familiar section of the castle. He smiled and turned toward his and Santon's old quarters.

Vered pressed his ear against the door and listened hard. The room had been occupied the last time they had checked. No interesting sounds came from within; Vered entered.

"Ah, a wardrobe still fit for the likes of a master thief." He threw open the wardrobe door and selected carefully. The clothing he had abandoned so many weeks ago still hung neatly in the cabinet. Vered decided a bath was out of the question, even if it did mean putting on decent clothing over a filthy skin. He preened in front of a full-length polished sheet of metal, then began searching the room in earnest for a weapon.

He found nothing. Cursing, he slipped from the room and made his way up the stairs at the end of the corridor to a small armory where he found his glass sword, Santon's glass shield, and enough other weaponry to hold off a small army. Vered gathered what he could and returned to his former quarters.

He dumped his treasure trove onto the floor and began sorting through it. He slipped four daggers into the folds of his clothing. Being caught unarmed did not appeal to him. He hefted the glass sword Alarice had given him and admired the way it fit his hand.

"Such a fine weapon. She forged well in glass." Vered started to thrust it through his belt when he heard the rattle of soldiers' gear in the hallway. He dropped the sword onto Santon's shield and shoved them under a pile of blankets just as the door burst open.

Vered used both hands to brush back his brown hair. In his most commanding voice, he demanded, "What is this? Do you always break into a lord's quarters in this scurvy manner?"

"Lord?" The soldier backed off. "Pardon. We search for a prisoner who has escaped from the dungeons."

"Do I look like any such prisoner? Begone!" Vered heaved a sigh when the soldier backed out and closed the door, still muttering apologies. The proper arrogance often carried the day.

He opened the door a crack and peered into the corridor. Satisfied, he slipped out—and froze.

A half-dozen swords pressed into his body.

"This is the one," came a cold voice. "Take him back to the dungeon and keep him separate from the others. Ruvary will interrogate him personally in the morning."

Vered struggled and held his arms high as he allowed them to prod him back down the steep flight of stone steps to the dungeon. His escape hadn't been as successful as he had hoped, but they had forgotten to search him.

The metal door to the cell clanged shut—and Vered still carried four daggers hidden on him. He would have to put them to good use. How, he couldn't say, but he would find a way. He always did.

"This solves one thorny problem, brother," said Dews Gaemock. "We no longer have to worry about Dalziel Sef."

Efran Gaemock stared down the river at the small boat working its way upstream against the heavy current and ice floes. He did not share his brother's confidence that Sef was soundly defeated.

"He's lost most of the army—*our* army," said Efran. "Does that make him impotent?"

"Hardly," said Dews. "But he no longer poses a threat to my command. Those who still rally against Lorens have only one banner to follow—mine."

Efran remained unconvinced. "Let's hear what he has to say. I cannot believe he was foolish enough to attack the castle."

"The scout reported it."

"We lack Lorens' information-gathering ability," said Efran. "I mistrust our source this time."

Dalziel Sef climbed from the boat and limped toward them. "Lords!" he greeted loudly. "Thank you for your hospitality!"

"Damn him," muttered Efran. "He begs sanctuary and we dare not betray the old customs, not when we need every man possible to replace the army he's lost."

"You worry too much about details, Efran." Dews Gaemock strode forward and extended his hand to Sef. "You've caused quite a stir with your attack," he greeted the rebel.

"My attack?" Sef shook his head and settled down into a proffered camp chair. He warmed his hands in front of the small fire and helped himself to some of the porridge gently boiling in a pot. He made a wry face as he burned his tongue on the hot food. Only then did he say, "Lorens attacked me. His troops came gushing out of the castle like a bucket with a hole in the bottom. We had scant warning he'd try such a bold move."

"He sees your every soldier. He listens in on your counsel. He can use the crown at every instant of the day. Why shouldn't he know his attack would succeed?" asked Efran.

"Your brother wasn't there, Dews. He cannot know of the storm."

"Speak directly to me or to no one!" raged Efran. He whipped out a slender knife and held it under Sef's nose.

The rebel leader looked at his reflection in the blade and said to Dews, "The storm was not natural. A wizard of great power conjured it. I think it was Lorens. He used it to shield his movement from my scouts."

Efran drew the blade back swiftly; a lock of Sef's hair fell, got caught in a gust of wind, and drifted away. Sef appeared not to have noticed. He turned back to his porridge, blowing on it until it cooled enough to eat.

"Good food," he said, wolfing it down. "We've been on the damned river for four days. Mostly eating raw fish. Hate fish. This is very good."

"You don't deny he caught your men sleeping?" asked Efran.

"Your brother's opinion of my talents as a commander are small. I tell you, Lorens sent the storm to hide his movement. We had no idea that an attack was planned. When he was alive, Duke Freow had been content to let us lay siege to the castle for months and months. Who'd think Lorens would attack us?"

"Lorens is mad," said Dews. "But in his madness he has outwitted you."

"A minor setback, nothing more," insisted Dalziel Sef as he helped himself to more porridge.

"How many of your men survived?" asked Efran. "We've heard conflicting numbers." For the first time, Sef stared directly at Efran, his eyes bleak.

"Few. Less than a hundred at a guess."

"What?" Neither Dews nor Efran believed this. "But you had over a thousand!"

"He gave no quarter. Any who were not killed outright were captured and slaughtered like sheep. I managed to escape through a quirk of fate. Some fool came riding through camp bellowing that we were under attack. My aides got me to the river and a boat."

"You left your army and fled like a craven." Efran Gaemock's anger mounted. Not only had Dalziel Sef usurped much of the rebel forces, he had turned tail and run at the instant his leadership was needed most.

"Would it have served any purpose for me to have died there, too?"

"Efran," warned Dews. "Do not harm him. We have need of every sword now—even his."

"Especially mine," corrected Sef. "I have survived Lorens' attack. Only I know his style of command in the field."

"He personally led his men?" Efran hardly believed this revelation.

"He ordered his archers to fire when I had barely begun rowing across the river. I'd know him anywhere—him and the glowing Demon Crown."

"This is worse than I thought," said Dews, scratching his chin. "As long as Lorens let his field commander lead the army, the royalists held back. Seeing their monarch in front of his troops might rally the peasants who were undecided."

"We might have difficulty getting supplies," summed up Efran. He stared at Dalziel Sef, with his cracked and yellowed teeth and wondered what went through the man's mind. He had almost single-handedly lost the war for them. A thousand men dead! He and Dews together led fewer than five hundred.

"We can bring together enough of an army to give him second thoughts on sallying forth into the countryside," said Sef. "A few bands of men along the roads will keep Lorens from travelling freely."

"We need to regroup. This is a major setback." Dews paced as he thought of a dozen different courses to pursue. Efran stared at Sef, trying to decipher the man's nonchalance.

It seemed as if this major defeat meant nothing to Sef. Efran saw the rebel cause dying, unless they were clever and bold. Lorens had not only destroyed most of their fighting force, he had swayed the populace to his side. When the royalists were penned in Castle Porotane, the peasants gave freely to the rebels without fear of reprisal.

That ended with Sef's crushing defeat. Lorens' troops could collect punitive taxes and burn out any farmer thought to be aiding the rebels. If Lorens had ordered the deaths of all rebels who surrendered, he had established the rules for the rest of the conflict.

No quarter asked or given.

Efran Gaemock shuddered. He had played at being court jester for two years trying to avoid such a war. Those following Lorens were not necessarily evil. Fear of the Demon Crown forced many to follow when they would otherwise resist. Now pardon for them was out of the question. Efran cursed again under his breath.

"We return to the oxbow above the castle,"

he heard Sef say. "We establish a camp and from there we spread out slowly. We need to establish our presence once more."

"A good plan," said Dews. "If we force the soldiers back into the castle and prevent them from establishing permanent bases in the countryside, we can triumph yet!"

Efran knew that his brother worked himself up into a frenzy before presenting this plan to the troops. He needed to be completely sure of himself and success or it would communicate to those listening—and doubt would cause even more the remaining five hundred to slip off into the night. With five hundred, they stood a chance, small but possible. With less, the rebellion against the royalists died on the spot.

"We must move downriver quickly," decided Dews. "The longer we allow Lorens to roam unopposed, even near the castle, the more difficult it will be to win."

Efran tacitly agreed. He sat, arms crossed and eyes fixed on Dalziel Sef. The other rebel leader had plans of his own. But what? Efran could not decide, but he would watch carefully. The years spent amid Castle Porotane's political maneuverings had not been wasted on him.

"Lorens should have interdicted travel on the river by now," observed Dews. "We've been able to set up camp so that he cannot pry us loose from our position."

"Unless we try another attack on the castle," said Efran. He stood on the rise peering down into the misty distance. Castle Porotane lay beyond the field of vision, obscured by distance and a feeble gray fog that had crept over the land.

"We can't attack. With luck we can accumulate and train enough men to lay siege to the castle again in the spring."

"We can certainly burn the crops to prevent supplies from reaching the castle," said Efran. He spoke of sieges and long-term plans but his mind turned over more immediate problems. Dalziel Sef had been too well behaved since the defeat. His words were conciliatory and his suggestions cautious. That did not match the personality of the man Efran had come to know.

All that he knew for sure was that the defeat had not broken Sef's will. The arrogance he had shown before when he had seized control of the forces in the Yorral Mountains remained.

"Dews?"

"What is it, brother?" Dews Gaemock pored over a map, drawing small arrows to show where raiding parties would best be used.

"We must not allow Sef to continue in a position of command. Send him to the western provinces to recruit a new army. Get him north to Claymore Pass."

"That is a poor idea," said Dews. "Remember the treaty he tried to sign with Ionia? If we hadn't discovered his perfidy and sent our own ambassador, he and Ionia would have seized the pass and mountains for their personal domains."

"My point is not lost on you, then," said Efran. "I do not trust him. Something more than obedience stirs in his wormy brain."

"He is courageous and skilled, in spite of the defeat he suffered."

"*We* suffered," Efran corrected. "His loss put the entire rebellion into jeopardy."

"We need all the skilled warriors we can find."

Efran clasped his hands behind his back and started to pace, his mind racing. The clatter of hooves brought him out of his reverie. He stopped and watched as a company of cavalry rode down a draw and vanished into the cold fog.

"Dews, where are they going?"

"Who?"

"An entire company is a horse. Where have you sent them? This is too large a group to commit. We'd agreed on that."

"I've sent no one anywhere. I ordered our sappers to fortify the roads leading to our camp and to do what they can to insure a good water supply. Perhaps you saw them leading a company of workers."

"These were armed cavalry." Efran spun and stalked off down the hill, found a checkpoint deserted, and proceeded angrily to find the company commander.

The bivouac was deserted. Campfires had been recently snuffed out. Only wispy columns of smoke rose to show that any soldiers had been here. Efran spun at a sound. Dews stood behind him, eyes wide.

"Where did they go?" Dews asked.

"We had regiment strength scattered about. Do any remain under our command?" asked Efran.

They raced back up the hill to their command post, alerted aides, and mounted, riding hard to find their field officers.

Most had left. Those that remained knew nothing.

Efran pointed and cried, "There! You! Stop!"

A solitary soldier struggled with a pack and

weapons. His left leg dragged slightly, making travel difficult.

"Yes, Lord Efran?"

"Where are your comrades? Where are you going?"

"Why, as you ordered. We're en route to the staging area."

"Staging area for what?" asked Dews, his voice cracking with strain.

"For the attack on the castle. Lord Dalziel leads it at dawn."

Efran and Dews exchanged horrified looks. "May the demons take him for all eternity!" exclaimed Efran. "He's doing the same thing again! The fool!"

They spent the next hour taking inventory of their supplies and the number of troops left them. Of five hundred, only one hundred remained—the one hundred closest to their command post. Dalziel Sef had cleverly taken only those at a distance to prevent the Gaemocks from knowing the full perfidy of his plan.

"Assemble the men immediately," Efran ordered. "We march after Sef. With luck, we can stop him. Without it, we might be able to rescue a few survivors."

He and Dews worked frantically to rally their remaining men. Of the hundred left them by Sef, fewer than eighty followed. Efran did not blame the deserters. When leaders had a falling out, the troops suffered—and died.

They marched hard all night and arrived behind Dalziel Sef's scattered lines to see that Lorens and the Demon Crown had again stolen victory from the rebel.

"He's allowed his ranks to be split by cavalry.

Less than two hundred on one side and . . . how many on the other, Efran? I cannot see well through the fog."

Efran checked with a scout. "Fewer than a hundred. The battle has only just begun and already he has lost more than a quarter of his total force."

"If we commit, we can save the smaller group." Dews looked at his brother, his expression grim. "Should we risk eighty to save an equal number? None might survive."

"What choice do we have? If we are crushed again, the rebellion is over for good. No one will follow you or me or any leader other than King Lorens."

"Then we attack." No confidence rang in Dews Gaemock's words.

"Death to the royalists!" shouted Efran. "No quarter! No quarter!" He put spurs to his horse and drew his sword, leading the all-out assault. Anything less would doom them all.

Even this drastic attack might prove too weak. If so, he would die with his men.

Chapter Sixteen

Birtle Santon pulled up the wool scarf and tried to keep the snow from getting onto his cheeks. They had already frozen—or so it felt. Dancing needles on his face kept him aware of continued life. Everything else assured Santon that he had long since died.

His body aches had gone away. The tingling in his fingers and toes had ceased. Even the nagging pain in his arse from being overlong in the saddle had vanished. His entire body, save for the incipient frostbite in his cheeks, had deserted him.

"We must rest," came Lokenna's plea. "To go on in this storm is madness."

"We have no choice," said Santon. His voice rang hollow and strange in his cold ears. It was as if another spoke. His mind floated free and looked back on his useless, frozen body. "There's no shelter, and without it we die."

"We die if we continue," argued Lokenna.

From Bane Pandasso there came only muffled grunts and peculiar whistles. He had long since ceased complaining and rode with his head bowed, more dead than alive.

"The storms shouldn't have been this vicious this early," Santon might speak the words but fact made a liar. They had ridden steadily and well across the plains to the ochre buttes lifting to the Uvain Plateau. Once they crossed the upper lip of the plateau the first freezing rainstorm struck.

Cold water had smashed into their faces; the rain froze on their faces and bodies almost instantly in the gusty, bitter winds coming down from the north. Santon had found a small cave along the plateau rim. For two days they had waited for the storm to lessen in intensity. Santon lied to himself for a third day that no blizzard could maintain such ferocity. On the fourth day it became apparent that no cessation would occur.

They had journeyed on, daring the elements.

That dare had become a curse. Santon knew the storm was not born from the natural actions of wind and wave. Only the Wizard of Storms' magic could produce such unrelenting cold and impossible tenacity. As effectively as if he'd stationed a thousand soldiers to guard the road to the Castle of the Winds, the cunning wizard defended himself with snow and fierce gale.

"Birtle," the woman said sharply. "We cannot go on like this. *I* cannot ride another instant." She reined in and stood, her horses shaking from the intense cold.

"Where do we camp?"

Lokenna had no answer. The flat plateau provided scant windbreak. The land had been farmed in such a way as to reduce elevations. The winegrowing regions that Vered cherished so for their alcoholic products had been devastated by the preternatural cold, stripping even vegetation from the ground.

"Fire," croaked out Pandasso. "There. Fire."

For a moment Santon thought Pandasso wanted only to start a fire. Then he saw the man painfully lifting a frozen hand to point. A desultory column of smoke rose, seemingly from the middle of a field as flat as the land over which they rode. Santon stood in the stirrups and tried to see the source of the smoke.

It might have been steam naturally occurring or it could have been due to a man-made fire. The former would save them. The latter might pose as much danger as freezing. The Uvain Plateau had been beleaguered by brigands for as long as Santon could remember. The civil war in lower Porotane had sapped the will of the monarch to patrol this section properly, and the rebels encouraged any breakdown in civil authority in nearby towns.

The result after twenty years of civil war had been to turn the plateau into a welter of small fiefdoms, each ruled by a brigand warlord. No visitors from lower Porotane were welcome. In this winter weather, Santon thought that *any* visitor threatening to take away heat and food from a local would be killed on sight.

"We ride to the fire," Lokenna said. "I know your objections. What matters it if we freeze into statues waiting for spring before rot sets in or we die with hot steel in our guts? That, at least, would warm us for an instant before we died." She turned her protesting horse toward the column of smoke. Pandasso followed.

Santon tried again in vain to identify the source of the smoke. He snapped the reins and got his horse moving after Lokenna. She had a point. Dying in one fashion as opposed to another meant little.

A hundred yards away, Santon saw a deep crevice cutting through the fertile farmland. That explained why he had been unable to see the source of the smoke—and smoke it was. Tiny embers rose and flared at ground level before turning to soot and ash. Only gray smoke rose above the ground.

"Can you see who lit the fire?" asked Santon, peering over the edge of the rim. Below he saw the campfire in the center of a tiny bivouac.

"No one," said Lokenna. She blinked her eyes. The eyelashes had frosted over and turned them into long snowflakes. This decided Santon. Brigand camp or not, they had to have shelter soon or die. This deep ravine gave it. They would never be able to fight for the right to stay, but even a hint of warmth might do wonders to restore feeling in their limbs.

"There. A way down. A narrow path. Can the horses stay on it?" Santon pointed to the rocky ledge hardly wider than his shoulders.

Lokenna said nothing. She dismounted and led her horse down. It stumbled and found footing difficult on the rock-strewn path but the escape from the cutting wind gave both animal and woman incentive to continue. Pandasso and a spare horse followed. Santon and the remaining spare animal brought up the rear.

By the time he reached the bottom of the ravine, Santon again felt pain throughout his body. The dancing needles had left his cheeks and now applied themselves to his hands and legs and any other portion of his anatomy that had begun to freeze.

"The fire is untended. What happened to the men who started it?" wondered Lokenna. She rubbed her hands together as she bent over the campfire. Santon threw on fresh wood and caused huge gouts of flame to leap skyward. The intense heat drove him backward. He knew how dangerous it was to thaw out quickly.

He skirted the camp, studying the blankets and other gear left behind. It seemed that the former residents had simply evaporated like the snowflakes falling into the column of rising hot air from the fire. Santon dragged out several of the blankets and gave them to Lokenna and Pandasso, then put one around his own shoulders. They had arrived on the plateau ill-equipped for the storms. With this camp's equipment, they'd stand a much better chance when they continued.

"I don't see any sign of them," Santon answered after a ten-minute pause. His teeth no longer threatened to chatter uncontrollably. "It is as if our unwitting hosts simply got up and left."

"I don't like it," said Pandasso. "It's not natural for men to leave like that. Not in foul weather like this."

"For once he said something I can agree with," said Santon. "The fire had not burned down. Whoever started it couldn't have been gone longer than fifteen minutes before we arrived."

"Perhaps longer," Lokenna said thoughtfully, "but where are they? We would have seen them if they'd departed in the last half hour. It took us some time to reach the edge of the ravine and at least fifteen minutes to come down."

Santon's green eyes scanned the sides of the rocky ravine for sign of ambush. No caves providing convenient hiding spots were evident. The question nagging at Santon was simple: Why leave camp, even if the former residents had intended an ambush?

Lokenna fixed their first decent meal since arriving on the Uvain Plateau from provender left by those now departed. The food rumbling in his belly, his arms and legs again working as well as they ever had, Santon went exploring. He didn't like what he found. Footprints went fewer than a dozen paces—then nothing.

It was as if the men who had been here simply evaporated.

"They must have been brigands. Look at this!" Bane Pandasso spilled out a bag filled with silver coins. In different times, Santon would have been interested. Now the piles of silver coin meant nothing. He wanted to tell Pandasso to stop weighing himself down with the useless coins he eagerly stuffed into his own pouch. Food mattered more than inert metal. Even if they encountered a farmer with grain or fresh meat, he would be unlikely to trade it for silver.

Food, not silver, meant survival in this unnatural winter.

"A storm is forming directly overhead," observed Santon. He watched uneasily as the lead-bellied clouds flowed past, giving him the impression that they stood still and he moved. He blinked hard and the illusion vanished.

But seeing more clearly did nothing for his peace of mind. Wispy tendrils of cloud formed on the underside. He and Vered had seen this before in the Yorral Mountains.

"The Wizard of Storms sent warriors from the sky in a similar fashion," he told Lokenna. "Why would he destroy an entire camp of brigands using his magical warriors?"

"My impression of him is sketchy and distorted," she admitted. "But there seems to be an overriding need for solitude. He can never achieve that when Lorens wears the Demon Crown."

Lokenna's eyes locked with Santon's. "The Wizard of Storms has brought all this down on our necks because he wants to be alone?" he asked.

"Who can say what a wizard's motives might be? I can think of stranger ones." She shuddered, and it wasn't from the cold. "My brother sought power through the crown. Now he seeks total domination of all Porotane."

"He's about got it," said Pandasso.

"No thanks to you," snapped Santon. He could not forget the man's betrayal, but he cut off this futile argument. What Pandasso had done was past—for better or for worse. Vered had not shown up and Santon could only assume his friend had perished.

"Take heart," came a soft whisper of wind that formed words next to his ear. Santon jerked upright, whirling around. A patch of gauzy white fog blew apart at his sudden movement.

"What's wrong, Birtle?" Lokenna asked.

"Nothing," he said. Santon started walking, carefully avoiding the drifting fog. In a low voice he called, "Alarice? Is that you?"

"My phantom, dear Birtle. Wait! Stop! You must not seek me. I find it hard to remain here."

"Show yourself. Please! You appeared to Vered."

"He still lives. Do not despair."

"Alarice!"

He called after the wind. The white fog he thought was her phantom drifted apart and blew damply across his face, leaving a thin film of moisture. He wiped away the droplets that intermixed with his tears.

"Birtle, are you all right?" came Lokenna's worried cry.

"I am. We must leave immediately." He looked upward and saw the tendrils from the clouds dipping ever lower. In a few minutes the cloud tails would sweep along the bottom of the ravine. He remembered all too well the power of the Wizard of Storms' magical defenders. The cloud warriors had decimated the ranks of Lorens' soldiers with little effort. What had driven them away, he could not say.

Whatever it was—the wizard's whim or Lorens' magic—it lay beyond his call.

"Get on your horses. We leave *now!*"

He vaulted into the saddle. His horse protested. He patted the mare's neck and tried to soothe the tired and frightened animal. "We must race the wind, you and I," he told her quietly. "We will not get a second chance."

The whites showed around the horse's fearful eyes. She tossed her head and looked at the long streamers of cloud that came from above.

"The clouds turn into warriors," marvelled Pandasso. "Look at them!"

"Those are what killed the brigands who camped here. We will follow them as phantoms unless we get out of this trap." Santon herded Lokenna before him and decided that Pandasso might finally serve a useful purpose by remaining behind as living decoy. When the first of the cloud warriors took form and reached out a vaporous hand in the man's direction, Pandasso let out a shriek of pure terror and frantically spurred his horse after Santon.

The trip up the side of the ravine took no longer than the journey down, yet Santon aged a hundred years. The cloud warriors lacked mobility. In the bottom of the ravine they reigned supreme but lacked the power to follow up the steeply winding trail.

Panting with exhaustion, the horses heaved themselves over the rim of the ravine and once more entered the full-blown snowstorm. To Santon it came as a breath of fresh air. The warmth of the ravine vanished, but he felt a freedom that had been lacking below.

"The clouds! They bring us more magic warriors," Pandasso shouted over the howling wind.

Santon saw the growing danger even as Pandasso spoke. New pillars of mist descended and solidified into warriors twice the height of a man. With footsteps that left behind frozen patches, the cloud warriors advanced on them.

"What can we do?" asked Lokenna.

"Unless your talents match those of your brother, all we can do is flee."

"I am untrained as a wizard. I know only what was revealed to me by the crown."

"Then we ride!"

Visibility limited, Santon chose the easiest path he could. They rode along the gentle contours of the land but the very flatness prevented him from finding adequate hiding places. The cloud warriors might not be able to climb steep ravine walls—but on this part of the Uvain Plateau they walked unhindered by anything larger than a fist-sized rock.

"They're catching up," wheezed Pandasso, still at the rear. The horse he led stumbled and fell.

Santon looked back in time to see one immense cloud warrior lift a bulbous hand and point a stubby finger in the fallen animal's direction. A shaft lanced forth. At first Santon thought it rivalled the lightning still dancing in the clouds above. Then he saw that the white shaft reflected light rather than produced it.

"Ice. The cloud warrior threw a spear of ice at the horse." Santon swallowed hard when he saw the massive ice lance pinning the horse to the rocky ground. The animal kicked feebly but life slowly drained from its dying body.

The nearest cloud warrior lifted a hand and made a sweeping motion. Hail pelted down on Santon with such force that he felt his skin bruising, even through the heavy layers of cloak and blanket circling his shoulders. One hailstone caught him a glancing blow on the side of the head. He wobbled and would have fallen from his horse if Lokenna hadn't reached across to steady him.

"There," she said. "Veer to the left."

Santon, dazed, did as he was ordered. He fell from horseback when the reins were yanked from his hand and the horse dug in all four feet to come to a skidding halt.

He lay on his back, staring up at the underbelly of the storm cloud spawning the magical warriors. Santon watched the cloud drift back in the direction they'd ridden from. He came up to his knees, then got to his feet ready to fight.

"They're ignoring us," he said in awe. "Lokenna! You used a spell to confuse them!"

"No, Birtle, I did no such thing. I saw a horse and rider through the fog and snow. By swerving from our course, the other acted as decoy. The cloud warriors are powerful but slow to react."

"You sent another to death to save us?"

"What choice was there?"

Santon dashed into the fog until he got a better look at the portion of farmland that had become a fierce battlefield. Not one or two riders had drawn the attention of the cloud warriors but a full dozen. From the way they fought, Santon knew they were not simple farmers.

Arrows arched into the cloud warriors and received answering shafts of pure ice. Swords flashed and tried to sever cloudy tendons. In return came monstrous fists laden with hail and searing lightning.

The fight was uneven and ended swiftly.

"Brigands," Lokenna said from beside him. "The Wizard of Storms seeks out brigands and methodically slays them."

"Why? I mean, the brigands are a menace to everyone on the plateau, but what does it matter to a powerful wizard? He is secure in his fine castle."

"Is he?" asked Lokenna. "The brigands are a

symptom of the problem in Porotane. The Demon Crown is the cause of the trouble."

"But the brigands have nothing to do with Lorens. I don't understand."

"The Wizard of Storms desires only solitude for his research. The civil war disrupts the kingdom for a score of years, but this affects him little," said Lokenna.

"It passed by him—until Vered and I returned from the Desert of Sazan with your brother and the Demon Crown."

"The crown disturbs the Wizard of Storms," she said. "He wants it sent back into oblivion, and if he cannot do that, and I think it likely his powers are not that great, he will kill Lorens."

"Our goals are similar."

"Not so," said Lokenna. "I have no love for Lorens, but he is my brother. I will not see him dead without purpose."

"Can you imagine him handing over the crown—or putting it aside?"

"No," she said in a small voice. "But he is all the family I have."

Santon looked back at her husband. Bane Pandasso cowered near the horses. Fate had dealt with Lokenna cruelly. A crazed tyrant for a brother and a craven for a husband.

"Can we use this need on the wizard's part to enlist his aid?"

"I have believed that for some time. We must reach the Castle of the Winds soon." Lokenna looked at the clouds and the warriors dropping to earth from them. "We have little chance of escaping the Wizard of Storms' minions."

"I wish Vered were here to enjoy this bit of

irony," Santon said. "The very one we seek to align ourselves with wants us dead."

"For all that, you sound cheerful," she said.

Santon smiled and indicated that the woman should mount and ride. How could he feel too sad when Alarice had told him that Vered still lived.

His momentary cheerfulness vanished when the storm lifted and he saw the Castle of the Winds perched high atop a rocky spire wreathed in fluffy white clouds.

Chapter Seventeen

"Fight, damn your eyes!" shouted Efran Gaemock. His cry rallied the small band of weary, frightened men in front of him. They doubled their efforts, firmed their attack line, and then surged forward. Lorens' soldiers were taken aback by such ferocity. The rebels under Dalziel Sef had retreated quickly.

Not so this band of berserkers. And of them Efran proved the fiercest. Ignoring a dozen cuts to his arms and legs and one large gash across his cheek, he always attacked and never retreated. Left and right he cut with his sword until he seemed to be a magical creation rather than human. When the blade became dull from cutting into bone and bouncing off armor, he cast it aside and picked up a fallen weapon. With this new sword he continued his battle until he stood alone.

"They're running like whipped dogs," he heard someone nearby say. For the first time since he had entered battle, he saw—really *saw*—what they faced.

Lorens had used the Demon Crown well to find the weaknesses in Dalziel Sef's troop deployment. The cavalry attack from the castle had split the rebel force and doomed the larger portion to annihilation. To his immense surprise, Efran saw that most of the smaller group had survived and managed to fight back effectively.

"Attack Lorens' flank," Efran heard ring over the battlefield. His brother sat on a massive black stallion—not the horse he had ridden into battle. From this majestic perch Dews Gaemock formed a new attack against the rear and weaker side of Lorens' now struggling, demoralized forces. If they had succeeded in keeping the rebel troops split, their earlier slaughter would have been duplicated, but this small rebel victory had doomed Lorens.

Efran's thrill of victory faded when he saw that he had rescued the eighty men—and lost the two hundred. Fewer than one hundred and fifty would survive this day in spite of their valiant fighting. The rebels, because of Sef, had gone from fifteen hundred to one-tenth that number in the span of a few days. Years of careful campaigning and building vanished because of one man's ambition.

"Dews!" he called. Efran waved his bloody sword and reflected light from its silvery blade to catch his brother's attention. When he did, he signalled for immediate retreat. Dews nodded, passed the order to his lieutenants, then jerked on the reins of his captured horse and vanished down the other side of the hill.

Efran began gathering those around him and slowly disengaging. Lorens' soldiers had been taken by surprise and retreated when given the chance.

That gave Efran's small band the opportunity to flee for the dubious safety of their base camp.

Efran supervised the pickup of wounded and the retrieval of what supplies they could.

"No!" he shouted when he saw a rebel start to cut the throat of a fallen soldier dressed in the uniform of Lorens' personal guard. "Let him be."

"He's one of *them*," the bloodied rebel protested.

"We can't take him prisoner. We let him be."

"If it had been the other way, he'd've killed us! Lorens ordered no prisoners left alive."

Efran looked down at the frightened soldier. One of the man's legs had been broken when a horse fell on him. "Take this back to your comrades. We do not slaughter helpless men and women. Think on who you would rather follow in the next battle."

Efran grabbed the rebel's shoulder and pushed him on.

"Wait!"

Efran turned back to the fallen soldier, his eyes bleak.

"Take me with you. I surrender. I don't want to go back to the castle. They . . . he'll order me executed."

"What?"

"King Lorens said that we either died on the field or walked back as victors. He'll have me killed as a failure." The soldier's plaintive tone told Efran that he spoke the truth.

To the rebel who had been intent on slicing the man's throat, Efran said, "See? We may not be superior in numbers but we soar above them in spirit."

The rebel grumbled and went to the stricken soldier. The soldier recoiled, then saw that he was being helped up. He turned pale and wobbled on his broken leg until the rebel hoisted him onto his back and started back to their camp with the injured man.

Efran smiled wanly. They had won a recruit this day. When the soldier healed, he would fight with twice the strength—and for the rebel cause. They would need many more such conversions, though, if they were to triumph.

Efran caught a horse to replace the one that had been cut from under him by a barrage of arrows. He rubbed his wounded calf; an arrow had passed through the fleshy part and embedded itself in his horse. He swung up into the saddle and wheeled about to get a better idea of their position.

His heart turned to ice. Sef had positioned well enough but had not considered Lorens' perfect intelligence-gathering. As a result, they would have to hasten their departure from the battlefield before Lorens turned the crown on them and saw how battered they really were. A quick thrust with a company of fresh cavalry and the rebellion would be crushed for all time.

"Dews," he shouted. "Can you keep them moving back to the river?"

"I must," his brother answered. Dews seemed unscathed by the battle but his paleness told of shock. Efran rode closer and saw the entire left side of his brother's tunic had blossomed with a bloodstain. Dews was losing blood by the bucket.

"Retreat, get them into barges and away downriver. Lorens might keep his troops close to the castle to consolidate his position. He won't come for us until spring."

"Yes, that is so." Dews leaned forward, winced at the pain, then said, "I ask a boon of you, brother." Their eyes met.

"I'm searching for him. He won't escape. I promise it."

"Good. We'll wait at the river. Join us quickly. There may not be time, if Lorens is in control."

Efran Gaemock turned his horse and rode quickly in the direction of the battlefield. Fog drifted through the wooded area. Already he heard the soft moans of phantoms escaping their mortal bodies. How many would remain phantoms, haunting this bloody patch of Porotane's once-fertile farmland? Too many, he decided. And it was all one man's fault.

Efran helped a few rebels orient themselves and begin the slow journey back to their camp. Many would die on the way but the few who would survive needed what he had to offer.

He found Dalziel Sef sooner than he'd dared hope. The other rebel leader sat with his back against a tree, his leg twisted under him.

"Efran! You've come for me. Hurry, I hear Lorens' men coming. They hunt out all the wounded and cut their throats—even their own!"

"Lorens considers it a sign of weakness to be injured in battle. I spoke with one of his soldiers." Efran stared at the man responsible for single-handedly destroying the rebel army.

"Help me, man. Don't just sit there on your fine steed." Sef cocked his head to one side and studied the animal. "You steal well. Your other horse was hardly worthy of a rebel lord and general."

"This one seems strong and ready to run all day."

"Then help me up and we'll be on our way."

"Help you I will." Efran dismounted and went to Sef's dead horse. He cut a length of leather harness loose and fashioned a loop. He tossed it over Sef's head and got it about the man's armpits.

"What are you doing?" Sef demanded.

"You're wounded. I wouldn't want you to be left behind."

"I can ride. It's only my leg that's injured. Now help me up!"

Efran fastened the leather thong to the saddle horn. He put his heels into the horse's flanks and took off at a trot, dragging a screaming Dalziel Sef behind. He did not seek out the rockiest areas to drag the rebel over, but he considered it. Rather, Efran chose the fastest route to the river where his brother and the remnants of their once-proud army waited.

"Damn you!" sobbed Sef when Efran finally reined back and came to a halt. "I'm all broken up inside." He spat blood and coughed. Pink froth showed at his lips. Efran thought Sef had a punctured lung, possibly from a broken rib.

Efran ignored Dalziel Sef and went to where Dews lay. His brother's condition had worsened. The paleness bordered on death itself, but the first words he spoke were what Efran expected. "Did you find him?"

"I'll bring him before you for judgment."

Efran tugged hard on the leather harness around Sef's body. Two others had to help him stand. They supported Sef before Dews Gaemock's litter.

"You are a fool," Dews said. "You have cost us years of careful work and turned hope into pain and fear."

"Who are you to say what I've done?" Dalziel Sef spat blood and coughed again. "You dared nothing! I almost won the castle after all your tedious years of laying siege. You are a coward, a weakling!"

"Tie him onto a horse and send him to Lorens," suggested a rebel at the edge of the assembled crowd.

"Hang him!" yelled another. Still another demanded torture.

"You hear the will of those you betrayed," Dews said. "I agree with their judgment in this. Execution!"

Dews rose painfully from the litter, a small dagger in his hand. A sudden flash of steel in the sunlight and then a tiny gasp marked Dalziel Sef's passing.

Efran wished he felt something. Elation. Revenge satisfied. Something. Nothing but a dark and abiding hollowness grew within him. He silently helped his brother onto a barge.

They had a long ways to travel before finding a safe encampment for the winter.

CHAPTER EIGHTEEN

"We can't go around them," said Birtle Santon. He studied the marching pillars of lightning-filled mist and saw nothing but death ahead. They had ridden through the storms and nearly frozen to death over the past week. But they had survived—somehow. Now that they had come to the base of the pinnacle holding the Castle of the Winds, he saw how futile their perilous journey had been.

"He uses the cloud warriors well," said Lokenna.

"There's only the one path to the summit," said Pandasso. "Let's forget this madness and go back to Fron. We can rebuild the inn and . . ." His voice trailed off when he realized that neither his wife nor Santon listened. Both drew small maps in the snow as they tried to figure out ways around the towering cloud warriors.

"We might lure them away," said Lokenna.

"Too risky," Santon told her. "We cannot see past this turning in the road. Others might stand sentry beyond. We sneak by these and we might find ourselves trapped, magical beings ahead and behind."

"I wish I had the crown," she said wistfully. "I could see what lies ahead for us."

"The road is not well kept. The horses will have a difficult time, even if we do get around the cloud warriors." Santon looked at the three horses, now half-starved and at the point of exhaustion. The other two horses had perished along the way. Santon wondered if they weren't the lucky ones. The Uvain Plateau emphatically ended at this spot. The pinnacle was sharp and jutted upward as if it could gouge out a piece of the sky. To follow that road winding around the peak meant a major expedition.

Santon was not sure any of them had the strength left for such a steep and treacherous climb. To fight the magical warriors made it all the more difficult.

"We can't sneak by. The Wizard of Storms would not post them here if they were deaf and blind."

"They might use other senses. After all," said Lokenna, "they are nothing but fog."

"Fog and magic," grumbled Pandasso.

"We might be going at this in the wrong way," said Santon, his mind racing in new directions. "Why do we assume that the wizard wouldn't be glad to see us? His magical minions have had innumerable chances to kill us these past few weeks."

"They seek out brigands," said Lokenna.

"They might ignore peasants—and we might seem so to them."

"*I* am nothing more than a humble innkeeper," said Pandasso. "I want to return to my village and ply my trade."

"What would we do if we did confront the wizard?" asked Santon. "We kill ourselves trying to get past his guards and then what? Does he reach out and send a lightning bolt into our mouths for daring to speak to him? What do we gain by that?"

"You have a point," admitted Lokenna. She stood and faced the nearest cloud warrior. The towering being of gray mist and burning red eyes turned slowly, as if not knowing who disturbed its sentry duty. A foggy hand lifted. Purple and green lightning arced between the fingers.

"We've come to see the Wizard of Storms," called out Santon, standing next to Lokenna. Bane Pandasso cowered behind a large boulder, not daring to show himself. "We have come far to see him—past brigand and royalist soldier alike."

"I am Lokenna, daughter of Lamost," the woman said. "My brother wears the Demon Crown."

The words caused thunder to rumble deep within the cloud warrior. Above scudded new storm clouds with underbellies of steel gray. They swirled and took shape overhead, trailing wisps of cloud stuff. New warriors dropped to the ground and formed a rank beside the guards already on duty.

"What do we do?" asked Santon.

Lokenna shrugged. "I have no idea. We can always die, if the Wizard of Storms refuses to see us."

"Th-they're coming for us!" Pandasso began scuttling away. Santon grabbed the man with his powerful left hand and jerked him to his feet.

"We stand together," Santon said coldly, but inside he quaked as badly as Pandasso did outwardly.

"I wish I knew a spell to utter," said Lokenna.

"Look. The warriors are . . . dissolving." Santon took a step forward to get a better view of the strange transformation taking place. The cloud warriors bent over, touching one another and forming an arch. The vague human forms turned into less animate walls.

"They still pulse as if life flowed in their veins," said Lokenna.

"Lightning still flashes and snow falls," Santon said, "but they've formed a tunnel for us."

"He wants us to meet with him. He wants us to go up the road to the Castle of the Winds!"

"No, not me. I'm not going—" Pandasso's protests were cut short when Santon heaved. Muscles rippled and sent the innkeeper stumbling forward into the cloudy arch. Pandasso screamed as lightning bolts speared down and collided with his outstretched hands. He bowed his back and continued to scream. Lightning touched his face and legs and bathed his entire body in an eerie purple and green glow.

Then Bane Pandasso disappeared.

"He was blasted into nothingness!" exclaimed Santon.

"No, Birtle, no, he wasn't." Lokenna walked forward with more confidence than Santon felt. She stood, arms aloft. Eye-searing flashes lanced toward her; Lokenna vanished.

Santon had to decide between turning to flee

like a craven or discovering Lokenna's fate. He walked forward, heart hammering fiercely in his chest. The darkness within the arch of clouds made him think that eternal night had fallen. Like the two before him, he raised his arms. His good one he held directly over his head. His withered arm rose only to shoulder level.

He swallowed hard when he saw the vivid, crackling magical energies mounting within the foggy walls of the tunnel. Then he screamed as the lightning reached down and touched his body. Every nerve within him shrieked in protest. Santon took an involuntary step forward and fell to one knee.

"Where . . ." He looked around in surprise. He knew he had to be dead, but this place resembled no hell he had ever heard described.

He stood in the center of a round room with comfortable furniture strewn about haphazardly. Santon ignored this. His full attention focused on the small rainstorms gathered at the walls. Each seemed a miniature of a full-fledged cousin outside. Rain pelted down to the floor and tiny lightnings crashed and crackled—and each time a discharge occurred, a window opened.

"Yes," said Lokenna. "He is able to look out over Porotane through the magic of his storms."

"Why else call me the Wizard of Storms?" asked a straight-backed, leathery, balding man. He pushed up baggy sleeves and revealed thin arms covered with burns and scars. When he saw Santon's frown, he said, "Every apprentice learns to cast spells." He laughed. "He also learns what *not* to do. These are my reminders."

Santon had believed the Wizard of Storms to

be all-powerful and even godlike. The man before him was just . . . a man.

"You seem disappointed." He turned and pointed a gnarled finger. The nimbus of magic around the finger formed a solid green rod that speared deep within the cloud on the southern wall.

"Efran!" cried Lokenna.

"Ah, you know the rebel. And his brother, too. Dews Gaemock is sorely wounded."

"By Lorens?"

"Indirectly," said the Wizard of Storms. "The direct cause was treachery by this one." The scene shifted slightly and showed Dalziel Sef's body strung up by its heels in a tree. Every gust of wind caused the corpse to sway like a clock pendulum. "His ambition proved stronger than the flesh of the rebel soldiers."

"What of Lorens?" asked Santon. "Can you show us the castle?"

"You want to know what has become of your friend Vered."

Santon blanched. This seemingly simple old man was truly a wizard.

"See what happens when I cast my scrying spell in that direction!"

Santon threw up his good arm to protect his eyes. Searing light burst forth from the tiny storm cloud. An instant later scalding water cascaded over him.

"The Demon Crown blocks my magic, even as mine blocks its power. I do not like this. Things were ever so peaceful when Alarice hid the crown and none dared wear it."

"You bring your storms to bedevil us," protested Pandasso.

The wizard glared at him. "I play with the elements. I enjoy fashioning works of kinetic art. Who else uses nature itself as a canvas? No one! Is there any soul in Porotane who claims to make music as potent as mine? Nowhere does anyone make such a false boast."

He threw back his sleeves and produced a crashing drumbeat of thunder punctuated by lightning and the boiling of clouds. "See? Hear? Feel? I produce art stimulating more than one sense. And now Lorens threatens my existence. I find this intolerable, just as I did when Waellkin donned that damnable crown."

"Why did you bring us here?" asked Pandasso.

"I? I did not *bring* you here. You came of your own will. Did I force you to ride across Porotane, across the Uvain Plateau? No! You are intruders on my serenity and as such will be destroyed." The Wizard of Storms pushed back his baggy sleeves again.

"Save the boasts and lies for another," cut in Lokenna.

"You do not think I can destroy you with a pass of my hand?"

"Of course you can—but you won't. You *allowed* us to come, even if you did not bring us here. Your cloud warriors could have slain us rather than the brigands."

"You fought well against my magic," admitted the Wizard of Storms.

"We need one another," the woman said.

"What? I? I am the most powerful wizard in the world! What do I need of you?"

"I can control the Demon Crown. My brother blots out your view. He ruins a masterpiece," Lokenna said shrewdly. "I can control the crown. Kill Lorens and the crown will destroy the world."

"You know." The Wizard of Storms sat down heavily and stared at her. "But you would. You wore the crown and saw what evil your brother has unwittingly unleashed."

"He is weak. I needed to know more about the danger, but he refused to tell me."

"What danger?" demanded Santon. "What are you talking about?"

"Lorens has fallen into a trap set by the demon Kalob three centuries ago. He is narrowing the gap between our worlds. The demons will pour through if my brother does not work to stop it."

"He won't," said Santon.

"He can't," corrected the Wizard of Storms. "He is untrained in the use of power. I warned Patrin about such things, but he'd never listen to me. Willful child."

"Patrin was your son?"

"Everyone is entitled to an indiscretion now and then," said the Wizard of Storms, shrugging.

"We need each other," repeated Lokenna. "We can work together. We want the same thing—peace in Porotane."

"You will guarantee the Demon Crown is rendered impotent after the removal of your brother from the throne?"

"No. I do guarantee that it will never interfere with your artistic creation."

"Impossible. The crown must be destroyed."

"It is a legacy of the realm. It cannot be."

Santon sat back in awe and listened to the argument. Lokenna pleaded their case well. He saw the Wizard of Storms weakening in his resolve to destroy the Demon Crown. As the wizard slowly came over to Lokenna's side, the storm clouds around the room lightened to fluffy white.

"It's agreed. I want nothing to do with your petty rulings after this is resolved."

"A temporary alliance, then," said Lokenna.

Birtle Santon wondered which one lied. From their expressions, he guessed both were. This conflict of magic would not end with Lorens' death.

Chapter Nineteen

Vered sat in the center of the cell trying to knock off the largest pieces of dirt soiling his finery. His trip to his old quarters had given him fresh clothing, for all the good that had accomplished. The dungeon was a filthy place and not the environment for maintaining a decent appearance. As he rubbed the dirt from his tunic, his sharp ears pricked up for any sound of guards.

He heard nothing. He continued brushing himself off and straightening the wrinkles in his tight vermilion and cobalt breeches. As he worked, his nimble fingers touched on the four daggers he had hidden before Ruvary's guards caught him. All were in place.

He went to the cell door and peered through the heavily barred grate. The dungeon was unnaturally devoid of activity. The guards had vanished and even the moans from tortured prisoners had died down. He shuddered. The other prisoners might have been put to death on Lorens' order. The wizard-king had shown no mercy for those less fortunate—or any who opposed him.

Vered touched the skin at his neck, wondering why the guardsmen hadn't simply slit his throat.

"They didn't, and that's my bit of luck." He dropped to his knees and examined the lock on this cell. His heart sank. The keyhole controlling an intricate lock, such as had been on his prior cell, gaped wide open. He thrust his finger through the hole and wiggled it.

The lock had been removed in favor of a heavy exterior locking bar.

Vered scowled. The other lock had fallen easily to his skill. This was another matter. He pulled out the dagger with the thinnest, longest blade and tried working it between doorjamb and door. It refused to enter the cramped space. He had to reach the drop bar outside or he would never be able to escape.

Vered thrust his arm out the small grate, winced as metal cut into his flesh, then tried to grasp the bar and lift it. His fingers curled just under the bar. Grunting with effort and pain, he got his fingertips securely under the heavy bar and heaved with all his strength.

The bar didn't budge.

"Won't do no good," came a voice from the next cell. "They got a cotter pin shoved through it. Takes more'n you got to get it free. Takes two good hands—from the outside."

"Hello there," called Vered, pressing close to

the grate in a vain attempt to see his fellow prisoner. "How is your door locked?"

"Got one of them fancy-ass locks on it. No way I can open it. Might as well have a bar like on yours, for all the good it does."

Vered cursed. If he had been in the other cell, he would be free in a flash. Sooner! The strongest lock made could not withstand his knowledgeable assault. And he was trapped in a cell with such a simple bar mechanism!

"Is there any way you could lift the bar on my cell door?" he asked.

"No way," came the answer. "There'd be nothing in it for me, even if I could."

"Nonsense," said Vered, wanting an ally, no matter who it might be. "We are in the dungeon together. That makes us comrades-in-arms."

"Comrades-in-prison is more like it," the other man said sarcastically.

Vered paced the cell, examining every corner. The wall around the door had been reinforced with a steel plate. Scraping through it would be impossible, even with his daggers. The back wall dripped cold water. When he pressed his ear to it he heard a loud rushing noise.

"There's water behind the back wall," his fellow prisoner called, as if he knew what Vered considered. "Supplies the whole damn castle, it does. Comes off an underground channel from the River Ty. That's why the rebels were never able to pry Freow loose with their sieges. The castle's got all the water it can use."

Vered laughed. "The rebels had intended to damn up the river to prevent the castle from getting water. That wouldn't have given them much of an edge, would it?"

"Don't reckon I can say. Been down here too long to know such things. That Dews Gaemock you're talkin' about?"

Vered's fingers probed the far wall. He used the handle of his dagger to tap the stone blocks. The solid sound worried him. To his fellow prisoner, he called out, "Am I in the end cell?"

"Last in the block, aye. You might tunnel out in the far direction from my cell, but you'd have to move a powerful lot of dirt."

Vered instantly discarded such a notion. Even if the guards failed to see the hole and the growing pile of dirt that would accumulate, such a tunneling operation would take considerable effort and would end up with him dirtier than a pig in a wallow.

"I'm going to take out a block or two in the wall between us."

"You that anxious for company?" asked the other prisoner. "I been down here well nigh two years. You haven't been in your cell for two hours."

Vered began working at the crumbling mortar between the blocks, gouging it out. "I can open the lock on your door and we can both get out of here."

"What makes you think I want out? This might be my idea of cozy."

"If you like it so much, I'll let myself out, then lock you in when I leave."

"No!" From the distress in the man's voice, Vered knew that isolation had worked on him overlong. "I don't want to stay here. I never meant to call Duke Freow a great fat cow. I'd apologize but one guard who talks to me on occasion says that the duke is dead."

"Baron Theoll poisoned him."

"I'll apologize to the baron. I want out!"

"Theoll's dead. Lorens killed him."

"Who's Lorens? Never mind. You can tell me when you get through the wall."

Vered worked steadily for hours, resting for a few minutes to get the cramps from his hands, then applying himself diligently to the task. One block slid through and crashed into the other cell. A grimy face with wild eyes and a thick, matted beard appeared.

"You are human. You're not a demon. I worried about that. Letting a demon into the cell might be my death."

"Help me get the next block free." Vered started to offer the use of a second dagger but he could hear Birtle Santon's voice warning him about his incautious ways. For the few minutes' work it might save, it did not seem prudent putting a weapon in the other man's hands.

He continued scraping at the mortar until a second block fell free. A third followed quickly. Vered scrambled through the tiny opening and brushed himself off.

"You're a weird-looking duck, aren't you?" the other said.

"High fashion dictates such a color match, though I am less partial to vermilion than I am to, say, a deeper, richer color. A wine red, mayhaps."

"What?"

"My clothes." Vered snorted in disgust. "Never mind. Let me get that cell door open. Shouldn't take long. I opened the last one with a lock in less than a minute."

Vered dropped to his knees and examined the sturdy lock. A slow smile crossed his lips. This lock was the twin of the other. He had already probed its depths and knew its secrets. Opening it with the tip of the dagger would be simple.

He began digging about inside when the man crouched behind him hissed like a stepped-on snake and said, "Stop. Listen. A guard's coming. You can't be caught. They'll put us both to death if they see you!"

The man grabbed Vered from behind and shoved him forward against the door. Vered grunted, the hilt of the dagger buried into his belly. Vered struggled and turned. The other prisoner attempted to reach around and pull the dagger from the locking mechanism.

Vered grabbed the other's wrist to stop him. They struggled, Vered falling back when the man showed surprising strength for one who have been imprisoned for two years.

The metallic tearing noise that resulted when the dagger broke off inside the lock hit Vered harder than the dagger hilt had. His stomach turned over.

"You fool!" he shouted. "You broke it off!"

"Silence. The guards!"

Vered shoved his face against the cell door's small grating and peered out. The dungeon remained as empty as before—but he did hear shouts and the clanking of arms and armor.

"The soldiers are running about on the levels above the dungeon. There aren't any guards stationed here." He almost added "you fool" but knew it would do no good. The damage had been done.

Vered dropped once more to his knees and looked into the keyhole. Not only had the tumblers been ruined, but also the dagger's point had lodged firmly in the cylinder.

"What are you waiting for? Open the door!"

"I can't," said Vered. "This door is sealed as surely as the one in the other cell—more. Not even a key can open this lock. The door is permanently sealed."

He sat down heavily, back against the cold metal door as he glared at his fellow prisoner. He still had three good daggers. One could be put to good use on this fool's throat.

Chapter Twenty

"I hate him! How dare he do that to my most masterful creation!" The Wizard of Storms clapped his hands together and produced a tornado that danced and hopped and slowly made its way to the rain cloud on the southern wall of the turret. The scrying cloud had darkened and the lightning had faded from it while the wizard had spied on Castle Porotane. The tornado whirred about its axis and disrupted the rain cloud, sending filmy tendrils of fog in all directions.

"Could he see us?" asked Lokenna.

"No, of course not. Lorens lacks such power, but he blocked my scrying spell."

"Did he—or was it the Demon Crown?" Santon had seen too much magic to be awed by this new spell woven by the Wizard of Storms. The tornado continued to kick up dust and debris from the turret floor. The scrying cloud had not reappeared and Santon doubted that it would. The small window in the center had shown the castle and the guardsmen walking their patrols along the battlements. The spell had carried them farther into the castle and then—words failed Santon.

The edges of the storm had turned green. He shivered at the memory of that peculiar color. The Demon Crown had glowed the same ugly hue when Lorens had worn it. He had become too accustomed to the softer, more cheerful green the crown emitted from Lokenna's brow. Being reminded of the darker side of the magical device's power chilled him.

"My best scrying spell and he ruins it, just as he's ruined so many of my finer pieces. Look," demanded the Wizard of Storms. "Isn't that the finest storm you have ever seen or heard?"

Through the scrying cloud dripping rain on the floor at the north section of the room Santon saw layered clouds interchanging lightning bolts of varying color. Purples and greens and vivid blue-whites dazzled the eye, but most beguiling was the sound.

Rumbles of thunder came in bass and were countered by higher pitched echoes off canyon walls. The entire range of the Yorrals became the Wizard of Storms' drum.

Santon had to admit that the primal, gut-stirring roll of thunder produced strange emotions within him. Not anger, he decided. Perhaps sadness. Even as he tried to identify the emotion, the timbre of the sound changed and his spirits lifted. Blue sky shone through the clouds and a double rainbow formed. Santon choked back an exclamation of joy and tears welled in his eyes.

"He ruins *that,*" complained the wizard. "He puts on the damnable crown and blackness oozes out like pus from some vile creature's wound and destroys the spells I weave. I won't stand for it!"

"You cannot look into the castle?" asked Santon. "Not at all?"

"No." The curt answer told Santon far more than he wanted to know. For all his skill and power, the Wizard of Storms stood helpless before the Demon Crown.

"We can do nothing against my brother," said Lokenna. "Santon has tried. I have tried. The rebels have tried."

She paused. The Wizard of Storms picked up what had become a litany of failure. "And I have failed," the wizard admitted glumly.

"Separately we fail. Together we might succeed. Isn't that why you allowed us here?" she asked.

"A truce between us might prove helpful." The wizard stroked over his white-stubbled chin with his gnarled fingers. He snapped the joints and nodded briskly. "I had been drifting along such a path. Your presence has confirmed my intuition."

"Efran Gaemock will be needed, too," said Lokenna.

Santon turned slowly and stared at the woman. Something about the tone she used told that her interest in Efran Gaemock transcended the military alliance against her brother. A certain breathlessness, Santon decided. He looked from the woman to her husband. Bane Pandasso had not noticed the excitement in his wife's voice.

"He is being summoned now," said the wizard.

"It will take a week or more for him to cross

lower Porotane and even if you do not hinder him with your storms on the Uvain Plateau, the trip is a long one. Can we afford to wait?" asked Santon.

The Wizard of Storms smirked. "Your dealings with those such as myself is limited. When a wizard desires something—or someone—it is easily obtained." He pointed to the scrying cloud dripping on the floor to the southeast.

"You've conjured a storm over the rebel camp," said Pandasso. "You send your rain on his head?"

"I send my cloud warriors for him. Look!"

Santon swallowed hard when he saw the filmy tendrils dipping toward the ground, dragging along, and then breaking off to form ten-foot-high soldiers of fog and lightning. The consternation in the rebel camp spread. A few tried to fight the magical warriors. They were brushed aside. The cloud warriors strode across the campground, their footprints drowning fires and their lightest touch giving death.

"Why not send them against Lorens? He cannot stand against such potent magic," Pandasso said, gawking at the cloud warriors' slow progress.

"He finally says something of worth," agreed Santon. "Why can't you send your legions against Lorens?"

The wizard's concentration faltered for a moment and the cloud warriors ceased their hunt for Efran Gaemock. In that instant Santon knew the answer. The Wizard of Storms might control one or two of the mighty magical warriors, but he lacked the ability to command the hundreds—thousands!—that he conjured. The Wizard of Storms could order them to march and march they would, but individual combat for each of his myriad lay beyond his skill.

"There," came Lokenna's excited voice. "There's Efran."

"So it is." The wizard made a small beckoning motion. A cloud warrior bent over and scooped up the struggling rebel leader. Efran fought against mist but was held by fingers stronger than steel bands. Another gesture from the wizard caused the cloud above to dip low.

As if being sucked aloft, cloud warrior and Efran Gaemock vanished into the storm.

"Gaemock will arrive shortly," said the wizard. He slumped into a comfortable chair, exhausted by his effort. Santon saw in this another reason the wizard had not sent his vaporous legions against Lorens. The strain of maintaining his magic must be immense.

"Can I get you anything?" asked Lokenna.

"Ah, the old habits die hard, don't they?" said the Wizard of Storms, smiling gently. Santon thought he looked like any other weary traveller in that instant, seeing a pretty barmaid.

Lokenna grinned sheepishly. "They do."

"I am Kaga'kalb," the Wizard of Storms said unexpectedly.

Santon stared at the wizard. For a sorceror to reveal his personal name meant that a large measure of control had been relinquished. The best and most effective spells were those naming the victim. Some wizards such as Patrin boasted that they were too powerful to worry about such secrecy, but Santon knew that inwardly they feared this personal revelation. When Alarice had revealed her name, Santon had known the complete trust this involved.

Of those in the room, only Pandasso did not seem to know the import of Kaga'kalb's revelation.

"We can share some food. It is not much, but these days I have little appetite. Lorens upsets my work too much." Kaga'kalb made a pass with his hand and mumbled a spell. Small storms appeared above glasses. The rain pelting down proved to be red. Santon sampled his filled glass and discovered the cloud had brought wine. Meat and cheese arrived in a more conventional manner; wind blew open doors and a wheeled cart laden with the food skidded across the room.

"Excuse my little displays of magic. I seldom have anyone to show off for," Kaga'kalb said. "I content myself with the beauty of the elements. The white of snow is such a lovely medium to work with, but I must admit I prefer the greens of spring. But then, each season carries its own secrets and beauties, doesn't it?"

A clap of thunder drowned out Santon's reply. Following the peal came loud cursing and a clattering on steps leading from the turret roof.

"Gaemock has arrived," said Kaga'kalb.

The rebel leader stumbled into the room. For a heart-stopping instant Santon feared that the man had died and only his phantom had come. Efran Gaemock was coated from head to toe in frosty white.

"He's frozen!" exclaimed Lokenna. She rushed to the man and threw her crude blanket-cloak around his shoulders.

"My, I forgot how cold it gets within a cloud. Do accept my abject apologies, Efran," said the Wizard of Storms.

"What is this place? Have I died?"

"You'll be fine," Lokenna assured him. "Rest for a while, and then we can talk. We are offering an alliance against my brother."

"Your brother? Lorens?" The rebel leader wiped melting ice from his eyebrows and studied her closely. "I see a resemblance. You . . . you're his twin! The one the Glass Warrior sent the two adventurers after!"

"And I recognize you as the jester Harhar," spoke up Santon.

"A disguise that proved of little use, it seems. How did you fare after you escaped the castle?"

"There'll be time enough for such gossip later," Lokenna said sternly. "You must get out of those frozen clothes and rest." She looked over her shoulder at Kaga'kalb. The wizard gestured toward a staircase leading down.

"Choose any room," he said. "I never have guests, so none are in use." He spread his hands out in front of him and made a motion encompassing the turret room. "This is my primary residence."

"You're the leader of the rebel army?" asked Bane Pandasso.

"What there is left of it."

"You didn't destroy Fron, did you?" Pandasso glared at Efran, as if challenging him to admit that he had.

"Dalziel Sef was responsible for many misadventures my brother and I never authorized. He has paid the final price for his indiscretions."

"You mean he's dead?"

Efran nodded.

"I'll help him down," the innkeeper offered. "You two make what plans you need with the wizard."

Efran looked at Kaga'kalb, who said, "He is right. A few hours will not matter. I apologize for not realizing that you would be in such a sorry condition as a result of my cloudy transportation."

"You're the Wizard of Storms."

"Kaga'kalb," supplied Pandasso.

Santon was pleased to see that this naming impressed Efran Gaemock, too. The rebel leader he had known as Harhar the court jester understood the trust involved.

"Help me to my quarters. We can talk soon." Efran cocked his head to one side and looked from Kaga'kalb to Lokenna as he added, "Alliance?"

"Yes," she said simply.

Pandasso put his arm around Efran's waist and helped him down the steps. Santon watched them depart, wondering at the innkeeper's sudden helpfulness. He turned back to the old wizard, but Kaga'kalb had summoned a new storm cloud and sat with his head wreathed by its miniature turbulence.

He silently ate of the meat and cheese and enjoyed the wine. No matter how he drank, the rain cloud kept it filled. This innovation would have appealed greatly to Vered, he thought.

To Vered.

Birtle Santon's mood turned morose once more. What had happened to his friend? Even Kaga'kalb's sorcery could not reveal that fate as long as Lorens wore the crown.

Chapter Twenty-one

The wizard-king clapped his hands over his ears to shut out the shrieks of pain. It didn't help. Lorens hesitantly opened his closed eyes and saw—nothing. His audience chamber was empty.

The moans and sobs of pain grew louder.

"Stop it, stop it!" Tears rolled down his cheeks as he tried to lift the Demon Crown from his head. It weighed a ton. Fire burned his fingers. It had somehow become fastened to his head. Millions of excuses flashed through his mind. Even as Lorens knew that all were lies, he stopped his attempt to remove the crown.

He sagged as he listened to the tormented souls crying out for surcease. Lorens blinked when the peculiar red-lit world of black rock and dancing figures again appeared in front of him. This time he felt intense heat radiating from the world as sluggish lava flows attacked the floor in front of his dais.

You are the chosen one, came the rasping voice he had grown to fear.

"Who are you?" Lorens cried aloud. The voice had not come from his chamber; it still echoed in the dusty corners of his mind.

Laughter mocked him. *You ask the wrong question, my king. What am I is the true question!*

"Stop," Lorens pleaded. A gust of hot wind seared his face and ripped at the flesh on the backs of his hands. He looked up and saw . . . damnation.

You only now get an inkling, my king? How strange. Even Waellkin, fool that he was, understood better what my purpose was in giving you mortals the Demon Crown.

"You're Kalob!"

I am Kalob and Prebeal and Septhion and Tabros and none of them. I am all, I am none.

"I don't understand."

Oh, my king, you do *understand.* The laughter threatened to drive Lorens totally mad.

He jumped to his feet and tottered on the edge of the platform. The sea of molten rock threatened him with instant and fiery death. Lorens hesitated, then jumped. He cried bitter tears when he landed squarely in the center of his audience chamber. Only cold stone lay under him. No lava burned away his flesh to rid him of the voices. Life continued in his tormented body, even if the door into the strangely terrifying world had shut.

"Majesty, are you hurt?" came a worried voice.

"Curse you!" Lorens shrieked. "Bring me the spies. The prisoners. Get them here at once!"

"Which ones, Majesty?"

"The spies in the barracks. The ones who tried to desert to the accursed rebels!"

"Oh, those." The squire swallowed hard and backed from the chamber. Lorens sat on the cold stone floor, fingers hesitantly probing in a vain effort to locate the sea of melted rock he had seen. In the distance he heard the squire's footsteps disappearing, then the clank of armed men returning.

Lorens picked himself up and dusted off his clothing the best he could. He had not changed his tunic in a week and his breeches had become stuck to his body with filth. He hardly noticed as he turned to study himself in a full-length polished metal mirror.

The image in the mirror wavered. Lorens saw a tall, handsome, well-groomed man worthy of being king. No fear showed on the face. Even as he began to smile, knowing that he was in command, that his destiny was to rule Porotane, the image changed and was replaced by that of a leering demon.

Lorens spun, hand going to a sheathed dagger. No one stood behind him. He was still alone in the audience chamber—but the ghastly laughter again rattled about inside his head, for only him to hear.

A sudden noise from his right caused him to swing around, dagger drawn. The guardsmen he had summoned herded the four prisoners to a spot in front of his throne.

"You are traitors," he snarled. "You are all traitors. You sought to abandon me and tell my secrets to Gaemock. Don't deny it! I see everything. With this"—he tapped the green-glowing

Demon Crown on his head—"I *know* everything. You will be executed!"

"Majesty, we have done nothing except serve you. There was talk of revolt in our ranks. *We* put down the mass desertion! We should be commended, not condemned."

"Liar. You think I cannot *see* what goes on in my own castle. I can *see* and *hear* anywhere in the kingdom!"

Lorens flopped bonelessly to the floor and let his senses cast forth like a hunting cat. He raced over the rolling hills of lower Porotane, to the upthrusting ochre cliffs that marked the beginning of the Uvain Plateau and onto the flatness of that grape-growing country.

The wizard-king cried in frustration when the storms began to form around his far-reaching magical senses. In seconds rain obscured his vision and thunder deafened him.

Your enemies do this to you, came the voice he loathed and feared. *You cannot allow the Wizard of Storms to block your magic. These soldiers are his spies. Slay them now!*

"Y-you are spies for the Wizard of Storms," Lorens gasped out. Half his mind still rolled along the ochre buttes. He had increasing difficulty collecting his wits after each of the magically thwarted outings. "You work for the Wizard of Storms."

"We know nothing of . . . aieee!" The leader who had started to protest bent double and clutched at his belly. The audience chamber turned suddenly silent. Then tiny popping and sizzling sounds echoed throughout. The soldier dropped to his knees, hands still at his belly. His lips moved but only pink froth came out.

He toppled to his side, his stomach gone and the cavity turned to smoking charcoal.

"I . . . I punish my enemies," said Lorens. Sweat ran down his face. He had done this. He had executed the traitor—but how? He did not know the spell. It had just . . . happened.

"Mercy. Have mercy on us, Majesty!" pleaded another.

Lorens lifted a shaking hand and pointed it at the man. "I do not like cowards who beg for their lives."

The soldier's head exploded in a bloody shower that caused the battle-hardened guardsmen to flinch.

Lorens stared at his magical handiwork in shocked silence. Deep within his skull came the soothing words, *You do well. Your skills as a wizard grow daily. There is much to be proud of.*

"There is?" he asked aloud.

"Majesty? What did you say?" asked the boldest of the guardsmen.

Do not let the other traitors escape your vengeance. Make examples of them so that others will know your wrath!

"Th-these two are to be . . . executed." Lorens stood up and touched the Demon Crown. Reassuring warmth flooded through him. Confidence returned and the voices in his head fell silent. "They are to be publicly executed. Everyone in the castle will watch or know my wrath!"

"Majesty, at once! We will get the executioner!"

Lorens motioned the guardsmen from the chamber. He took some delight in seeing that they were as fearful as the two condemned prisoners.

He would maintain discipline in the ranks if he had to kill them all!

"I don't need them. I am more powerful than any rebel army. Let the Wizard of Storms come down from his mountain. He cannot stop me. I am Lorens, King of Porotane!"

In the courtyard he heard the trumpets sound the call for all to assemble. The crowd noises rose, then fell as the two traitors were executed. Lorens did not go to the window to watch. He had no need of mere eyes.

He used the Demon Crown.

Faint laughter welled up deep within his mind, laughter that had been denied release for three hundred years.

Chapter Twenty-two

"How long can he stay like this?" Santon asked nervously. He wanted to shake Kaga'kalb and see if he could rouse the wizard from his deep trance, yet he feared the consequences. The clouds that orbited his head produced no rain, but the lightning was intense for such small puffs of mist.

"I am no wizard. I cannot say, but he does not seem to be in any danger," said Lokenna. Her eyes kept straying to the staircase leading down to Efran Gaemock's quarters. Santon wondered at her interest in the rebel. While he and Vered had been in Lorens' good graces after giving him the Demon Crown and installing him on the throne, he had come to like the court jester—Efran. He had seen more in the comically wild gyrations and reckless talk than any of those who schemed and killed within the castle walls.

"Why does the storm cloud stay over his head?" Santon asked, pulling his attention away from idle speculation and back to the matters at hand. His mind turned over the possibilities. "If the storms along the walls allow him to see at great distances, mayhap this storm is for scrying closer at hand."

Santon fell silent, realizing that he put words to his own private thoughts. His curiosity would not be assuaged until he learned what business Bane Pandasso had with the rebel lord. That Pandasso had something important to say had been apparent from his attitude. The innkeeper would not last a single day in the machinations of a royal court; his every emotion played on his brutish face.

"He's had time enough to rest from his trip," said Lokenna. "I'll see how Lord Efran fares."

"There is no need," spoke up Kaga'kalb. "I hear his boots on the steps now."

Santon wondered at this. It took his keen ears several long seconds before he heard Efran and Pandasso returning. The rebel had donned dry clothing and a fur-lined cape to ward off the worst of Kaga'kalb's elemental masterpieces raging outside.

"Do you agree to an alliance, Efran?" asked Kaga'kalb.

"What are we each to gain from this? You are a wizard. If we join forces and defeat Lorens—Lokenna's brother"—he bowed in the woman's direction and received a bright smile in return—"how do the oppressed people of Porotane benefit? Are we exchanging one wizard's rule for another's?"

"Kaga'kalb cannot wear the Demon Crown," said Santon. "Only Lokenna can."

"Then there is a new element introduced. Are we substituting one tyrant for another?"

"You're talking about my wife!" protested Pandasso.

"You know my part in getting Lorens onto the throne," said Santon, feeling the weight of forging the alliance resting heavily on him. He was no diplomat but knew he had to convince all parties that defeating Lorens was in their best interests now and later.

Then he had to convince himself. He had seen how the crown had changed Lorens. Lokenna had worn it and not been perverted, but what would a year of exposure do to her?

"Aye, that I do. You're responsible for the condition of our proud kingdom."

"That's a bit harsh on Birtle," defended Lokenna.

"But true, my queen," Santon said before Efran could argue. "Kaga'kalb has no desire to leave his Castle of the Winds. He wants only to work his magic and create his natural art with the storms. Is that not so?"

The Wizard of Storms nodded.

"And," Santon rushed on, "you want peace. Lokenna can give it by uniting the warring factions. Those royalists who have fought so long will follow no one but a monarch wearing the crown."

"I want only what is best for Porotane," said Efran.

"This can work," insisted Santon. "Kaga'kalb is left alone—and leaves the ruling of Porotane to Lokenna."

"She *is* of the royal blood," said Efran, rubbing his chin. "I entered the castle as jester two years ago in hope of installing a member of the family on the throne. That is where I parted company with my brother Dews."

"He is sorely wounded," said Kaga'kalb. "You are the one who must decide for the rebel army."

Efran snorted. "There is no army. Not much, at any rate after Lorens was finished with us."

"Dalziel Sef betrayed you," said Lokenna, softening the sting of the self-criticism Efran had administered.

"We all gain—if we defeat Lorens," said Santon.

"What of you?" asked Pandasso. "You argue well, but what do you gain from this?"

"Aye, you have the look of a thief about you. Even after I learned of your alliance with the Glass Warrior, I wondered how you became embroiled in this."

"Politics is usually the farthest thing from my mind," said Santon, "but Lorens holds my friend in his dungeons. I want him freed."

Santon was acutely aware of the look that went around the room between Lokenna, Efran, and Kaga'kalb. They knew he had scant chance of seeing his friend alive again, but he had to believe. Alarice had told him that Vered lived. Her phantom would not lie to him. Ever.

Even if she had not come to him, hope would have stirred within him.

"We all stand to gain what we hold dearest." Efran glared at Pandasso in a manner that startled Santon. What had happened between the two men? Before he could speak, Efran went on. "Then we should prepare for the assault on Castle Porotane as soon as possible. If you can return me to my camp, I can begin assembling my army. By spring we can—"

"No." Kaga'kalb's single word caused a heavy silence to fall on the room. Even the minor thunderings in his scrying clouds died.

"But we . . ." Santon's voice trailed off when he saw the utter determination written on the wizard's face.

"We fight now. We can go to the rebel camp, if you need to assemble your troops there, but they will hardly be needed if we can destroy Lorens."

"They are needed," insisted Lokenna. "The castle forces must be committed, separated from Lorens. That will give us the best chance of defeating him. Kaga'kalb might not be able to summon many of his cloud warriors—human ones will be needed to bear the brunt of the battle."

"Very well." Kaga'kalb motioned for them to go to the roof of the turret. They silently filed up the stairs. Santon pulled his rude cloak tighter around him when the fierce, bitter cold winds clawed at him. Kaga'kalb herded them into a small circle, then lifted his arms.

Santon tried to scream, but the words jumbled in his throat. He felt impossibly strong hands lift him, yet those hands were composed of fog. Winds buffeted him and snow pelted his face. Lightning of unbelievable intensity crashed around him as he tumbled and fell head over heels.

His arm and legs became numb with the cold. Frost formed on his eyelashes and threatened to freeze his eyelids shut.

At the instant he thought he would surely die, he stumbled and dropped to one knee on the muddy banks of the River Ty. The distance that had taken them weeks to travel on horseback had been traversed in Kaga'kalb's storm in the wink of an eye.

"Assemble your troops. Get them into the field," ordered Kaga'kalb. "And hurry. I . . . I do not like being exposed like this."

"What do you mean?" asked Santon.

The wizard tensed, then seemed resigned. "I have given you my name. I might as well bare my final secret. The storms I have created are all I can do unless I return to my Castle of the Winds."

"You mean you can't summon *any* of the cloud warriors unless you're in your castle?" asked Lokenna.

"From these storms, I can—a little. I cannot conjure new storms. My powers are severely limited."

"Then return to the Castle of the Winds," said Efran. "Let us prepare on this front. We will need all your skills, all your spells."

Lokenna held up her hand. "Wait," she said in a choked voice. "He knows. My brother knows we are here."

"The crown has betrayed our presence," said Santon. He knew, though, that it required no great spell for Lorens to detect their arrival. The prodigious thunderhead rising above them marked something unusual. He hoped that Kaga'kalb had conjured enough in the way of storms.

"Send the soldiers out," ordered Efran. "Use the ambush tactic we discussed." His lieutenant looked skeptical, then rushed off to obey. Santon's heart froze when he saw how few rebels rode out to engage Lorens' troops.

"Only a hundred are left in fighting prime," said Efran. "We will keep them from retreating unscathed, if only they are overzealous in attack."

"You intend to hide and take their riders off the perimeter of their force?" Santon knew that a direct confrontation would destroy the rebel army. Lorens could afford a two-for-one or even a five-for-one loss and still emerge victorious on the ground.

"Aye," said Lokenna, again seeming to have accurately read his thoughts. "The true battle occurs above us."

"I cannot see Lorens. The crown obscures him and those around him, but it will not matter. I will show him magic!" Kaga'kalb thrust his arms upward and made gestures as if trying to grab the clouds between his fingers. A purple nimbus of energy formed around him, then arched up to the thunder cloud in a blinding flash.

"What can I do?" asked Santon, feeling useless.

"There is nothing either of us can do," said Lokenna. "We must let Kaga'kalb and Efran carry the battle to Lorens. Afterward, *then* it will be our time."

Santon paced restlessly, trying to keep the snow and rain from running down his neck. The wind came up in powerful gales, then died as the power was redirected toward Lorens' troops. Through the ebb and flow of the storm, Santon saw Bane Pandasso arguing with Efran.

He edged closer. The rebel leader showed obvious distress at what the man said.

"We can do it, I tell you. It's for the best. He would never harm his sister—or the one who ends this madness!"

Efran Gaemock cried something that vanished in a clap of thunder and pushed Pandasso away angrily. The rebel spun and stalked off, every muscle tense. Pandasso waved a fist at him. When he saw that Efran had vanished into a small tent, the innkeeper looked about. The set of his body warned Santon that Pandasso sought a fight.

He ducked behind a tree and waited for Pandasso, intending to follow him and see what the man did next. The pounding of a horse's hooves startled him. Pandasso rode past his place of concealment, a sword in hand and a look of grim determination on his face.

Santon blinked in surprise. He shook his head in wonder and returned to the low hill where Kaga'kalb mustered his elemental magics for the assault. Lokenna stood to one side, ready to aid the wizard should he require it.

"Lokenna," Santon shouted over the din. "I owe you an apology—and to your husband."

"What? What are you saying?" She turned to him, eyes wide.

"I just saw Pandasso riding out to join the rebels. I misjudged him. I'd thought him a coward."

The sudden cessation of lightning and thunder struck Santon harder than any body blow. One instant there had been peals of thunder and eye-searing aerial discharges. The silence made him feel as if he had become deaf and blind.

Kaga'kalb's cry of outrage put those ideas to rest. "What has that craven done now?"

"Pandasso?" asked Santon, confused. "I was apologizing to Lokenna for thinking her husband was a coward."

The flush of anger that rose on Kaga'kalb's

weathered face cut off any further words. The Wizard of Storms said fiercely, "He will *not* betray you again. I swear it!"

"Wait, what are you saying?" Lokenna clutched at the wizard's sleeve. He jerked free. "I demand to know. He is my husband! What has Bane done now?"

Kaga'kalb clapped his hands. The small cloud that Santon had seen in the Castle of the Winds again formed around the wizard's head. This time the swirling mist expanded to include both Lokenna and him. Santon staggered. Only Lokenna's strong hand steadied him. He expected to see nothing but gray fog.

The world opened for him. Every sense sharpened. He saw. He truly *saw* and realized what allure the Demon Crown had. His ears heard and *heard.* By turning slowly, he was able to witness events happening within a few hundred yards.

"The scrying spells operate at great distance. This works only for a short way. You see the darkness where Lorens—the Demon Crown—blocks the magic."

Santon saw tiny darting black motes in the direction of the castle. Of Castle Porotane or its inhabitants he saw nothing.

"There he is," said Kaga'kalb. The anger had not died in his voice.

"Bane," Lokenna said in a choked voice. "What have you done?"

"Nothing. He tried to get Efran to turn traitor and sell out to Lorens. Efran refused."

"Why didn't Efran say anything . . ." Santon's objection drifted away. He knew the answer. He had seen the look in the rebel's eyes—and it had matched that in Lokenna's.

"He rides to betray us to Lorens, thinking the tyrant will return all things to the way they were. The unutterable fool!"

"Kaga'kalb, no!" Lokenna tried to stop him but the spell had already formed on the wizard's lips.

A lance of lightning caught Bane Pandasso's sword tip. For an instant the man stiffened—then he simply vanished. No trace remained of rider or horse.

"You didn't have to do that," sobbed Lokenna. "He was my husband."

"He was a demon-cursed fool and a traitor. And a coward. Only you can know what else he was—or wasn't." Kaga'kalb spun around and the scrying cloud vanished.

Again came the eerie silence. Santon stood, feeling helpless in the face of such power and heartache. The crescendo of thunder drove him to his knees. He had no idea where the lightning stroke touched down, nor did he care. Such magic sickened him. Better to die of a clean sword thrust. At least that way you saw your killer.

"Lokenna!" he called, seeing the woman rushing off. He got to his feet and followed her. He overtook the woman outside Efran's tent. "Where are you going?"

"I cannot stay. Not after he . . . he killed Bane!"

"Your husband tried to betray us. Lorens can't see the rebels any more than Kaga'kalb can see into the castle. Magic protects both sides. If he had given Lorens our exact numbers and location, your brother would have killed us all!"

"He was my husband. Why did I ever leave Fron? I should have listened."

"Was he good to you?"

"As good as he could be. In Fron everything was simple. The inn required no great work, and that suited Bane. Me, too."

"It wasn't my fault that you were born to wear the Demon Crown."

"It was your fault you found me!" the woman flared.

"No," came a whispering voice. "Destiny treats us all poorly. We must do what we can—what we must."

"Alarice!" cried Santon. He stepped forward and reached out. His hand passed through the misty patch that was the Glass Warrior's elusive phantom.

"You have done well, Birtle, my love. Now you must show even more courage. Vered still lives—or so I believe. The crown dims what vision remains with me."

"Alarice, I . . ." The phantom passed through him and now faced Lokenna.

"Your husband died because he could not accept change. You will die, also, unless you realize your true position in the kingdom. Be strong, Lokenna."

"This phantom is the Glass Warrior?" asked Lokenna. She reached out. For an instant the mist firmed into a warm human hand that squeezed hers. Then the phantom drifted apart on a small gust of wind from the storm raging above.

Santon stared into the light snow falling all around to catch some small glimpse of Alarice, but she had gone.

From inside the tent came Efran's voice. "You are sure? There is no doubt?"

Santon went around to the front flap and saw that a messenger had arrived. He feared the worst, even though Pandasso's traitorous mission had been cut short by the wizard's spell.

"We've done it!" The rebel leader pushed through the flap and caught Lokenna up in his arms and spun her around. Almost guiltily he put her down and smiled. "Sorry. I couldn't help myself. We caught Lorens' personal guard in the woods. They were overconfident, as I'd hoped. With Kaga'kalb's storm giving us magical cover, we attacked from ambush. We routed them!"

"You defeated them totally?" asked Santon.

"Not that, but we are giving chase. The wizard's storms cut them off from easy retreat. We pursue—cautiously. If we can meet them on our terms in battle just once more, we can crush them."

"What other force does Lorens command?"

"That I don't know, but to send his personal guard tells me that he is not as well armed as we'd thought."

Santon considered this and agreed with Efran. A monarch as insecure as Lorens, even with the Demon Crown, would keep his most highly trained and trusted guardsmen to protect him. If he'd had another regiment, he would have sent it into the field. Even if he had one and did not consider it well enough trained, he would have fielded it.

To be left in the castle with possibly mutinous troops while his personal guard fought and died in the field would be a situation Lorens would avoid at all costs.

"We have him!" cried Efran. "We can push through the remnants of their force and take the castle!"

Santon looked to the south and west. Kaga'kalb's storms hammered at the castle's battlements but did little damage. Lorens was a wizard in his own right—and he still wore the Demon Crown.

What evil power had that accursed crown unleashed in the untrained wizard-king?

Chapter Twenty-three

Vered's hands shook uncontrollably. He licked at his dried, cracked lips and tried to remember the last time he'd had a good drink of clear, clean water. He couldn't. The deep rumbling that had bothered him so when it had started he now ignored—it was his belly complaining about the lack of food.

"How long has it been?" he asked his fellow prisoner. The skeletal prisoner slept fitfully at the far side of the cell. Even when awake, he showed little sign of intelligence now.

Vered answered his own question. "Too long. What's happened to the jailers? Do they think to starve us to death?" The rattling and creaking in the castle told him that the guards had been drawn away from such futile work as guarding and feeding prisoners in the dungeons and put to defense on the castle battlements. He knew a huge battle raged above—but who attacked? And who won?

Vered hoped that Santon and Lokenna had not forgotten him. He went to the wall holding back the underground river and began licking at the damp stone. He had considered working free a tiny bit of mortar to let the river water flow through, but he remembered what had happened when he was a small child playing along the coast.

His village had built dikes to reclaim part of the western ocean. One hot summer afternoon he had idly worked a long steel rod into the dike, not knowing or caring what would happen. The first trickle had amused him. When he could not stop it, he had been concerned but not frightened. When huge chunks of the dike began cracking away and the sea threatened to inundate the entire lowland farm, he had rushed off for help.

Only a few acres had been lost back to the sea—but the lesson had stayed with him. Vered knew that he would drown in the cell before the pressure of the water burst open the cell door.

Tongue raw from the rock but his thirst quenched momentarily, he went back to the front of the cell. He had pulled down most of the stone blocks and found only steel plate. In the other prisoner's cell—he had never learned the suspicious man's name—the steel plate had been even thicker. To the rear of the cell ran the underground tributary to River Ty and to the far end of the cell he had found only solid rock. That left the other wall, the far wall in the distant cell.

A half-dozen heavy stone blocks had been pulled free before Vered had given up. It seemed too thick and he grew increasingly weak from lack of food.

He lay on his belly, the third of his four daggers dragging around the flagstone to pry it loose. Vered cursed the loss of his first dagger; its point permanently jammed the lock on the other door. His second dagger had worn down to a nub from working through so many miles of mortar and block.

The third dagger bent at crazy angles as he used it. He knew it would break soon. Vered rolled onto his back and closed his eyes to rest. He should save the final dagger for a quick end.

"I refuse to die of starvation. May all the demons take you for this, Lorens!"

"We are already demon food," said the other prisoner. He propped himself up on an elbow and stared at Vered, his eyes glazed over and unfocused. "This Lorens you curse so. What is he like?"

"He's the kind of ruler who would put a prisoner into a cell and then starve him to death," said Vered. Changing the subject, he asked, "Did you ever make any attempt to escape?"

"Once, then I reconsidered my plight. They tortured others who tried. Me, they left alone. I never questioned that."

"The ship with the smallest sail takes the longest to arrive," said Vered.

"How's that? You from the coast?"

"The ones they tortured are out of their misery," explained Vered. "You evaded death for this."

"Slow death instead of quick," the man said, as if the concept had never occurred to him.

"Haven't seen any guardsman lately, have you? I had a dream."

Vered didn't want to hear about it. He began scraping away again at the flooring. Getting the dagger tip under the large, flat block, he heaved. The knife blade snapped off but he exposed the hard dirt beneath. Hope returned. He drew the fourth dagger and began scratching at the packed dirt.

"What good's it going to do to tunnel under the steel plate?" asked the other man. "You'll still have to tunnel up through the stone floor outside."

"Gravity will work for me then. A small chamber is easy to cut in dirt. A bit of sawing at the block and it falls into the chamber and we can climb out."

"You can climb out," said the other. "I am too weak."

Vered refused to let hope die. He felt as weak as the other prisoner sounded. It had been almost a week since their last meal. Dining off his boots had not helped much, but it had provided bulk for his stomach to work on. Beyond this, he'd eaten nothing.

He lay flat on his stomach, thinking rather than working. What the other man said might be true. In his debilitated condition it might not be possible to perform the ambitious tunneling required for escape.

And what then? What if he managed to get free and into the dungeon proper? He was too weak to engage a soldier in combat. Vered wasn't sure that he could even wield his dagger properly from ambush. How was he to get free of the castle and past the rebel lines to rejoin Santon?

He rested his forehead on the cool stone and thought back on his days with Birtle Santon. Life in the village had been brutal. Soldiers and rebels alike had burned and massacred constantly. Santon had taken him, a young and clumsy thief, away from that and shown him the vastness and beauty of Porotane.

He owed the older man much—his life and more. Who could put a price on the friendship they had shared over the years?

"I can get the blocks removed and begin tunneling under," he said more to himself than to the other prisoner, who again had fallen into a half coma. "I can *start* the tunnel, then pull out a block and let in the river. Let the water cut the rest of the tunnel. It would push away the stone flooring with ease."

He began to dig with more determination now that a plan had formed in his feverish mind. Vered worried if he would be able to survive the time between the cell filling and the water finishing the tunnel under the steel wall.

"I can hold my breath long enough," he mumbled. "And if I can't, it might be just as well. I've always travelled with a full sail—and a big one!"

The only sounds in the cell came from the knife blade scraping on dirt and the distant trumpets and noises of battle.

Chapter Twenty-four

"Look at them run," crowed Efran Gaemock. "They run like cravens!"

"No," said Santon. He had no wish to defend those soldiers who had cast their lot with Lorens, but he felt obligated to point out what no one else wanted to. "They are not cowards. They run because they lack leadership. Where are the officers?"

"We cut them down first. We had to," said Efran. He watched as the squads broke into pairs of men and the pairs split into single soldiers seeking escape. "I see what you mean, though. They have no spirit, no need to fight."

"Consider how many surrender—and what they say. Two surrendered to me," said Lokenna, still somewhat startled at this. "They begged me not to kill them."

"Lorens has taken to executing his own troops if he feels they have not lived up to his expectations. I spoke with one prisoner," said Santon. "They had orders to take no prisoners and had been told we did the same."

"They came into the field thinking they would roll over us as easily as they did before," said Efran. "If only Dews could see this with his own eyes."

"Hearing it from you will be as good," Lokenna said, her hand on Efran's arm. Santon noticed how the rebel leader moved closer to her without seeming to move at all.

"I still cannot penetrate the castle with my spells. The Demon Crown blocks me. It . . . I feel more. My head. *My head!*" Kaga'kalb shrieked and clutched at his temples. Santon grabbed him with his good arm to keep the wizard from falling face forward into a snowbank.

"What's happening?" asked Efran.

The peculiar expression on Lokenna's face told Santon that the woman knew. She turned slowly, as if in a trance. Facing the castle, a look of utter horror began to spread over her lovely face.

"My brother has released a demon. Demons! The crown has somehow opened the door and demons flood into our world!"

"But they were banished," protested Efran. "King Waellkin accepted the crown as proof of their—" The look of horror spread over him, too, as he realized the depths of Lorens' perfidy.

"Lorens has invited them back to this world—to Porotane? He has unleashed the plague of demons upon us again?" Even Birtle Santon, who had come to believe the worst of Lokenna's brother, found this outrageous and frightening.

"He had no choice. He . . . he did not know what he was doing. The crown has perverted him. The lure of power made him believe he was invincible. When his scouts reported back that we had routed his personal guard, he accepted the demons' offer of aid."

"What can we do to stop them?" Santon had fought the best and won, even though he had but one good arm. In a fight such as this, he felt totally helpless.

"Let me up." Kaga'kalb struggled and got to his knees. The wizard's face was haggard and drawn. Santon saw that he had aged a hundred years—more—since this battle of magics had started. "I am not done. They cut me off from my Castle of Winds but I will show them. I know their secret. I advised Waellkin not to take the crown, but I know their secret."

"What?" Efran, Lokenna, and Santon chorused.

"There might seen to be legions of demons, but if you defeat one, they are all defeated."

"You mean there's really only one of them?" asked Santon. He preferred simpler fights. Man against man; ax against steel sword; that was his kind of battle.

"Whether there is only one or many matters naught," said Kaga'kalb. "All we need do is defeat one and the rest vanish. Then we must close the door through which Lorens has invited them!"

"How do you fight a demon?" asked Efran.

Kaga'kalb got to his feet. "Magic. They block me from the center of my power, but they underestimate me. I am still strong. I will drive them back to where they come from!"

Thunder rolled across Porotane in response

to the wizard's battle cry. Kaga'kalb threw back his sleeves and brought down bolt after vivid lightning bolt until the earth turned molten and flowed. Winds came up and blew the superheated liquid away.

Revealed in the center of this cauldron of molten rock stood a smirking demon.

"So, Wizard of Storms, you again oppose us."

"Again I will send you back!" Kaga'kalb clapped his hands. An ice storm of bone-chilling severity blew across the land and swirled around the demon. The demon struggled and fought, but his movements slowed. Kaga'kalb brought down freezing rain, then whipped up a tornado. The ice accumulated faster around the demon, turning him into a statue of gleaming white and blue ice.

Within the cold sheath Santon saw the malevolent dark eyes, the ruddy pallor of the creature's face, the sharp, angular bones that threatened to rupture skin, the emaciated body—and always he returned to those haunting, dark eyes.

"Do not gaze into his eyes," warned Kaga'kalb. "They will steal your will."

"Kill him," muttered Santon, captivated by those infinitely evil eyes. "I have to kill him." He hefted an ax he had taken from the rebel camp and advanced on the ice-encrusted demon.

"Wait, no, Santon, stop!" He heard Efran's warnings. Lokenna's joined the rebel leader's. Even when the Wizard of Storms barked out a command to halt, Santon could not. He had to kill the demon. He had to stop this magical invasion and return Porotane to humanity.

The muscles on his powerful arm knotted with the effort of bringing the heavy ax back and driving it directly for the demon's skull. One swift, powerful stroke would end this invasion.

The ax struck the ice. The explosion caught Santon up in an invisible and supremely powerful hand and cast him backward through the air. He landed in a snowbank, the air gusting from his lungs.

The cold, the gasping for breath, the sight before him, all broke the spell the demon had cast on him.

The demon lifted spindly arms and flexed wiry muscles. The sneer curling his black lips mocked not only Santon but all humanity. "Weakling. I played on your basest desires. I have no fear of this Wizard of Storms. His petty spells cannot harm me. I toy with him!"

Santon rolled from the snowbank, got to his feet and charged, his ax already coming around in a vicious circle that would end with the ax blade sinking deep into the demon's sunken chest.

The shock that rolled along the blade, along the haft, up his arm and to his powerful shoulder rattled Santon's senses. He staggered away, staring numbly at the ax. The edge had shattered against the demon's rib cage.

"You cannot harm me. No mortal can!"

Laughing, the demon plucked the ax from Santon's feeble grasp. He hefted it, then laughed even harder as he cast the ax in Kaga'kalb's direction. The wizard sidestepped the spinning blade.

"You are nimble for an old man," complimented the demon.

Santon turned and saw the demon's trick. The heavy ax had missed Kaga'kalb—but it swung in a wide circle and now returned of its own volition, the heavy blade coming directly for the back of the wizard's skull.

Even before Santon could shout a warning, a lightning bolt crashed down from above and destroyed the ax.

"I *am* nimble, Kalob."

"You misname me. I am not Kalob. I am another." The denial rang false in Santon's ears.

"Kalob will do as a name." Kaga'kalb began an assault of the elements so fierce that Santon struggled to get up the slope and back to where the wizard, Efran, and Lokenna stood. Lightning even more intense, winds of hurricane force, tornadoes swirling in tight circles and sucking up everything in their center, rain and snow and even dust tore at the demon. The ground around him bubbled and boiled and froze and spun as Kaga'kalb varied the type of elemental assault.

During it, Santon closed his eyes and listened. An order came through the Wizard of Storms' attack. It was as if he heard music. Soft here, louder there. Building to a crescendo, then slipping away into a more soothing beat. Kaga'kalb created a natural symphony of death to destroy Kalob.

"He . . . he tries to escape. I must maintain this level of attack to pin him here. Go," urged Kaga'kalb. "Go before I tire. Get the Demon Crown away from Lorens. It is our only hope."

"What?" Santon turned to Lokenna. "Do you know what to do with it if we can wrest it from your brother?"

"I think so. The few times I wore it gave me great insight into its use—and misuse. I know nothing of how Lorens brought the demons here, and I do not know if I can drive them back. But I must try!"

Santon looked from the maelstrom where Kalob was pinned by the elemental forces commanded by Kaga'kalb to the castle. "We ought to try getting in now," he said. "Lorens will be blinded by so much magic. It'll worry him, infuriate him. We have to take advantage of his confusion and fear."

"Wait here. I'll bring horses." Efran Gaemock rushed off. Lokenna turned to say something but he had already gone.

"There is no need for him to go with us," she said, her face lined with concern. "We can do this alone." Lokenna turned and looked into Santon's green eyes. "*I* can do it by myself. There is no reason for either of you to endanger your lives."

"You love him, don't you?" he asked.

She nodded her head slightly. "When I wore the crown the first time, I spied on him. For hours I watched and listened and he never knew." She bowed her head. "I am so ashamed of myself. I was *glad* that Bane had died."

"Glad or relieved?" asked Santon. "There is a difference."

"Relieved. My choices are not easier, but—it does not matter," she said abruptly. "We have much to do. If I fail, my feelings for Efran mean nothing." She laughed weakly. "I dare hope too much. He cannot even like me. My brother has visited upon Porotane the worst plague since the days of King Waellkin. And . . ." Her face hardened.

"And what?" Santon demanded.

"Kaga'kalb is unable to summon his cloud warriors. I sense his dismay. His storms are all he can muster. His nearness to the crown robs him of his most potent weapons."

To this Santon said nothing. Matters became increasingly complex. He had seen how Efran looked at her when she was not aware of his interest. Still, Lokenna was right about them having much to do, and it was all dangerous. Their love lives could be straightened out afterward.

If there was an afterward for any of them.

"You do not have to go, Birtle. It is too risky."

"Vered's alive in the castle. Alarice believes this, and so must I."

Before she could answer, Efran rode up leading two horses. He tossed the reins down to Santon and Lokenna. "We must ride like the wind. We dare not hope he can maintain this level of exertion long."

Santon saw that Efran was right. Kaga'kalb weakened visibly, yet any less effort on the wizard's part would release Kalob from the pen of wind and fire that held him.

Santon clumsily mounted, rubbed his withered arm, and flexed his good hand. The cold had begun to take its toll on his joints, yet he wished he had the security of the battle-ax on a leather thong weighing down his wrist again. There was no time to replace the ax; they had to ride directly to the castle.

"I know a way in," said Efran. "From my days as jester, I poked into every passageway until I found all Baron Theoll's secret tunnels and spy holes."

Santon had to chuckle as they rode. Again he entered Castle Porotane and it was not by the main gate. He would learn every secret tunnel into the place before he used the way most entered.

"The brambles," said Lokenna. "They can hold back any attacking army." She studied the thorny tangle. "I see why my brother is so frightened of Kaga'kalb. The cloud warriors could pass through unharmed."

"Or descend from the sky. Or even be formed within the castle, if Kaga'kalb could see where to cast the appropriate spell," said Efran. "I have given him a map showing the layout of the castle, but he said he needs his scrying spell to work before he can send his magical warriors."

Santon and Lokenna exchanged glances. Kaga'kalb lied to Efran to bolster his spirit. There would be no cloud warriors. Santon settled down and watched closely for patrols as they rode. He saw none, even on the castle's battlements. If he had not known better, he would have thought Castle Porotane to be deserted. They dismounted when they came to a particularly heavy patch in the bramble wall.

"Here?" asked Lokenna. "There's no way to crawl through without being cut to pieces."

"Therein lies the beauty of this tunnel," said Efran. He poked around for a few minutes until he found what he sought. A loud *click*! sounded and he worked to push away a heavy door covered with camouflaging brambles. "Inside and hurry. It is not far to the innermost courtyard, but I do not want our king spying on us."

"What does it matter where we are when he sees us?" asked Santon. "With the crown, walls—or tunnels—mean nothing." He remembered the brief glimpse through the magics of Kaga'kalb's scrying spell. To *see* and *hear* like that all the time would be a boon second to none!

"This tunnel is equipped with special . . . traps. It has floodgates built in near the castle proper. Should we be seen while in the tunnel, those gates can be opened." Efran took a deep breath and exhaled, sending silvery plumes into the frigid air. "We would be drowned like rats in the bilge of a barge."

"A cheerful notion," said Santon, diving into the hole. The darkness stopped him. He felt as if he had walked into a midnight black curtain. His eyes adapted to the darkness and he saw faint pinpoints of light along the roof.

"Special holes cut through to provide guidance, but be careful," warned Efran. "If you see a red light, stop and let me know. That marks a special deadfall that must be skirted."

Santon walked slowly, carefully picking his way in the muddy tunnel. He followed the twinkling pinpoints of light until he came to a red one. He called out the warning.

"Turn to your right and walk forward two paces," ordered Efran. "We're following. Now turn left and continue. That should avoid the tripwire."

"What would it trigger?"

"Who can say?" answered Efran. "I have been down this tunnel only once, and that was from the other direction. On rare occasions, I slipped away from the castle to meet with my brother to see how the war progressed."

"I see a brighter light," interrupted Santon. "What does that mean?"

"It means we have come to the end—and now the real danger confronts us." Efran and Lokenna pressed close as Santon made his way up a slippery ramp to a stone door. He slipped his hand through the rusty metal ring and heaved. The door opened slowly and silently. Efran slid past, hand on his sword.

"It's safe. No one in sight."

Santon hung back a pace and let Efran and Lokenna precede him. When they reached the courtyard, he motioned for them to stop.

"What is it, Birtle?" asked Lokenna. Her face was pale and drawn but he thought she held up well to the danger. "My brother is . . . in the throne room," she finished. "I can *feel* his evil presence. The blackness fluttering around him is like a veil."

"I can do nothing against such magic," Santon said. "I want to seek out Vered. With another sword and his quick wit, perhaps we stand a better chance of defeating Lorens."

"Lorens is leaving the throne room," said Lokenna. She turned as if she watched him. "He is climbing stairs, going to the battlements." Lokenna stepped out into the courtyard, oblivious to the cold rain against her upturned face. "There. He is there."

Santon saw nothing where she pointed; the storm clouds obscured vision beyond a few score of yards.

Efran Gaemock looked from Lokenna to the hidden Lorens and back to Santon. "Go, find your friend. I remember Vered with fondness. I wish you both well." He clapped Santon on the shoulder.

"I'm not abandoning you—*we're* not," he said, speaking for Vered, too. "We'll join you when we can."

"Hurry," said Lokenna. "Kaga'kalb weakens and Kalob is fighting his way free of the storm prison. We must get to Lorens quickly. Only the crown can drive Kalob back into his netherworld." She started off, not waiting to see if Efran or Santon followed.

"Luck," Santon told Efran, "and save some of the good times for us. We'll be there. I promise."

Efran Gaemock squeezed Santon's shoulder in a comradely grip and then hastened after Lokenna. Santon stood in the cold, driving rain and wondered if he had lost his mind. Vered might be dead; hunting for him would take time and endanger Lokenna's chances of besting her brother. They ought to remain together.

Santon watched Efran and Lokenna vanish into the castle. He turned and ran for the door leading to the dungeons. Bare-handed he would fight his way to the torture chambers and get his friend out. *Then* they would help Lokenna against her brother.

To Santon's surprise, he encountered no guards as he spiraled down the stone staircase to the dungeon. The heavy metal grating barring entry into the cell block was easily opened. A departing guard had carelessly tossed aside the key. Santon jerked open the grating and dashed into the dungeon.

Silence greeted him. He peered in one cell after another and saw the same sight. Bodies. Decaying humans. Emaciated corpses. The prisoners had starved to death. Hope died with each cell and left only drifting gauzy white phantoms.

He came to the end of the cell block and peered in the small grate. An obviously dead prisoner sprawled in the back, but Santon's attention came to the hole through the wall into the next cell. He rushed to this door and peered in.

Empty.

He fumbled with his key ring and then saw it wasn't necessary. This door was barred, a heavy pin holding the locking bar in place. He jerked free the cotter pin and drew the bar.

Santon stepped into the cell and yelled as he fell into a hole. He turned in the hole and looked back through the open door in time to see the flagstone in the floor rising. He jerked his right hand in an instinctive motion designed to get his ax into hand.

No ax. No weapon. He struggled to get free of the pit.

The flagstone slid back and a head poked through. "You've picked a fine time to open the door for me," said Vered.

Santon leaned against the cell door and shook his head. Alarice had been right. Vered was a survivor.

All they had to do now was survive the battle with Lorens and the Demon Crown.

Chapter Twenty-five

"Are you going to help me up? I am so giddy I can barely stand." Vered crawled onto the cold stone floor and held out his hand for Santon to give him a boost. Santon's meaty hand closed around Vered's thinner one and heaved. Vered shot to his feet. "There. That's better. Except for my finery. All ruined." He made a futile brushing motion to dislodge the worst of the caked dirt.

"You hardly needed me. You were already
of the cell."

"It took you so long getting here, I d
not to wait." Vered wobbled. Santon ha
port him.

"You appear a bit the worse for t
patience."

"Food stopped coming . . . a w

"I noticed its effect on the

The stark silence in the dungeon emphasized Santon's epitaph for the others. "How did you survive?"

"I was stronger. They had just put me in when the food stopped." Vered looked at his bare feet. "I need new boots."

"Easily done. There is a rack of guards' clothing. They had to change after torture."

"Bloodstains are difficult to conceal when you must attend state dinners," agreed Vered. He walked on unsteady feet to the small wardrobe Santon had pointed out. He found a pair of boots that almost fit. He stuffed in a few rags to make up the difference.

"Food is what you need."

"I need more than that," said Vered, a twinkle in his eye. "And so do you." In a conspiratorial whisper he said, "I know where to find your shield and the sword Alarice gave me."

"Where?" barked Santon. He calmed. "I'm sorry. Food for you, first."

"Not much. It would make me sick. Let me build up slowly. Then I'll demand a full banquet."

…ther they left the dungeon and made their
…rted kitchens. Food was scarce;
… to be overfed. Santon's
… of food, too, but he let
…nted before sampling of
…h, wormy meat.
…know how to set a fine
…s he finished off the last
…a gristle and rubbed his
… minutes for the food to
…ber our old quarters?"
…

… Look under the pile of

blankets near the bed. And while you are rummaging about up there, bring me back another change of clothing. These rags simply will not do if I am to appear before a king."

"Keep eating," Santon said. "You need to fill out that form. You always were a trifle on the skinny side, even if you did eat like a team of mules."

"If I eat any more, I might explode." Vered poked at the maggot-infested meat. "Then again, if I don't eat it, it might decide to eat me."

Santon left and hurried through the corridors, wondering where the castle residents had gone. The entire time he had been inside he had seen no one. Even by straining, he had been unable to hear anything more than the crash and rumble of Kaga'kalb's storms.

The thought of Lokenna and Efran facing Lorens alone added speed to his journey. He raced along the empty halls until he found their old quarters. Inside the room, he dived and slid on his belly to look under the blankets. He gusted a sigh of relief. Ax and glass shield supported Vered's sword. He drew out the bundle and carefully fastened the shield onto his withered arm until he could maneuver it as he had in the past. His ax felt good in his grip once more.

With Vered's sword thrust through his belt and an armful of clothing snatched from the wardrobe, he returned to the kitchens.

"What was that hideous sound?" he asked.

"I belched. I'm not tolerating this so-called food very well." Vered belched again and wiped his mouth with the back of his hand. "Starvation might prove a more humane death than what this is doing." He stood and came to the door. Santon noted the familiar spring in his friend's step. He would be weak when it came to a fight, but his condition had improved greatly from the tainted food.

"Ah, my precious sword. And you have your shield," said Vered. "Let's not dally. Let me get into the clothing you fetched—your color sense is abominable, dear friend—and we shall be off to do . . . what?"

Santon tersely explained the situation as Vered changed his clothes. "Kaga'kalb cannot hold Kalob prisoner much longer. When he weakens, the demon will be free again."

"So Lorens let the demons back into Porotane." Vered shook his head. "I never thought he showed any common sense. Too much power too soon and you sell out to the netherworld. It's an old and sorry story."

"You'd have done the same thing. I saw how the Demon Crown affected you."

"Of course I would. I admit to avarice and a fine lust for power. I've never pretended otherwise. Now where is the battle taking place? I've seen no one around here."

"I encountered no one in the upper corridors, either," said Santon. "I find it strange."

"Has Lorens slain everyone?"

"It is possible, but he would have left bodies littered all around—or he would have stored the prisoners in the dungeons."

"There's only one solution to this small riddle. Let's ask the whoreson ourselves!" Vered pushed past Santon and went back into the courtyard.

"There," said Santon. "There's where Lokenna said her brother had gone."

"You can see through this storm? Snow, fog, rain, what isn't falling on our heads?" Even as he spoke, a clap of thunder sounded and a vibrant bolt of lightning lashed through the clouds to the uppermost turret.

"There's Lorens."

Santon and Vered made their way through the empty passageways and to the throne room. Lorens' audience chamber contained a few bodies, some blown apart from the inside and others that had perished from severe sword wounds.

"Unless I misinterpret this," said Vered, "Lorens has survived a castle revolt. Those poor wights with the blown-out guts tried to seize power. The ones with the swords defended—until Lorens made his wishes in the matter known magically."

"He killed them all," said Santon.

"The crown did it."

They silently left the audience chamber and found the spiraling stone stairs that led to the upper levels. From here they heard the raging storm outside. Snow piled up at the end of a corridor, blown from above.

"What an invitation," muttered Santon. "They've left the door open for us."

Vered pulled his cloak tighter around him. He still shivered. With a small flourish, he drew his sword and waved it about. "Standing here does nothing to help Lokenna and Efran." Vered looked at his friend. "Is Efran as clever and witty as he was when he pretended to be a jester?"

Santon didn't bother answering. He made certain his glass shield rested easily on his arm, flipped the battle ax into his grip, then advanced. The biting wind cut at his face and arms, but he left the warmth of the castle and ventured onto the battlements.

Behind him he heard Vered panting and puffing with exertion. The man had yet to recover his full strength—Santon knew it would take days before that happened. It was their destiny that they were thrust into the fight before either was ready.

Birtle Santon swallowed hard and wondered if he would ever have been ready. The sight before him told the answer.

Lorens stood on the highest point in the tallest tower, his arms outthrust as if daring Kaga'kalb to bring down his lightning bolts. The Wizard of Storms did just that. Santon lifted his shield to protect his eyes when the prodigious blue-white bolt struck Lorens. The wizard-king staggered, but other than this small indication of weakness showed no injury.

The Demon Crown had drained the brutal thrust of Kaga'kalb's energy.

"Where are Lokenna and Efran?" asked Vered.

"I don't see them."

"Then we should press on. We can't let Lorens stare at the scenery overlong. He might get to enjoy it too much to stop."

They started forward, the cold wind buffeting them. They hadn't advanced ten paces when Santon sensed movement to one side. He spun, his shield coming up to protect his head. A heavy cudgel landed and drove him to his knees. As in prior fights, when one was attacked, the other countered.

Vered came around the side with a long lunge that spitted Santon's opponent neatly. The glass tip entered the guardman's armpit far enough to kill with the single thrust. Vered recovered and let Santon stand in time to deflect a sword attack.

"Lorens' personal guard," muttered Vered.

"Green soldiers. Efran routed the personal guard outside the castle walls."

"Why didn't you say so? These younglings will fall quickly to a master swordsman such as myself!" Vered launched a flurry of thrusts, ripostes, and parries. Santon joined him, knowing that his friend's strength would soon fade in the face of such opposition.

Vered drove one guardsman over the battlements to his death. Santon used his shield to catch another under the chin; the soldier's head snapped back and made a crack so loud they heard it over the thunder. A third guardsman tumbled to the inner courtyard when Santon's ax bit deeply into his thigh.

"This is all Lorens has left to protect him? How absurd. We can fight them all day long!"

Santon saw that Vered boasted. This minor skirmish had drained him of strength. Vered stumbled as they made their way forward. When they reached Lorens, Vered would be unable to lift even his light glass sword.

"Guard my back. Here come two more!" Santon rushed the guardsmen rather than letting them choose the battleground. He upended one and sent him tumbling over the stone battlement. He heard the poor wight's screams of agony as he was impaled on the thorny brambles outside the castle wall. The second soldier fought more cautiously, avoiding direct blows from Santon's mighty ax and turning to keep Santon's shield out of position.

"You, soldier," called Santon, his voice

sounding faint and distant in the storm. "We have no quarrel with you. Is that the man you want as king? Up there?"

The guardsman cast a quick glance over his shoulder. Santon stepped back, both to give the young man a chance to study his liege lord and to rest. The cold robbed him of vitality faster than he would have liked. He worried at what this fight in the frigid wind did to Vered if he felt this drained himself.

Lorens shrieked and ranted and made gestures in the direction of the rebel camp. Santon did not know if the Demon Crown allowed the wizard-king to seek Kaga'kalb or if Lorens merely vented his wrath in the most convenient way. The expression on his face defied description. He had once been a handsome enough youth. The lines furrowed into his leather-skinned forehead were those of someone carrying the burdens of the world. His hair had turned white, either from frost or strain. Most telling of all was his frame. He had been well muscled when they had arrived in Porotane.

He now stood as gaunt as a demon, his cheekbones protruding and his eyes dark pits. Lorens shook all over as magical spells tumbled from his lips.

"Is *he* your monarch?" repeated Santon.

The young soldier looked back. "He has killed my friends. He has destroyed most of the people within the castle walls. He has done what the rebels were unable to do in twenty years of fighting."

The soldier lowered his sword and waited. Santon turned, putting his back to the battlements and motioning the man by. The soldier cast his sword into the courtyard and then rushed past Santon and Vered, obviously glad to put this to an end.

"So much for inspiring loyalty," said Vered, watching the young man descend the icy stone steps and vanish into the castle.

Santon wasn't listening. He stared at Lorens, wondering if any shred of humanity remained in that fragile-appearing husk. It didn't look like it.

He and Vered made their way to the steps leading to the platform where Lorens muttered his spells. The wizard-king's attention was focused elsewhere. He took no notice of them.

"Can we kill him this easily?" Santon said, his voice a whisper.

"Trying is the only way to find out." Vered wiped the snow from his eyebrows and gripped the hilt of his sword so hard his knuckles turned white with strain.

"Wait!"

They spun, ready to fight. Lokenna motioned them away. She had taken refuge in a small guard post at the base of the tower.

"Birtle, Vered, please!"

Santon backed from the steps leading to Lorens. The king remained oblivious to their presence. Attacking him now might be their best opportunity for victory. Even knowing this, he motioned Vered to join Lokenna, then ducked into the guard post.

The small room was crowded with two. With four it made for a closeness Santon didn't want. Efran hunched over, holding his side. A bright red stain showed where a heavy sword blade had slashed through his light armor.

"He will be all right," said Lokenna. The look on her face assured Santon that she did not speak simply to bolster Efran's spirits. She truly thought he would live. "We must wait before we go after my brother. The crown gives him power beyond belief."

"Can Kaga'kalb wear him down?" asked Santon. "That *is* what you're waiting for?"

The stricken look on the woman's face gave Santon his first hint that the battle of magics did not go well. Without his cloud warriors, Kaga'kalb had to rely solely on his storm-bringing ability—and this was limited by nearness to the Demon Crown.

"There is so little I can do. Kaga'kalb must carry on the fight while I stand and watch. The last of Lorens' guard is gone. Beyond this . . ."

Vered poked his head outside into the storm and held up a hand to shield his eyes from the rain. He ducked back in and said, "Lorens shows no sign of weakening. If anything, he seems to be turning aside the worst of the storm."

"What can we do?" asked Santon.

"I . . . I don't know. When we came up here, I thought I could deal with my brother."

"He'd never listen," cut in Efran. "He is crazed with the crown's power. Trying to reason with him was foolish on our part."

"He killed almost everyone within the castle," Lokenna said in a choked voice. "I hadn't known that until we . . . until we came across the rooms where the bodies are stacked."

Efran moaned, then bit his lower lip to keep from crying out again. Santon knew that they could not remain here indefinitely. Efran needed help desperately. Vered was still weak from starvation. Kaga'kalb's power waned as the spell battle raged on. The fight had to be carried directly to Lorens.

"Santon, where are you going?" asked Vered. Santon pushed his friend back and stepped into the storm. In front of him moved a patch of fog that flowed and took shape.

"Alarice?" he asked, not daring to hope.

"The demon comes. Lorens has worn down Kaga'kalb. You must act now, dear Birtle. Do it now or all is lost!"

Lightning flared across the sky and drove away Alarice's phantom. Santon gave the leather thong on his wrist a quick jerk and brought the ax to fighting position. He went to the stone steps and started up. He hesitated when he felt a presence behind him.

"Vered, don't," he said, then stopped. With Vered was Lokenna and Efran—and behind them wavered a phantom.

"We all go or none do," said Vered. "It is only fair. Why should it be any different from the way it's always been?"

Lokenna nodded her agreement. Efran hefted his sword and held his ribs, anxious to engage. Behind them Santon saw Alarice's face with its gentle smile. He turned and raced up the stone steps.

The turret had protected him from the worst of the wind. When he got to the top, storm winds buffeted him from all directions. Santon wavered for a moment, then plunged ahead, ignoring cold and snow and wind. Lorens and the Demon Crown became the center of his universe.

With a bull-throated war cry, Santon swung his ax directly at Lorens' throat. The heavy blade struck its target—and rebounded. Santon yelped in surprise as the shock worked its way back along his arm and into his shoulder.

Fighting instinct saved him. He threw up the glass shield as if to ward off a blow. Energies beyond any mere steel blade boiled on the rounded shield's surface. Santon swung again, hunkered down behind the shield. This time he aimed at Lorens' legs.

The impact again knocked him back. It also brought Lorens to his knees.

"Who dares attack me in this manner?" The voice came from Lorens' mouth but the hollow, ringing quality to it was not human.

"You are Kalob, not Lorens," accused Santon.

Ghastly, shrill laughter drowned out the thunder. "Kalob is my ally. I have allowed him to enter this world again. He fights the traitor Kaga'kalb."

"You know his name!" Lokenna gasped.

"The Demon Crown reveals all to me!" Again Lorens laughed. This time Vered and Efran attacked him, one from each side. Efran's steel sword failed to injure the wizard-king, but Vered's glass blade dug deeply into Lorens' side. Black blood trickled out of the wound.

"He's not human," muttered Efran. "He has become a demon, too!"

The three men attacked simultaneously, but failed to penetrate the ring of Lorens' spells. Whatever magic he used now proved effective and kept them at bay.

"I know this spell," Lokenna said in a small voice. "Attack him again. *Now!*"

The three men reacted as one. Vered swung at the man's eyes. Santon's ax drove deep into Lorens' right thigh and produced a new artesian well of the inky blood. Efran lunged directly for the wizard-king's heart. All three felt their weapons strike and wound.

Lorens screamed in pain, clawing at his injured eyes, hobbling on his leg, and geysering blood from a ruptured heart.

"No man can survive those injuries," marvelled Vered. "He cannot be human!"

"Human or not, he dies!" Santon stood over Lorens, ax raised for the killing blow. As powerful as the downward blow was, the hand grabbing his wrist and lifting him off the turret was stronger. Santon struggled in the impossibly strong grip, twisting to see his attacker.

"Kalob!" he gasped.

"Kaga'kalb fights himself." The demon sneered, black lips pulled away from bloody fangs. "I have escaped his traps. I stopped him from conjuring his cloud warriors. Now I must rescue my puppet. Lorens has allowed me back into this world. He will serve me well when the new order is established."

Santon kicked and fought but could not free himself from the demon's grip. Both Vered and Efran had collapsed on the turret, exhausted from the fight with Lorens—or under Kalob's spell.

Only Lokenna remained on her feet. Beside her glowed the patch of mist that was Alarice.

"There is a way of forcing you back," Lokenna said in a voice unlike her own. Santon ceased his struggles for a moment and stared at her. She had reached out. Alarice's phantom sent out a glowing tendril that rested on Lokenna's palm. "I know what it is. When I wore the crown, I knew it. My brother knows, also, but he is too weak."

"*You* are weak, bitch!" roared Kalob. With a contemptuous gesture, he threw Santon across the turret roof. Santon skidded and managed to keep from falling to his death below at the last instant by clutching at Vered's leg. Vered twitched weakly and moaned. He showed no other sign of life.

'There is a different power, one I can use," Lokenna said. "I have always known it—all my life."

"You fear it, bitch. You cannot use it because you are weak!"

"I could not use it because I lacked the power, not the will!" Lokenna spun and reached out to take the Demon Crown from her brother's head. Lorens jerked away.

Santon saw that Lokenna needed the crown if Kalob was to be forced back into his netherworld. Santon rolled and swung the edge of the glass shield at the back of Lorens' neck. The impact knocked the wizard-king's head forward. In a smooth motion, Lokenna snared the falling crown and held it.

The transition from ugly, corrupt green to the verdant emerald came abruptly. Kalob roared in anger as Lokenna put the crown on her head and began muttering the spells that would break the demon's power.

Kalob fought. He reached out with his spindly arms and skeletal hand and caught Santon by the throat. He lifted and held the struggling man over the edge of the turret.

"Give Lorens the crown or I drop this feeble worm!"

"You cannot open your hand," Lokenna said. Santon gagged as the demon's fingers tightened on his throat. His feet kicked above a drop of two hundred feet—and hidden below in the swirling clouds lay the treacherous brambles. The six-inch-long thorns would kill him, even if the fall did not.

"Bitch! Do not oppose me in this. Return the crown. Now! Do it now!"

Lokenna stood for a few seconds, bathed in the vivid green glow of the Demon Crown.

"Release him," she ordered.

Santon felt the demon's claws opening. He grabbed for the spindly arm; he had no desire to die, but if he did, he would take Kalob with him.

The demon discarded him as if he were a piece of offal. Santon screamed as he fell away from the turret, tumbling over and over, falling to his death.

The wind he had hated for so long cut against his face, caught at his clothing—lifted him. Like some ungainly bird, Santon flew on the powerful currents. He swooped low over the deadly brambles and blasted upward into the sky. Clouds drifted under him and supported him with their misty substance. Lightning flared around him, lighting his way through the rain and snow and dust.

As light as a feather, the winds put him down in the edge of the turret again. The sight of the human returned from certain death shocked Kalob. He tried to utter a spell, to finish the job he had begun, but Lokenna's voice cut deeper than any blade.

"Your legs are numb. Your vision fades. Kalob, your senses are being taken from you. Blind, deaf, without feeling, you are slipping away. There is no taste or odor in this world. Only yourself, only you, and you are growing weaker."

"You cannot do this to me! I beg you! You have no idea how terrible it is in my world!"

Lokenna stepped forward. The crown sat on her head and drew every lightning strike. She was not the target of destruction; she was the center of power. As she moved, her lips worked on the spells needed to banish the demon.

Kalob shrank in size. The fragility of his body increased. Santon moved forward and used the edge of his shield against the demon's neck. Kalob's head flew into the storm. Lokenna pointed and a bolt of lightning vaporized the skull. She reached out and lightly touched the still-wiggling body. It tumbled off the turret.

Santon saw it vanish as if it were mist evaporating in the morning sun.

"He is banished," Lokenna said. "The gateway opened by my brother is closed—and will remain so."

Santon sank to his knees, thankful for the respite. He started to speak and then saw the determination on the woman's face.

"Lokenna, no, let me!"

Santon's warning came too late. Lokenna went to her brother, who hopped on one leg. As she had done with Kalob, she reached out and gently shoved. Lorens shrieked as he lost his balance and tumbled backward off the turret.

Santon fell belly down and peered over the brink. No bolt of lightning vaporized Lorens. His body cut a tunnel through the clouds. Santon got a long look at the wizard-king's twisted body impaled on the deadly thorns before the storm closed the pathway to death.

"There is no need to worry about me, dear Birtle," she said, touching his cheek. "He was my brother, my twin, but he was also venal and . . .

evil." She straightened. "As my relative, it was my duty to do what had to be done."

Lokenna turned from Santon, then fainted, falling face forward. He tried to catch her and only partially broke her fall. He lay beside her on the turret, too weak to move. Above, the storm began to abate. Within minutes blue sky arched above and soft, almost springlike winds blew.

Santon remembered the rainbow before passing out.

Chapter Twenty-six

Vered stretched and leaned back in the cushioned chair, hiking his feet to the table in front of him. He took a morsel of bread and carefully ate it as he stared out the slit window in the room. Behind him Birtle Santon moaned softly.

"Are you awake, Santon?" he called.

"Awake? What?" The man came fully awake, hand reaching for his ax. Santon groaned again and got out of bed. Standing beside Vered, he said, "You're looking plump. You must have been gorging yourself to put on so much weight in . . ." His voice trailed off. Outside the trees tried to put on leaves and the grass had turned green once more. The snows had gone and the day looked like a perfect spring.

"No, you've not slept *that* long. But three days is a long time."

"Three days!"

"A little over. Much has happened while you've been dreaming away your life."

Santon grabbed Vered's shoulders and spun the man around. "Tell me what's happened."

"First of all, you seem well enough after your sleep. Have some food. Nothing wormy in this scrumptious food. Efran sent for his brother and the peasants robbed their winter larder to provide decent food for the conquering heroes—that's us."

"Winter?" Santon went to the window and felt warm breeze against his skin. Tears came to his eyes. He had not thought to ever see spring again.

"It *is* winter, but this is Kaga'kalb's coronation gift to Lokenna."

"Is he in the castle?"

"He returned immediately to his Castle of the Winds. He was even more drained than you, but Efran and Lokenna would not let him go until they'd forged a strong treaty. He can create his masterpieces of clouds and his symphonies of thunder and lightning as long as he does it in the Yorral Mountains. No more of this perpetual winter, even though we are barely into autumn."

"Then we will see winter again?"

"Soon, he said. But it will be natural and not the product of his magic. This unusual warmth is a reaction to the magic he used to defeat Lorens and the demon."

"They are gone?"

Vered shuddered. "Lokenna has the way of a queen about her. She refuses to allow her brother's body to be taken down from the thorns. He's to remain until the crows pick his skeleton clean. Then she's decreed that his bones be broken and sent to every corner of Porotane and put on display."

"The crown?" Santon was hesitant to even suggest that the Demon Crown also corrupted her.

"No. She considers this justice for what he had done to Porotane." Vered shrugged. "Mayhap she is right. The peasants seem to enjoy the thought of looking on the tyrant's bones and spitting on them. But then you know how peasants are."

"How can I have slept through all this?"

"You were exhausted by the battle. You of all, save for Lokenna and Kaga'kalb and perhaps Efran and myself, expended the most to save Porotane." Vered popped another choice tidbit into his mouth and chewed contentedly.

"Then all is well in the castle?"

"As smooth as silk," said Vered. "The formal coronation is slated for this afternoon. Most of the principals have recovered from the battle. Lokenna thought it was a reasonable time. She dares not wait too long or the kingdom will fall apart again and the petty warlords will stir up armies in opposition."

"What of the Gaemocks?"

Vered laughed. "She has them firmly on her side." Vered laughed even louder. "With Efran, she has more than this. She has him firmly in her bed."

"From the looks he gave her when they were together, he is not complaining," said Santon.

"Far from it. The court jester has now become the court favorite. It would not surprise me if she decides to make him more than consort. He is a valuable resource at this court. And if things do get dull, he can always cut a caper or two and liven them up. I suspect life will soon enough become dull here."

"He knows the politics of rule," agreed Santon. "And his brother? What of Dews' ambition for the throne?"

"He is a strange breed of man, that Dews Gaemock. He always avowed that he had no desire to sit on the throne, that he opposed Duke Freow simply because he wanted to see someone competent ruling the kingdom—and not necessarily himself."

"So he has bowed out?"

"Hardly. Lokenna would be suspicious of him if he had not exacted some post from her. He is now Marshal of Armies entrusted with maintaining order throughout the kingdom."

"In certain ways, this is a more powerful position than monarch. He collects taxes."

"He collects taxes and maintains the army against brigands, but Lokenna need have no fear of perfidy when he's off in the provinces. She still wears the Demon Crown."

The information worried Santon. Lorens had not been the evil fiend when he first donned the crown. He had been weak and from that weakness came the evil. The Demon Crown was a potent symbol, a magical relic of immense power. The potential for abuse and destruction was also great.

"Lokenna," said Santon, "uses the crown in a fashion different from Lorens. Therein lies the safety of the kingdom."

"She can still see or hear—spy on!—anyone anywhere she pleases. Except in the Castle of the Winds. That was part of the agreement between her and Kaga'kalb."

"His magic prevents such use, anyway," said

Santon. "No, she does more than spy. She looks into a person's soul and ferrets out emotion." He remembered the times she had seemed to read his thoughts—and she had not even been wearing the crown.

"I'm not certain I want a ruler who can do that. There is blackness lurking within that I refuse to face. Why should someone else know what I cannot about myself?" Vered's words hung heavy but his attitude dispelled any gloom.

"Will you stop eating for a moment?"

"Why? I am still famished. The time in the prison was awful—and be sure to remind me to always buy a high quality of boot. The leather in my old ones was well nigh inedible."

Santon stared into the countryside and saw a steady stream of people coming into the castle for the coronation. He asked Vered, "When is Lokenna to be installed as queen?"

"Soon. Get yourself into what rags you wish to be seen in publicly. Myself, I feel quite comfortable in these old things." Vered stood and pirouetted to show off his finery. Santon noticed the tunic and breeches less than he did the gleaming daggers Vered had hidden away in the folds.

"Expecting a new war to break out?"

"They saved me once. Call me superstitious. I intend to always carry four daggers with me. And my glass sword, of course." He tapped the hilt. Santon shook his head and went to dress. To his surprise the wardrobes overflowed with clothing that fit him as if tailor-made.

"I've had to do something to occupy my time. Choosing suitable clothing for you gave me some small respite from boredom."

Santon thanked him and stood before the polished metal sheet to study himself. He cut a fine figure, he decided, even though he would never tell Vered. His friend carried the "better things in life" to extremes. Santon preferred to be astride a strong horse with the stars above. Even a wind in the face as he rode would not be amiss.

"Hurry, Santon. The ceremonies begin without us."

Santon hitched up the glass shield and slung his ax in a belt loop. Crowning or not, he, like Vered, did not feel comfortable without weapons. They made their way down the back ways of the castle and came into the throne room through a side door.

"Isn't she lovely?" whispered Vered.

"Aye, she is. A regal bearing for a true queen." A catch came to Santon's voice when Lokenna took the Demon Crown from a plush pillow and placed the gold circlet on her head. A hush fell over the assemblage as the crown turned a light green, then began to shine with a clear, pure emerald light.

Santon let out pent-up breath he hadn't known he was holding. He had feared the crown would be the same ugly color it had been on Lorens' brow.

"Can you hear what she's saying?" asked Vered.

"Not well. She's thanking everyone. Kaga'kalb. Something about the alliance with the Wizard of Storms, blah, blah, blah. Dews Gaemock is Marshal of Armies." Santon smiled. "Your rumormongering is accurate, it seems."

"I hear something about Efran. Surely she is not appointing him court jester?"

"Nor consort. They've announced an alliance

more binding. This is a coronation and a wedding."

"A better choice than Bane Pandasso. She has learned quality in men, though why she chose him over me is something I will never understand."

Santon looked around the large chamber and saw the rapt faces. Rebel soldiers stood next to royalists. Peasants mingled with the few nobles remaining in the kingdom. There would be much rebuilding. New orders of nobility awarded, a settling into peace that might stretch for years.

Porotane needed the healing. The civil war had been too destructive for too long.

"Do you feel it, too?" asked Vered.

"What?"

"Sadness. It is over."

Santon considered, then nodded. "There is one item that remains to be done."

"I have no wish to stay in the castle and have them force baronies or even duchies on me. You know how I loathe it when beautiful women fawn on me and thrust riches into my hands."

"I've noticed," said Santon. "Shall we do what must be done?"

"Of course."

Long before Lokenna, Queen of Porotane, came to their names on the lists of nobility, Birtle Santon and Vered had departed the castle.

One last obligation had to be met.

Chapter Twenty-seven

The dust storm cut at their faces and hands and forced Santon and Vered to stop too often. Even worse than the biting dust was the freezing cold.

"I thought deserts were supposed to be hot. This is terrible." Vered huddled behind his horse in a vain attempt to find shelter from the storm raging across the Desert of Sazan.

"It's winter. There's nothing to keep the heat in. Do you see anything but rocks and sand?"

"It wasn't much warmer in the Iron Range when we came through the passes. Won't this ever get any better?"

"Not until summer. Then the heat will fry your brains inside your skull."

"I remember all too well," Vered said glumly. "I think that's already happened. There's no other reason for us to be out here exposing our precious bodies to the elements."

They had left Castle Porotane, taking horses and supplies for their long journey. Not bothering to consult with Lokenna had speeded them on their way. As Santon pointed out, the new ruler of Porotane could find them easily if she desired. All she had to do was don the Demon Crown and *look* for them.

The black, angular peaks of the Iron Range had brought fierce winter storms and bands of brigands who had not heard of the new law in the land. Each group they eluded or outfought reminded them that Dews Gaemock would not tolerate such thievery—but bringing law to this portion of the kingdom would take months or even years.

The Inquisitor had finally risen at their backs and the barren Desert of Sazan stretched before them.

"How are we going to find it?" demanded Vered. "I can't see ten paces in this dust."

"We'll find a way. We must."

Vered grumbled a bit, then said, "We owe her much. It's a pity her phantom cannot aid us now." No phantom could locate the body from which it came. No one had been able to give a reasonable explanation; Santon and Vered had aided more than one phantom in Claymore Pass and other battlegrounds to find eternal rest. For Alarice they could perform the same service.

Without her, Porotane would not have a decent queen on the throne and peace for the first time in over twenty years.

"Patrin's City of Stolen Dreams was near this spot," said Santon.

"How can you tell?"

"I've not lost my tracking sense. We found it before, when Alarice led us here. I can always retrace my steps."

"I've heard of birds being able to perform such a feat," muttered Vered, pulling his cloak up to protect his nose and mouth. He took a step forward and stumbled over something buried in the sand.

"What's that?" Santon pounced on the broken pot.

"It looks like one of Patrin's dream jars. Do you think it remained when his entire city just . . . vanished."

"It might have. If so, that means she is near—her remains are near," he corrected, his voice choked with emotion. Vered rested a reassuring hand on his friend's shoulder.

"There is much desert to search and the sands will have drifted over her," said Vered as gently as possible. "It might be the work of a lifetime finding her skeleton. This storm makes it even more difficult to do."

"I'll do it."

"We'll do it," said Vered.

They began their hunt until both dropped to the ground in exhaustion.

"It's so cold and the demon-damned wind never stops," said Vered. "How can we be sure that we're not simply searching the same spot over and over? I'm so turned around, I cannot tell where I am."

"We've been . . ." Santon's voice trailed off as the wind died. In the distance he saw huge pillars of cloud rising to form black anvilheads. Lightning crashed within the clouds.

"Those look exactly like the storms Kaga'kalb conjured," said Vered.

"Quiet. Listen!"

"Music!"

"The thunder. It . . . it's a song!" Santon stood and made his way to the top of a sand dune. From here he was able to get an unobstructed view of the two towering columns of lightning-filled storm.

"The winds still rage except down the corridor," said Vered. "Do you think Kaga'kalb is aiding us?"

"He is," came Alarice's faint voice. "I cannot help you to help me. But Kaga'kalb can—and so is Lokenna."

"Lokenna?"

"The Demon Crown. She can see anything no matter where it is!"

Santon said, "The cloud warriors—look. Kaga'kalb sends one toward us."

"Lokenna guides it, Kaga'kalb sends it," came Alarice's voice, hardly more than a whisper in the desert.

"I see no remains of Patrin's city," said Vered, "but the cloud warrior must. He's stopped and is pointing."

Santon rushed forward, Vered following. They approached the cloud warrior cautiously. The huge, nebulous figure pointed to a spot in the desert. Santon dropped to his knees and began digging frantically with his good hand. Vered took the shield from his friend's left arm and used it as a giant scoop to move even more sand.

"A skeleton," Santon announced. He gingerly pushed away the sand until the entire body was revealed. "The ants have stripped off the flesh and there is no clothing left—the elements have done them in. How can we know this is Alarice's body?"

"By this," said Vered. He had continued to dig and had found a long glass sword. He held it up so that it gleamed in the bright sunlight and reflected a beam down to a rocky outjutting.

"There," said Santon, pointing to the rock the light beam selected. "We'll entomb her there."

"That's a major undertaking. It's solid rock. How can we—'

Vered and Santon were blown backward by the lightning bolt that struck the rock prominence and burned a cavity in it.

"Kaga'kalb," saluted Vered. He flourished the long glass sword in the direction of the distant Castle of the Winds. "Thank you."

They carried the bones and put them into the crypt. Santon took the glass sword from Vered and gently laid it across Alarice's skeleton. The Glass Warrior had found her final resting place.

"Rest in peace, my love," he said.

"Thank you, dear Birtle," came the phantom whisper.

Santon and Vered stepped back when the cloud warrior motioned them away. Another bolt from the twin storms at the edge of the desert fused the stone over Alarice's remains. Santon quietly recited the ceremony that would lay Alarice to rest for all eternity.

As he finished a cold wind blew choking dust in his face.

"Kaga'kalb has done what he can," said Vered. "We again have miserable winter storms in this miserable desert to plague us. Let us find somewhere cozy and warm to spend the winter. You mentioned an hospitable town to the south?"

"Let's see what we can find," said Santon. "It's been too many years since I've been in that direction. Porotane holds no real challenge for us."

Vered mounted and began singing a bawdy ballad he had learned in a western province seaport tavern. Birtle Santon did not listen to the off-key song. In his ear he heard the faint whispers of his lover.

Then they were gone.

He joined in Vered's song and did not look back.